T0316213

# Bello:
# hidden talent rediscovered!

Bello is a digital only imprint of Pan Macmillan,
established to breathe new life into previously published,
classic books.

At Bello we believe in the timeless power of the imagination,
of good story, narrative and entertainment and we want to use
digital technology to ensure that many more readers
can enjoy these books into the future.

We publish in ebook and Print on Demand formats
to bring these wonderful books to new audiences.

### About Bello:

www.panmacmillan.com/imprints/bello

### About the author:

www.panmacmillan.com/author/rcsherriff

# R. C. Sherriff

On his return from the First World War, R. C. Sherriff settled in London, working as an insurance agent and writing plays in the evening. *Journey's End*, inspired by Sherriff's own experience of fighting, was his sixth play but the first to be given a professional production. It was an immediate, outstanding and phenomenal success. Thirty one separate productions ran concurrently around the world and it was translated into twenty six languages. Its success, however, was both a boon and a burden – while it allowed him to give up the day job and devote himself full-time to writing, it often overshadowed his later work or was used as the yardstick against which it was measured unfavourably.

Fortunately for Sherriff he was not only a playwright but also a novelist and a screenwriter. He wrote a best-selling novel, *A Fortnight In September* in 1931, and the screenplays for *The Invisible Man* (1933), *The Four Feathers* (1939) and classic films such as *Goodbye Mr Chips* (1939), for which he received an Oscar nomination, and *The Dambusters* (1955).

Although Sherriff was occupied as a playwright and screenwriter he did not lose his urge to write novels and he followed the success of his first novel with *The Hopkins Manuscript, Chedworth, Another Year* and others. Now, while *Journey's End* continues to define Sherriff's reputation, much of his work remains ripe for rediscovery.

*R. C. Sherriff*

# THE WELLS OF ST MARY'S

BELL◎

First published in 1962 by Heinemann

This edition published 2012 by Bello
an imprint of Pan Macmillan, a division of Macmillan Publishers Limited
Pan Macmillan, 20 New Wharf Road, London N1 9RR
Basingstoke and Oxford
Associated companies throughout the world

www.panmacmillan.com/imprints/bello
www.curtisbrown.co.uk

ISBN 978-1-4472-2104-3 EPUB
ISBN 978-1-4472-2102-9 POD

# Chapter One

As I write this evening in the quiet library of my country home I look back upon a day that should have been the proudest of my life.

I have been overwhelmed with honours. This morning I was enrolled as the first Freeman of St Mary's for outstanding services to the town. I was presented with my portrait in oils and a silver inkstand: a gift from the people in token of their gratitude for what the Mayor described as my 'surpassing generosity'. At the official luncheon in the Casino a Cabinet Minister paid tribute to me as 'a man whose devotion to his fellow citizens will stand as a shining inspiration for generations yet unborn'. At nightfall I saw my portrait illuminate the summer twilight in the form of a large, impressive firework, and heard the cheers that greeted it. I have been told in confidence that I shall almost certainly receive a knighthood in the New Year's Honours List, but even as I record these things I listen for the sound of a police car in the drive, and the arrival of the men who will begin the inquiry that will send me to penal servitude.

The truth about St Mary's Casino is bound to come out sooner or later. It may happen tomorrow, or it may not be for years, but one day it is certain that some trifling accident will uncover this wretched affair that has taken me from my peaceful country life and made me what I am today: Chairman of a fraudulent Company and an accessory to a shameless murder.

I will call this a confession, but God alone must be the final judge of whether I was right or wrong. If the truth comes out before my death, then my written confession will not be needed, because I shall come forward in person to explain the facts and take my punishment. But if the discovery is not made until some distant day when I and the present Directors of the Company are no longer living, then this must be our silent testimony, and I hope we shall not be judged too harshly.

I shall leave it in a sealed packet, in the safekeeping of the Company's solicitors, inscribed: 'To be opened by the Chairman only in grave emergency.' I can say no more without giving the whole thing away, and must hope that it will never, by unfortunate mishap, be opened prematurely.

My name is Peter Evelyn Joyce: a local magistrate and retired Army officer, born sixty-five years ago in this same house where I now spend my last unhappy days.

Minston Manor, the home of my family for centuries, stands on the southern slopes of a pleasant valley a few miles from the ancient country town of St Mary's. In days gone by we owned a thousand acres of this fertile land with seven prosperous farmsteads, but piece by piece we have had to sell, until now the Manor House and the Home Farm alone remain in my possession, with a few outlying cottages.

I need say little of my Army career. It is of small interest and of no concern to the events I am going to relate. From Sandhurst I was commissioned in the spring of 1914 to our county regiment, the Suffolk Fusiliers. I fought in France and Mesopotamia, and at the close of hostilities was posted to the Second Battalion, then stationed in India.

Retiring with the rank of Major in 1936, I was re-employed at the outbreak of the Second World War, promoted Colonel and given command of a regiment on coastal defence in Norfolk.

A very ordinary career, but I was a soldier by tradition rather than desire. By nature I am a countryman, and during those long years abroad my thoughts were never far away from this beloved old house in Minston Valley.

It is a big house: far bigger than I need today, and sadly in want of painting and repair, but I never tire of the beauty of its surroundings, and the fine views from the hill crest that stretch on a clear day to the Norfolk Broads and the distant sea.

We were hit badly by the war and forced to sell a good deal of our remaining land, but we made ends meet as best we could. We bred turkeys for the Christmas market, grew fruit and early vegetables, and on the whole we rubbed along quite happily.

My wife died five years ago. We had no children and as I could no longer afford to entertain, I was often lonely in the Manor House: specially through the long dark winter evenings.

I tried to overcome my loneliness by taking an active part in the affairs of St Mary's. I became a Member of the Town Council, a Governor of the Grammar School, and a Magistrate. But these things, in so quiet a town, took relatively little of my time, and many of my evenings were spent alone.

It was in fact this loneliness that made me write the letter to my old friend Colin that was to have such fatal consequences.

I need say little of Colin here, because the name of Lord Colindale, statesman and millionaire newspaper proprietor, will not be forgotten, even if this chronicle remains unopened for many years.

We were at school together and close friends for some time afterwards until we took our different ways: mine to obscurity and his to fame.

Colin was always a rebel. He was nearly expelled from school for running an unofficial magazine lampooning various masters. His father was a Bishop who had hoped for his son to follow him into the Church, but Colin disgraced himself in the eyes of his family by cutting loose from tradition and taking a job as a reporter on a small weekly newspaper in a seedy Midland town.

The rest is too well known to be recounted. In a few years he was editor, then owner of the Batley *Herald*: by 1940 he was in control of a chain of newspapers across the length and breadth of Britain: Lord Colindale, and still a young man.

In the wartime Government he became a national figure: a burly John Bull, with supreme confidence, in himself and in everything he did, capturing the public imagination with the sheer exuberance of his personality and physical endurance.

To everybody's surprise he retired from politics in 1945, announcing that his duty to the State was done, and that his widespread business interests called for his return. It was, in my private opinion, the carefully judged move of a vastly ambitious man. Foreseeing the temporary eclipse of his party, he withdrew from public life during their years out of power, and returned, with a considerable blast of trumpets, when the Conservatives came back in 1951. By taking a minor office he displayed a modesty that disarmed suspicion and paved the way towards the power he sought. Everybody was glad to see him back: his public appearances drew the crowds, and his speeches made headlines even in the newspapers that he didn't own. He was a leading personality on television: people enjoyed his downright views and sturdy defence of all things British: they admired his abounding energy, and he was tipped on all sides for one of the highest places in the next Government.

And then the mysterious fade-out. Without warning and without explanation Colin disappeared completely from public life.

Buried away, as I was, in my house in the country, I had followed the career of my old friend from a distance, but with pride and admiration. He had paid me a few visits during his years from politics. He was a keen angler and enjoyed a day's fishing in the river that ran through my small estate. But on his return to the Government his time was entirely taken up, and it seemed as if our long but sporadic companionship was finally over.

In a sense I never lost touch with him because he was always in the news. I read his speeches in the morning papers and looked forward to his appearances on television. I watched for his photograph in the illustrated magazines and never missed his talks over sound radio. His comings and goings were so fully reported that I could almost have kept a diary in his name. So when the mysterious fade-out came it was as if a long, unbroken personal companionship had suddenly ended.

I might better call it a 'slow fade-out' because it was not a sudden disappearance. I came gradually to notice that his photograph no longer appeared in the magazines. There were no more appearances on television and his public speeches grew few and far between. There was an occasional recorded talk on sound radio when I thought that his voice seemed strained and tired, then finally silence: complete and absolute.

It puzzled me because I knew that nobody enjoyed the limelight more than Colin and nothing but sheer necessity would keep him out of it. I watched the papers for some explanation, but it seemed as if the press, by one accord, had agreed upon a conspiracy of silence.

If my life had been a busy one I would have thought less about it, but in the quiet evenings, alone in my library, I began to brood over it and wonder more and more what had happened to Colin. He was after all a very old friend. At school we were inseparable, we spent our holidays together, walking in the Highlands, sailing on the Broads, exploring the Continent on our bicycles. Even when our ways had parted, he had still found time for that occasional brief visit to the Manor House and had always written afterwards to say how much he had enjoyed it.

A full year passed. The silence remained unbroken beyond one brief paragraph stating that Lord Colindale had left that morning for a holiday abroad, and a similar paragraph a few months later saying that he had returned. But there had been no photograph of him leaving or coming back: nothing on the television newsreel: not even a clue to where he had been.

There was no mutual friend to seek information from, and one evening the impulse came to solve the mystery myself. I sat down and wrote:

Dear Colin,
    It is a long time since you came down here for a few days' fishing and golf: nearly five years since I last saw you. There are plenty of fish in the river this season, so what about it?

Things at the Manor House are very much as usual: old Fred the butler and his wife are still with me, and we'd love to see you again.

I'm always here, so you only have to give the word and your old room will be ready for you.

I made it short and casual because I didn't want him to think I was being inquisitive about his mysterious disappearance from public life. I posted the letter without much expectation of getting a reply, but an answer came with surprising promptness:

Dear Peter,

I was delighted to get your letter reminding me of those happy days at the Manor House and nothing would give me more pleasure than to see you again.

So I will take you at your word, I will be with you this coming Friday in time for a cup of tea, and I hope, if I may, to stay for a long week-end.

His letter was so normal and cheerful that I felt rather foolish for allowing my imagination to build up such grim forebodings about my old friend. It occurred to me for the first time that Colin might have deliberately effaced himself from the public eye to carry out some confidential work for the Government as he had frequently done during the War. If it concerned foreign affairs, then that would account for his long absence abroad so guardedly reported in the papers.

The news caused considerable excitement with Fred and Amy. Colin had always been an honoured guest and Amy's niece came from the town to help spring-clean the bedroom that Colin had always used on previous visits. There were discussions about food and I spent some time with Fred in the cellar deciding which wine should be served from my sadly depleted stock.

All was in readiness in good time on Friday, and shortly before five o'clock I saw the big car swing through the gates and come slowly up the drive. My reassurance about Colin increased as the car drew nearer. It looked so sure of itself: so comfortable and prosperous: so characteristic of the man himself that all my remaining concern for him was gone. I noticed that a stolid, bowler-hatted man was sitting beside the chauffeur. It was the first time that Colin had come to see me while a Member of the Government and I remembered that it was customary for Ministers in responsible positions to travel with a private detective. It occurred to me that I ought perhaps to have asked the Chief Constable to station a policeman at the gate during Colin's stay.

My feelings of reassurance made the shock the greater when I realized that the man in the bowler hat was not a private detective, but a nurse attendant.

I had waved to Colin as the car drew up. Colin, in his seat behind the chauffeur, had leaned forward and waved back. But before I could reach the car, things happened quickly, and the whole pitiful truth revealed itself.

The man in the bowler hat jumped out almost before the car had stopped, and pulled two crutches from beneath the seats: rubber-ferruled crutches with elbow supports. The chauffeur climbed smartly out: hurried round to help, and the two men, clearly well accustomed to their duties, almost lifted Colin from his seat.

Waving the crutches impatiently aside, he stood stiffly and painfully, supporting himself against the door of the car, as he took my hand and shook it warmly. Then the crutches were placed in position and I stood helplessly by as Colin struggled slowly up the steps, the nurse and chauffeur close beside him to save him from mishap.

When he was at last made comfortable by the drawing-room fire, and Amy was serving tea, I had a private word with the nurse while the luggage was brought in.

'We had prepared a room for Lord Colindale on the first floor,' I said; 'the room that he has always had on previous visits. But there is one downstairs, quite a nice room facing the park, that might be more convenient.'

'I'm sure that Lord Colindale would appreciate it,' replied the nurse. 'Stairs are very difficult for him.'

There was a hasty conference with Fred and Amy: running about with bedclothes, towels and hot-water bottles, and by the time tea was finished the downstairs room was ready for our guest, who went to rest for an hour before dinner.

Alone in the drawing-room, I sadly reconsidered the plans I had made for Colin's entertainment. There was to have been billiards after dinner, because Colin had always enjoyed a game on his visits in the past. But billiards was obviously out of the question. All that remained was cards and television: possibly a game of chess. There were not many card games for two players: I could not remember whether Colin played chess, and a glance at the television programme offered a choice between boxing and music hall.

But these problems were of little account beside the shattering discovery of Colin's condition. If he had been a frail and delicate man by nature the tragedy would have been far less, but his robust physique and exuberant energy were almost a legend. In television newsreels he never went up steps at less than two at a time, cartoonists drew him as a strong man lifting enormous weights: as a giant striding through the labyrinth of politics, head and shoulders taller than Big Ben – and there he was lying – a pitiful wreck – in the twilit bedroom down the passage. He had barely mentioned his infirmity when he had arrived: 'I suppose I ought to have told you about this,' he had said. 'But there's nothing to be done, so let's forget it', and with an impatient gesture it was dismissed.

He had grown much stouter since I had last seen him on television more than a year ago: no doubt from lack of exercise. His cheeks were pouched and heavily flushed. My first impression was that he had had a stroke, but his eyes, though tired and haggard, had all their old command, and his voice was strong and clear. More probably, I thought, a collapse through overwork. He had always driven himself with ruthless energy, but now it was pitifully clear that he had driven himself beyond the point of no return.

As things turned out, I need not have worried about Colin's entertainment, for at dinner, with the distasteful crutches pushed away in a corner, he became his old exuberant self again. He was enthusiastic about Amy's excellent cooking and he praised the claret that Fred had carefully decanted. His cheerfulness, at times, seemed forced and artificial, but there was no doubt about his pleasure at being once more in the surroundings that he had enjoyed so much in days gone by.

He asked me a hundred questions about the farm: what crops I grew; what stock I reared; the costs; the marketing and profits. He wanted to know how I passed my leisure time: my hobbies and interests in every side of country life.

At first I imagined that Colin was asking all these questions to keep the conversation away from his own affairs because he had never shown much concern for such things in the past, but gradually I began to see that he was genuinely and deeply interested. He listened intently to everything I had to say, and came back with new and searching questions, some of which were rather beyond the capacity of an amateur farmer.

It was only later when the crutches had been recovered from their corner, and the slow and painful journey back to the drawing-room completed, that Colin began at last to talk about himself, and of the calamity that had overtaken him.

'These things don't just happen,' he said. 'They don't just drop suddenly out of a blue sky. I imagine it all began at school, when I grew a head taller and a stone heavier than I ought to have done for my age: playing rugger for the school at fifteen: boxing heavyweight at sixteen: doing weight-lifting in my spare time to show off. Naturally I showed off, because I was proud of being big and strong.

'In my last year at school I went down with rheumatic fever. They didn't know much about such things in those days. The doctor put it down to a chill, hanging about in wet clothes after rugger, but of course I had outgrown my strength and was paying for it, I should have taken things easy at least till I was twenty-one, but

I was back on the rugger field in a month and playing as hard as ever.

'I got a blue at Cambridge, but it was a hard fight because even a small injury would leave me stiff for days when a fellow of my age should have thrown it off by the morning. There were plenty of red lights, but I never saw them. I don't imagine we do at that age.

'But everything seemed to clear up and I was all right for years: strong as a horse. You know that from the climbing we used to do in Cumberland.

'It wasn't until the war that it began to catch up on me. I was working eighteen hours a day, travelling all over the place under the worst conditions. I began to get pains in the back and legs. I fought it off in one way or another and kept quiet about it because I was the strong man of the team and it wasn't in the rules for me to go sick.

'Things went on like that for years. I didn't get better and I didn't get worse until last spring – when I went down with a bad dose of 'flu.

'I was in bed for a couple of weeks – and when I tried to get up I felt as if somebody had rammed a couple of rusty iron bars down my leg bones and another down my spine.

'I thought it was just the after effects of 'flu. I'd had it before, but not so bad, and I tried my usual remedies. But this time they didn't work – and the irony of the whole thing was that just before it had happened the Prime Minister had told me that if we won the next election he was going to set up a new Ministry and put me at the head of it. It was what I had hoped for all my life: a brand-new Ministry starting from scratch: an exciting job that was right up my street.

'When I hobbled in to see the Prime Minister after that attack, he gave me a lecture about working too hard and told me to take it easy till I was well again. There were nearly two years to go before the election, and I hadn't a doubt that I'd be right again by then.

'That's when I faded out of the news. I set about my plans for beating this damn thing like organizing a campaign. I had the money and I reckoned I could buy a cure. I began with London specialists who gave me shots and filled me up with medicine and plastered me with liniment; I had massage and electric shocks and ray treatment and God knows what else; but after six months I was as bad as I was before I started, if not worse.'

'Did they find the cause?' I asked.

'That was the devil of it,' said Colin. 'If it had been some obscure bug, then one of those brilliant fellows would have run it to earth and got rid of it. But it's just plain common or garden rheumatism: a thing they know everything about except the cure.

'When the London doctors failed I began roaming round the Continent seeing specialists at every Spa in Europe. I drank the waters and had mud baths and more shots and more massage, and after a year of it, I knew I was beaten. It was no good pretending any longer. I just had to face the facts. I saw the Prime Minister last week and told him how things were. I told him not to consider me any longer for the new Ministry after the elections. I said I would have to retire from public life, and that was the end of it.'

There was a silence. Colin moved painfully in his chair and I tried to think of something to say. He had told me the whole tragic story so calmly: with such resignation that anything I said would sound pointless and banal.

'It's your brains and experience they want, Colin, not your legs.'

Colin smiled and shook his head. 'That's what others have said,' he answered. 'But there's a lot more to it than that.

'In the old days a Public man didn't need a colourful personality because the majority of the people never saw him, but in these days of television and newsreels and all the rest of it you've got to establish yourself as a character. People demand it. You've got to play a part, and once they've accepted you in that part, you've got to stick to it. You can't suddenly appear as a new character, any more than a comic actor can suddenly appear as Hamlet or Macbeth.

'The part I had chosen for myself was "strong man", I enjoyed it because it suited me, and people enjoyed watching me play it. I've played it for so many years that it's become a sort of institution: people just couldn't conceive me in any other way. So what do you suppose would happen if they saw the strong man come doddering on to the stage as a cripple? They would be shocked, of course: maybe sympathetic – but they wouldn't want me any more. They'd reckon I was finished: just hanging on for the sake of authority and power.'

'I'm sure they wouldn't think that,' I said. But in my heart I knew that he was right.

'What people think,' went on Colin, 'wouldn't matter so much if it wasn't true, and the truth is I *am* finished – at least for the work the Prime Minister had in mind for me, and that was all that mattered. It would have meant hard travelling: inspections, visits to industrial plants that would have needed all the activity and strength I ever had.'

He was silent for a while. 'I didn't make the decision hastily, Peter. God knows I went on fighting it – even after the doctors said there wasn't any hope. I'm only sixty. I could have reckoned on ten good years and done great things . . . but I'm not going to drown you in self-pity. I've had a good life and been luckier than most men.'

He roused himself and turned to me with a flash of his old vigour and enthusiasm.

'And do you know the luckiest thing that has happened to me since all this started?'

'No?'

'Your letter.'

'My *letter*?' I looked at him in astonishment. 'Honestly, Colin – I hardly expected an answer.'

'I'll tell you something I wouldn't say to anyone else.' He took a cigarette and played with it before he lit it: hesitating as if in second thoughts about what he was going to say.

'You probably won't think much of me when I tell you – but on the night when I told the Prime Minister I had given up, I damn nearly took a bottle of sleeping pills to make an end of it.'

'I can understand how you must have felt, Colin.'

'I wonder if you really can? – You've always had a hundred things to interest you. If one dried up you had plenty to fall back on. But last week, when I gave up politics I suddenly realized that I had nothing: utterly and absolutely nothing – except a couple of crutches and a wheel-chair. If I'd married it might have been different. I had a fine house in London, but it wasn't a home. My whole life had been built around the keystone of being somebody who mattered. The keystone had gone – and everything with it. I knew a thousand people: pretty well everybody who counted for anything, but there wasn't one that I could reckon on as wanting a has-been in a wheel-chair. That's self-pity with a vengeance, Peter! But it's the plain, blunt truth!'

'There's your business,' I said. 'The Colindale Press. That's something to be proud of – and something that needs you.'

'There's that,' replied Colin. 'But it's hard to explain. Big things wear out quicker than small ones. Five years ago when I came back to politics I picked out my best men and put them in charge of my business affairs. They've done a fine job, and between ourselves, if I never went back, the shares of the Colindale Press wouldn't fall by sixpence. I control the policy, but even a thing like that wears out when you've done it for more years than you can count.

'When I got home after handing in my resignation, I lay in bed thinking of life as it was going to be from then on: life on hotel verandas looking into space: life on the decks of cruising liners looking at the sea – always somebody in the background whispering to friends: "You know who that is? – poor chap – quite a tragedy." The only friend I had that night was my bottle of sleeping pills: nearly full: a new bottle. I began to consider whether I'd chew them up or swallow them whole: whether I'd wash them down with water or brandy. I was still considering the most effective technique when I dozed off – and when I woke up, there was my man by the bedside with my morning tea – and your letter on the tray.'

'I'm glad,' I said, rather lamely, because for the life of me I couldn't see what use my letter could have been.

But Colin was warming up. 'It came like a breath of fresh air, Peter, a revelation! – a new lease of life! I was amazed that I had never thought of it before! I never had a place in the country: never had time for it – but I love the country, even though I know nothing of farming or country life. You see now why I bombarded you with all those questions at dinner?'

I began to see – and was glad to have something constructive to talk about: something I understood so well myself.

'Do you know of a nice place round here?' asked Colin. 'I always liked this part – ever since I first came to stay with you.'

'I'm certain we could find something,' I said. 'Farrell would know. He's the Estate Agent in St Mary's. I'll go down and see him in the morning.'

'I could have a special car built for getting around in,' said Colin, 'a good bailiff and staff. I'd breed stock; grow fruit; try out methods of crop growing. I might even run a small research organization of my own.'

He was glowing with enthusiasm. Politics; newspapers; even his infirmity was forgotten.

'And the joy of it,' he said, 'will be the clean break into something I've never done before! New things to learn! Back to school again! By next summer I'll be wondering why I was fool enough to waste all those years on politics!'

The nurse came in to remind his master that it was past his bedtime: doctor's orders. But Colin waved him away and told him to come back in an hour's time. 'I'm a farmer now!' he said. 'Farmers don't need doctors to tell them when to go to bed!'

It was past midnight before Colin went to his room.

I stood in the hall, watching him struggle painfully down the passage with the nurse beside him. There was something very pathetic in the way he drew his shoulders back and tried to hold himself upright, and I felt more pity for him at that moment than at any time since he had arrived.

I had shown all the enthusiasm I could for his brave defiant plans to start a new life in the country, but in my heart I could not bring myself to believe that it could possibly succeed.

Long years of experience had told me that the men who succeeded on the land were those of infinite patience and immune to disappointment: deliberate, calculating men who ploughed in a ruined crop to fertilize the land for another year and planted young trees to protect a windswept meadow for their grandsons.

But patience was one of the virtues that Colin had never had, and disappointment, to him, was proof of failure. If he spent enough money and hired the best men he would expect success, and nothing but success – and things just didn't happen that way in farming. I dreaded to think of Colin's reaction to the inevitable disillusionment that lay ahead, but I was resolved to do all that lay in my power to help him: if only to stave off to the last possible moment the final tragedy of his disillusionment.

# Chapter Two

Early next morning I drove into St Mary's to see Farrell, the Estate Agent.

I told him that a friend of mine was looking for a nice property with about 500 acres of good land suitable for mixed farming. Without divulging Colin's name, I hinted that expense would not be a major consideration and that funds would no doubt be available for renovations and rebuilding if the property demanded it.

Mr Farrell was extremely interested. Enquiries of this kind rarely came his way, because most people nowadays were looking for small places with a minimum of upkeep. Several nice properties were available: some vacant and ready for immediate occupation: others still occupied by owners who would gladly move out upon completion of the purchase.

In some cases illustrated booklets were available: in others the particulars were typewritten. I selected half a dozen that seemed most promising and drove back to the Manor House.

Colin was sitting on the terrace with a rug around his knees, waiting impatiently for news, and was delighted to hear that so many interesting possibilities were open to him.

'I'd like a house with some character and history to it,' he said. 'If it's in bad repair all the better. I'll enjoy having it restored by a good architect, and maybe I'd open it to the public for a couple of days a week.'

From what I knew of several big houses in the neighbourhood I felt reasonably sure that Colin would have no difficulty in finding a place in bad repair. I suggested a quiet morning discussing the various properties that the Estate Agent had suggested, then a drive round to look at them in the afternoon, but Colin was bursting to get going, so I told Amy to pack a picnic lunch and we were off by eleven o'clock.

To avoid attracting attention Colin decided to leave his big car in the stables and travel in my old station wagon. It wasn't built for comfort: much less for cripples, but with the help of some cushions for his back and a hassock for his feet, we made him reasonably comfortable.

It was a lovely spring morning, and we were soon back in the past again, reminding one another of the tours we had made together in the days before the War. Colin was buoyantly happy, and declared that he would be content to spend the rest of his life ambling through the country lanes in a station wagon.

I had not had time to look for the various properties on my map and plan a methodical tour, so we drove here and there, covering more miles than we needed, spinning it out to make a leisurely day of it.

To save Colin getting out of the car we examined the properties through binoculars from various vantage points. I knew most of the houses fairly well: I had known some of the past owners and visited them, so was able to give Colin a certain amount of information beyond the range of the glasses.

After the first few inspections, Colin's enthusiasm began to wane. Most of the houses were vast in size: uglified by Victorian extensions, and some of the land was dull and featureless: scarred with the remnants of wartime camps or the runways of deserted airfields. In some cases the timber had been ruthlessly cleared to replenish the waning incomes of owners who had not troubled to replant, or even to remove the forlorn, upturned roots. Everywhere we saw overgrown spinneys and gardens choked with weeds.

Colin cheered up at lunch, when we ate our sandwiches and drank a bottle of wine in a pleasant wood beside the road. It brought back, he said, happy memories of the past. Too many, I thought, as I began to feel that he was deliberately raking up these memories to avoid the distasteful business of discussing the houses he had seen. He wasn't good at concealing his thoughts, and it was plain that he was disappointed. I could scarcely wonder at it, for how he would pass the long winter evenings in a ghostly, isolated, rambling country mansion I could not imagine. Yet I dared not contemplate the total collapse of his desperate bid for happiness.

Fortunately the first house we saw after lunch was the best: an attractive Tudor Manor House: not over-big, with well-kept grounds, and a small farm that looked to be in sound condition.

I suggested a closer look on the following day. Colin agreed, but as he was getting very tired and beginning to suffer from his cramped position in the car, I felt it best to cut out the other houses on our list and make for home.

It was five o'clock, and the sun was beginning to go down when the incident happened that was to have such profound effects upon Colin's future and such disastrous ones upon mine.

We had just driven through the old town of St Mary's and were within a few miles of the Manor House when Colin, who was obviously suffering increasing pain from his cramped position, said he would have to get out and stretch his legs to get the circulation back into them.

I drove the car on to the green verge and helped Colin to climb out. We walked together, slowly to and fro. At first he could scarcely move, but gradually the gentle exercise relieved the pain.

We walked as far as a corner where a by-lane branched off towards some distant farm buildings: the country was quiet and deserted, for we were on an old road, rarely used.

At the junction stood a decayed, lop-sided signpost pointing down the lane, but the inscription had been almost obliterated by time and weather.

Colin peered up at it. 'To the Wells of St Mary's,' he read. 'You never told me you had any wells round here?'

'I wouldn't recommend them!' I laughed.

'What are they?' he asked.

'As a matter of fact they belong to me,' I answered. 'A sort of family heirloom.'

Colin was interested, and I told him all I could about them.

Away back in the distant past, somewhere in the thirteenth century, the Nunnery of St Mary's was established here. Judging by the massive walls that still survive, it must have been a place of considerable wealth and importance, and after the dissolution in 1539 the deserted buildings, together with a wide area of the surrounding land, fell into the hands of Emmanuel Joyce who thereby became the founder of our family fortunes.

Emmanuel was a somewhat shifty and disreputable official of the Royal Household who rendered the King good service and received the property in reward. His grandson Evelyn pulled down most of the remaining Nunnery in 1608 to build the Manor House, and for nearly three centuries our family lived in wealth and affluence.

But even after the Nunnery buildings had disappeared the tradition survived that the wells supplying the establishment had miraculous curative powers. It was no doubt the familiar superstition of the 'Holy Wells' that surrounds the remains of many religious buildings of the past, but early in the nineteenth century one of our family tried to cash in on the prevailing boom in medicinal waters. By that time only one of the wells survived, and a strange octagonal building like a dovecot was put up to enclose it. It was advertised in the London newspapers, but St Mary's had none of the attractions of famous Spa towns like Bath and Harrogate, and the venture fizzled out.

The place became derelict and almost forgotten until circumstances made it necessary for us to begin to sell our land. The farms were easily sold, but the site of the ancient Nunnery was a problem. The ruined surrounding walls still remained, enclosing about fifteen acres useless for grazing or cultivation on account of the foundations of the buildings still beneath the soil.

The result, of course, was that the property remained on our hands, but my father, who was then alive, felt that he ought to do something about it.

The ruins were mentioned in the guide-books and always attracted a few tourists in the summer who were free to go into the well house and drink the water if they wanted to. So my father repainted the old sign-board, cleaned the place up and put a man named Henry Hodder in charge.

Henry had worked on our land since he was a boy. He was lazy and too fond of drink to be much use, but instead of discharging him, my father gave him a cottage to live in near the well, and allowed him to keep whatever he could collect from chance visitors in return for looking after the place and keeping the well house clean.

I went in to see him once or twice a year. He was now an old man over seventy, dirtier and blearier than ever, and I never stayed longer than I could help. I never asked how much he collected from visitors, but in the summer it must have been £2 or £3 a week, so with his old-age pension and a free cottage he got along all right.

Colin wasn't greatly interested in all this, and if things had happened in a normal way, that would have been the end of it. We should have got back into the car, driven home to the Manor House and our misfortunes would never have happened.

But it was a fine warm evening. There was time to spare, and as Colin felt much happier outside my car than in it, he suggested walking down the lane to see the well.

I wonder whether Colin himself ever looks back upon that evening, and thinks what that chance visit was to mean to him? Our way was down a narrow rutted lane bordered by hedgerows so rampant and neglected that in places we had to push our way between them. I was annoyed that Henry had allowed them to become so overgrown and decided to send my gardener down to help him cut them. It was hard going for Colin, but when he had made up his mind to do a thing he never gave it up, and luckily we found a fallen tree-trunk to take a rest on.

Nor was it very encouraging when we arrived. There was a weedy cobbled yard with some ramshackle old wooden sheds in it; a small chicken run with a few forlorn hens scratching for fleas and the gaunt, octagonal building that housed the well: an incongruous structure of pale brown brick with a broken slate roof. Upon the closed door of the building hung a tattered piece of paper inscribed:

*WELLS OF ST MARY'S*
Renowed health giving waters.
*Apply at Cottage.*

Colin sat on a bench outside the building while I went off to find Henry.

The old man was digging in his small patch of garden when I arrived, and seemed, at first, resentful at what he took to be a surprise visit to catch him out. But he was willing enough when I told him I had brought a visitor because it meant a fee.

He got the key from his cottage and came down the lane with me to open up the building.

It was damp and musty inside, darkened by the dirty windows and filled with a sickly tomb-like odour. But despite the neglect of recent years there were still signs of the care that had been given to it in the past. The large blocks of polished granite that paved the floor were finely laid and the oak benches round the walls had been carved by a skilled craftsman.

The building had been constructed so that the well should be exactly in the centre, its grey stone parapet, obviously much older than the building, rising about three feet above the pavement.

The spring was evidently still in full vigour, for the water level was considerably above the surrounding pavement and would have overflowed the parapet of the well if an open stone culvert had not carried the surplus water into an ancient stone cistern by the wall. This cistern was of very ancient origin and probably dated back to the days when the Nunnery was built. It was shaped rather like an oval font, and carried a constant running supply of the spring water that poured into it from the well at one end and out at the other by a lead pipe through the wall of the building and down a drain.

Except for the surrounding oak benches there was nothing in the building beyond a large cheap china jug and a thick glass tumbler that stood on a dusty window-sill.

Henry looked up at the cobwebbed roof and began to recite some stuff which he had no doubt learnt by heart, but constant repetition over the years had made it almost unintelligible.

It was obviously something to do with the history of the well and a description of its beneficial waters, for when it was over, the old man took the china jug off the window-sill, filled it from the cistern and poured a glass for Colin.

Colin looked at it distastefully. He had drunk in the luxurious surroundings of the famous Spas of Europe and was not likely to enjoy the waters of St Mary's from a dirty glass.

'It's all right,' he said. 'I won't bother about the water. I just came along to see what the place looked like.'

Henry was hurt. Apparently it was part of the routine for visitors to drink a glass before they left, and he no doubt thought that Colin was refusing in order to avoid the fee. 'The waters are renowned, sir,' he said.

'What for?' asked Colin.

Henry was caught. My father had evidently omitted to pass this information on to him and he had no answer. The best he could do was to begin chanting his stuff all over again, but I cut him short by saying I would try a glass of the water myself. I had not drunk from the well since I was a boy, when I used to come here with friends to play among the ruins.

The first taste was unpleasant. It had a flat, metallic flavour: slightly fishy, with a vague suggestion of garlic. It had a brownish tinge, but it was cool and obviously fresh because it was constantly running, and after the first reaction, I rather enjoyed it.

'You ought to try it,' I said. 'It really isn't bad. Not bad at all.'

And so it came about that because Colin was thirsty from the wine we had drunk at lunch he took a full glass of the water, and another half glass because the flavour intrigued him. 'There's something about it that reminds me of the Karlsbad waters,' he said. 'And something of Vichy – but it's softer than the Continental springs. I would say there's a good deal of the sulphates in it.'

The sun had set. It was twilight outside, but the gloomy building was almost dark. It was eerie and ghostly, with no sound but the steady trickle and splash of the water as it ran down the gully from the well.

We went out and Henry locked the door and said: 'Goodnight.' He was astonished when Colin gave him a ten-shilling note. I imagine he had never had more than a shilling from a visitor in his life, and he was so moved that he took off his greasy cap and said: 'God bless you, sir.'

Colin was exhausted by the long day and could scarcely drag himself up the steps into the house.

His nurse was waiting to help him to his room, and half an hour later came out, very worried, to ask me whether there was a doctor who could be called at short notice, if required.

'Lord Colindale is not at all well,' he said. 'I am afraid he has done far more today than he should have done.'

He looked at me as if it were my fault, and no doubt, to some extent, it was. I should have persuaded Colin against the rough walk to the well, and brought him straight home when he was so obviously tired. I said that Dr Nugent was the best man in St Mary's, and that I would telephone him at once if the need became urgent.

'Lord Colindale is a heavy man,' explained the nurse. 'The strain of walking taxes his heart. The doctors had warned him to take great care.'

The nurse was inclined to be arrogant and possessive. He annoyed me when he tried to prevent me from going in to see his master, and I had to remind him that I had known Lord Colindale for nearly fifty years. 'Considerably longer,' I said, 'than you and his present doctors have known him.'

Colin was lying on his bed in his dressing-gown. He certainly looked very tired. He had a hectic flush and his breathing was bad, but he contemptuously waved aside my suggestion that he should have his supper in bed.

'Craddock fusses,' he said. 'He's a good man, but he's fussing all the time ... never happy unless I'm ill. All I want is a good glass of that excellent claret of yours ... and a brandy and soda afterwards.'

Colin knew better what was good for him than the nurse did. He brightened up after a glass of wine and ate a good dinner, but I watched him anxiously, ready to hurry out to the telephone in the hall if the doctor was needed. Will-power alone kept him going that evening: a feverish burst of conversation was followed by an exhausted silence. Little was said about the houses we had seen. I tried to persuade myself that his lack of interest came from his exhaustion, but I had a nagging fear that the whole thing was over, that the desolate houses we had seen that day had destroyed his impulsive ambition for a country life. When I reminded him that we would take a second look at Kingleigh Manor next morning, he scarcely answered, and changed the subject.

I dared not imagine what the rest of the long week-end would be like, now that the chief purpose of Colin's visit had proved a failure, and I felt sure that his alarming condition of weakness was in some part due to his disillusionment and disappointment.

Much as I liked him, I began to count the hours that remained until he would leave on Tuesday morning.

We watched television after dinner, but he fell into a heavy, unnatural sleep and was still sleeping an hour later when the nurse came to help him to his bed. I remember the relief I felt when he woke up, because he had snored so hard that I had feared it might have been the prelude to a stroke or heart attack.

I scarcely slept a wink that night. I heard the nurse go several times to Colin's bedroom, and I could not rid my thoughts of the tragedy that faced my old friend now that his last, forlorn endeavour had ended in such failure.

# Chapter Three

It was my habit, in the spring, to do an hour's gardening before breakfast and, on the next morning, still tired and heavy-eyed from a sleepless night, I was working in the rose garden when Fred the butler came hurrying down the pathway from the house.

My concern for Colin's health was now so great that anything unusual was bound to fill me with foreboding. I waited with my heart in my mouth, dreading the news that Fred might bring, for in all his years at the Manor House he had never come out into the garden to see me before breakfast. Was it the dreaded overdose of sleeping pills? – a heart attack? – a stroke? – I felt almost sure that Colin had been found dead in bed.

Fred was disturbed and out of breath. 'The nurse has sent a message, sir ... from Lord Colindale. Will you kindly go to his bedroom at once.'

'What's happened?'

'I don't know, sir.'

'I'll come.'

It was a relief at least to know that Colin wasn't dead. But if he were seriously ill ... All manner of problems ran through my mind as I hurried to the house. The local hospital was small and not very well equipped. It would mean getting Colin to Chelmsford – fifteen miles away. If he couldn't be moved, we had no facilities in the house for the care of such a distinguished invalid.

To my great surprise Colin was sitting on the edge of his bed, in pyjamas and slippers, with a strange look in his eyes: a sort of dazed excitement.

'Look!' he said – and he slowly stretched one leg to its full extent, then gently drew it back, bending the knee until his foot was against the bed.

'And look at this!' Like a child proudly showing off its toes, he carefully stretched the other leg until it was nearly straight, then drew it back and lowered his foot to the ground as if it were made of fragile china. When this was done he looked down with a kind of incredulous wonderment, as if doubting whether the legs that had just moved were in fact his own.

It took time for me to adjust my mind to a scene so totally unexpected. I had been prepared to find Colin prostrate, labouring for breath, or inert and helpless from a paralytic stroke. My first reaction was that something even worse had happened: that Colin had had a complete mental breakdown, and had become like a child.

But he was talking: whether to me or to himself or to his nurse was not quite clear, for he stared in front of him with a vague, faraway look in his eyes.

'I knew something was happening,' he said. 'It had just gone three. I heard the clock strike in the hall. It was time to turn over on to my left side and I prepared myself for the wrenching pain of it. But when I moved . . . I drew my knees up . . . quite easily . . . I thought I was dreaming. It's always that kind of dream: running but scarcely touching the ground; jumping and floating on and on. I went to sleep believing that I'd wake as I always do . . . the dream over.'

He looked at me and spoke with a strange humility, quite unlike his usual self.

'But it wasn't a dream!'

And once more he repeated the movement of his legs.

'Eighteen months,' he said . . . 'eighteen months since I could bend my knees like that!'

There was a silence. I was still trying to collect my scattered thoughts. Colin looked up at his nurse, nodded a curt dismissal and turning again to me spoke almost furtively:

'Do you think it could have been that water?'

In my anxiety of the previous evening I had forgotten all about the water we had drunk at the well. I could scarcely believe that the water from our obscure and humble well could touch a deeply rooted infirmity that had defied the most distinguished doctors and famous Spas of Europe. I replied cautiously, fearful of raising false hopes but careful not to destroy any seeds of faith that might be germinating.

'It's been known for centuries as a curative spring,' I said. 'I don't think the tradition would have survived so long if there hadn't been something in it.'

Colin began asking searching questions. He wanted to know everything possible about the well: its origins; when its curative waters were first recorded; the nature of the water; its analysis and source – and so on. I could tell him little beyond what I had told him on the previous evening. As a family we had never taken the well seriously, and personally I had never bothered to go into its history, but I promised to find out all I could.

After breakfast Colin wanted to go back to the well. He was burning to get back: he could scarcely contain himself. But with all his impatience he was anxious to avoid making a scene or doing anything that might lead to unwanted publicity.

'That old man,' he said. 'That old caretaker ... can you get rid of him? – I don't want him hanging about – telling stories round the town.'

Henry was easily disposed of. When we got to the well I went up to the cottage and told him that my friend was interested in historical buildings and wanted to study the well house at leisure. There was a spare key which I promised to return when my friend had finished his studies.

Henry looked bleary and smelt strongly of liquor: a condition no doubt connected with the ten-shilling note of the previous evening, but he gladly surrendered the spare key in hopes of further handsome tips, and we didn't see him again during Colin's visits, although Colin sent him a pound note when he left.

27

Alone with me in the ghostly, twilit building Colin began to take stock of things with his usual thoroughness. His first exultant excitement had given place to a suppressed, tormenting anxiety. Was it a mere coincidence? – A mere stroke of chance? – Or could it possibly have been the water? He was disappointed, on arriving, to find himself as stiff as ever. He could barely move when he got out of the car, but I tried to reassure him by saying that he was bound to feel a reaction after bending his knees fully for the first time in over a year.

It was a slow and painful struggle up the lane, but once inside the well house Colin began to revive. He took the jug from the window-ledge, washed it and dried it with his handkerchief and drank a full glass of the water.

He made a careful inspection of the well and its surroundings. Although the house was fairly modern, there was no doubt of the antiquity of the well itself and the paving surrounding it. The stonework was beautifully tooled and fitted, though scarred by age and thickly covered with moss and lichen. The open culvert that carried the water from the well to the stone trough, and the trough itself were, in Colin's opinion, mediaeval, possibly twelfth century, but the heavy paving slabs appeared to be of later date.

'If I were to make a guess,' said Colin, 'I'd say that it's the work of half a dozen different periods. Various people from time to time have rescued the well from neglect and built things up again.'

After an hour's rest and discussion about the well, Colin took another glass of the water and filled his thermos flask with sufficient to provide a drink for the evening and first thing next morning.

We drove back to the Manor House for lunch. In the afternoon Colin went to his room to rest and I drove down to St Mary's to find out what I could about the well from Mr Philpot, the Town librarian, who was by way of being a local historian.

At Colin's request I did not mention his name, merely telling the librarian I had taken a friend to see the well, and that he was interested in its history.

Mr Philpot was pleased to tell me all he could.

'The Romans were no doubt the first people to make use of the spring,' he said. 'The military highway from London to Norwich passed close by, and they established a camp or posting station there to take advantage of a good supply of water. The ancient earthworks surrounding the camp are still to be seen.

'Nothing more is known of the wells until the thirteenth century when the Nunnery of St Mary's was built on the site of the Roman settlement, no doubt to take advantage, as the Romans had done, of the good spring water.

'It was one of the foremost establishments in England of the Franciscan Order,' said Mr Philpot. 'It flourished for more than two hundred years, and by the time of the disestablishment the water of the wells appears to have attained some reason for its curative value, because contemporary manuscripts refer to distinguished visitors coming long distances to drink it.'

With the disappearance of the Nunnery, the wells again fell into disuse, and Mr Philpot had been able to discover no further reference to them until 1825, when my great-grandfather Oswald Joyce, inspired no doubt by the popularity of the wells at Droitwich and Buxton, had built the well house and made his effort to exploit the water.

'By that time,' said the librarian, 'only one of the wells existed: the one that remains today. By tradition it stood in the outer courtyard of the Nunnery and was used by visiting pilgrims who came to seek their health from it.'

The rest, of course, I knew. Mr Philpot had told me nothing of great interest, but one significant point came out when I asked him whether there was any evidence to show that the Romans had sunk the well.

'Certainly,' said Mr Philpot. 'The most conclusive evidence, because when the well was cleaned out in 1825, the workmen discovered a large number of Roman coins at the bottom of it. They were mainly silver denarii, but types that spanned a very long period, from the Emperor Hadrian almost up to the close of the Roman occupation at the end of the fourth century.'

'Suggesting,' I said, 'that the well was held in high esteem by the

Romans, who made votive offerings in gratitude for being cured by the water?'

'Possibly,' replied the librarian. 'More probably because the spring was dedicated to the god who protected travellers. People would throw in their offering as thanks for a safe journey, or in anticipation of a hazardous journey to come.'

'Are there any known cases of people being cured of anything?' I asked.

The librarian laughed. 'The only people who drink the water nowadays,' he said, 'are young men on bicycling tours who call out of curiosity, or hikers and occasional motorists. Henry gives them a glass of the water as part of the routine, but whether it cures them or what it cures them of, I don't know – because they continue on their travels and never come back.'

'Nobody in the town has ever taken it?'

'Nobody that I've ever heard of,' replied Mr Philpot. 'I doubt whether people ever do drink medicinal waters in their own towns. They only seem to cure people who come long distances to get them.'

I thanked the librarian and drove back to the Manor House.

Colin listened keenly to what I had to tell him. He was very pleased about the find of the Roman coins because to him it was proof that the Romans had gained such benefit from the waters that they thought it worth paying for in cash. 'The Romans were astute people,' he said. 'They wouldn't have paid like that unless they had got their money's worth.'

I think what pleased him most was the news that nobody in recent times had taken the waters seriously, that nobody had attempted a methodical 'cure', by drinking the waters every day. He saw himself as the discoverer of a priceless but long-lost treasure. Had I produced evidence of recent dramatic cures he would not have been so excited, because Colin would have disliked the idea of merely being one of a crowd. It appealed to his sense of drama, and his personal vanity was stimulated by the thought that this remarkable discovery should have been made by him, and by him alone.

But these reactions came gradually: only in fact when his steady improvement had assured him beyond doubt that it was a genuine recovery, and not merely a temporary relief that he had sometimes experienced in the past.

During the first few days he was subdued, almost humble: He was keeping his fingers crossed, touching wood, scarcely daring to breathe a word about his improvement for fear that a word of over-confidence might break the magic spell. And there were moments of bitter heartbreak and disappointment. On rising from a period of rest, his legs and back were acutely painful, more so than at any time during his long illness. But as time went on he began to understand that this was the natural result of bringing long disused muscles into play again.

We followed a regular routine. At eleven o'clock every morning we drove down to the well house and Colin would take a full glass of the water which he drank slowly as if he were savouring a rare vintage wine. After lunch he rested on his bed, and at six o'clock we returned to the well so that he could take another glass and fill his thermos flask to provide a drink at bedtime and another first thing in the morning. I suggested that we might take a more attractive jug and glass with us from the Manor House, but Colin stuck to the old thick tumbler and cracked china jug that he had used on his first visit as if these themselves must also hold some magic properties.

He had already telephoned to his London home, saying that he was extending his stay with me indefinitely, but he gave no hint of the true reason for it. Every morning he had long telephone conversations with his office concerning his newspapers, and sometimes the editors would call him in the evenings for their instructions.

For the first ten days his progress was slow and painful, with some nerve-racking setbacks. I was still very doubtful whether the well water really had anything to do with what happened. It was a case of familiarity courting contempt because to my family the Nunnery ruins and the well itself had always been a tiresome nuisance or a mild joke. I couldn't honestly bring myself to believe that the water was any good. It seemed more likely that a chance improvement in Colin's condition had come by a mere coincidence on the morning after he had first drank the water and that faith had done the rest, and because I could not convince myself that faith alone could possibly effect a total cure, I lived in a state of acute suspense: waiting for the tragic day of relapse.

But during the third week his improvement became so rapid, so truly astonishing that I could no longer doubt the miraculous powers of our obscure and humble well. As movement became easier Colin's fine constitution began to play its part. One morning he walked in to breakfast without his crutches, a few days later he was playing croquet, and by the end of the fourth week he was walking with me around my farm; even climbing the hill crest for a view of the sea.

I noticed that as his condition steadily improved, his interest in taking a country estate gradually waned and finally disappeared. I knew of course the reason. With his health restored nothing stood in the way of his return to public life, and that, to Colin, was the breath of life itself.

In all he stayed five weeks with me, but during the final week he was as strong and as well as he had ever been. It was simply a case of making assurance doubly sure. He never ceased in his routine of taking the waters.

On the night before he left for London he made, what I felt at the time, a strange request. He asked me to promise on my word of honour not to say a word about what had happened to anybody: not even to my fellow Councillors at St Mary's.

He was so earnest and insistent that I had to give my promise, though I must admit that I considered it ungrateful of him and very selfish.

He had told me on the night of his arrival that he had kept his infirmity a secret from the public to avoid destroying their conception of him as the 'strong man'. He would probably cook up some romantic explanation for his temporary disappearance, and so preserve the legend that his physical powers were unassailable.

In other words, it seemed that the rest of suffering humanity was to be denied the miraculous waters of our well to satisfy the vanity of Lord Colindale. It was to be his well and nobody else's.

I discovered later that he had even given Fred and Amy a handsome present as a bribe for their silence.

I could scarcely conceal my indignation and disgust when he sent his chauffeur into St Mary's to buy a dozen large bottles of beer, which were emptied and cleaned and filled with the well water to provide his daily dose on returning to London. He even had the nerve to say that his chaffeur would drive down once a week to have them refilled.

He departed after lunch on the Monday of the sixth week of his stay with me. The luggage compartment of his car was packed with bottles.

He was so excited about the surprise in store for his London friends that I doubt whether he even noticed the coolness of my farewell.

He had incurred a telephone bill running into several pounds, had drunk the best of my remaining wine and barely said 'thank you' as he stepped jauntily into his car and drove away.

I was left to ponder, sadly and bitterly, why Colin's ruthless ambition and lust for power had destroyed all sense of courtesy and gratitude.

# Chapter Four

As the days went by without even a brief note of thanks I began to fume with indignation at Colin's extraordinary behaviour. In the past, even after a short week-end visit, he never failed to ring up or drop a line, and it was almost beyond belief that a man could ignore without a word of acknowledgement a five-week holiday that had so miraculously restored his health.

I have never been a man to nurse a grievance, but it began to rankle so much that I lay awake for hours at night, thinking out the stinging letter that I would write, telling him plainly what I thought of him. I had come to the firm conviction that Colin was so obsessed with the national importance of his return to public life that the cause of it was now a matter of complete indifference to him – his only concern was to conceal from the public that the 'strong man' had ever been ill at all.

Towards the end of the week I could stand it no longer and began to put my letter on paper. I stressed his selfishness in asking me to keep secret a discovery that might bring such lasting benefits to the people of St Mary's. It was a poor town, I told him, with no modern industries to support it, and the news of a remarkable cure, specially of a man so famous, was bound to attract visitors to the advantage of our trades-people.

I ended by saying that I considered it his moral duty to release me from my promise of secrecy, and that if he refused, I would consider it my own duty to ignore my promise on account of my obligations to the people of the town.

It was a tricky letter to write because I didn't want to suggest that I was using the townspeople merely as a cloak to cover a selfish desire to cash in on the well myself. I wrote several drafts and tore them up, and the unfinished letter was still on my desk when the event happened that was to change the fortunes of St Mary's beyond my wildest imaginings.

I shall never forget that extraordinary, chaotic Saturday. It began so camly and peacefully: just another ordinary, routine day at the Manor House.

It was a fine morning in early April, the sun was warm and I was sitting on the terrace reading my paper after breakfast.

We took two morning newspapers: *The Times* and the *Daily Gazette*. It was customary for Fred and Amy to have the *Gazette* while I took *The Times*, and Fred used to bring the *Gazette* into my library during the morning so that I could glance through it before lunch. It was one of the Colindale papers, and had the sensational, racy flavour about it that characterized Colin himself and had given it such a wide circulation.

But on this memorable Saturday morning the *Gazette* was not destined to appear on my library table in the usual way, because Fred suddenly appeared with it on the terrace, in great excitement.

'Look at this, sir!' he exclaimed, and held up the leader page to show me an enormous headline inscribed: 'THE WELLS OF ST MARY'S'.

On first sight I could scarcely believe it. It seemed unreal, fantastic for the name of our obscure, almost forgotten town to appear in huge capital letters, and when I had recovered from my astonishment I began to read what must surely be one of the most sensational personal testaments ever written by a famous public man. It occupied the whole leader page, and I discovered later that it was published simultaneously in every provincial paper under Colin's control.

I will not repeat it here in detail, for a framed copy hangs today in the entrance lobby of the town hall.

It began by revealing for the first time the secret of Colin's mysterious, unexplained disappearance from public life: how, at the height of his career, he had been stricken, and become a helpless cripple. With surprising frankness he described his dread of appearing publicly in a condition that would have shattered the tradition of his physical strength: how he had hidden himself and lived in isolation and seclusion during his desperate fight to regain his health. He described his fruitless journeys to the Spas of Europe; his endless treatments and visits to specialists.

He described in moving terms his feelings upon the day when he had seen the Prime Minister and told him of his enforced retirement from public life; the end of a hopeless struggle and the desolate prospect that lay ahead. He even mentioned his thoughts of suicide, and how the letter 'from an old boyhood friend' had arrived, as it were, like a message from providence.

Then followed, in dramatic detail, an account of his visit to the Manor House and the events that led to our walk that evening to the well. He described in vivid words the miraculous results: how day by day his strength and vigour had been restored to him.

'It has been left,' he said, 'to the waters of an ancient spring in the heart of the English countryside to achieve what the greatest specialists and the most famous Spas of Europe found impossible; to the small, forgotten town of St Mary's in Suffolk I owe a debt of gratitude that can never be repaid.'

It was a fine piece of sensational journalism, but its most impressive feature was the genuine feeling and deep sincerity that lay beneath it.

Other factors added to its significance and made a deeper impression upon the public mind. In the course of his long and successful career as a newspaper proprietor, Colin had never before published an article from his own pen with a facsimile of his signature beneath it.

There were two photographs to confirm the authenticity of the miraculous cure. One showed Lord Colindale as he was before his visit to St Mary's: a tragic, stooping wreck of a man, hobbling on crutches towards a waiting car (a photograph previously suppressed); the other showed him on his return from St Mary's; a fine, upright figure, the embodiment of exuberant health as he stood on the steps of his London home.

As I read the article Fred stood by, beaming with pleasure because Colin had mentioned 'my friend's butler' and it was the nearest approach that Fred had ever made to appearing in print. But the old man hadn't the remotest conception of what it was all to lead to. He merely thought it was nice of Lord Colindale to write so gratefully about his visit; and nice to see St Mary's in the news for once, because the town was hardly ever mentioned in the big London papers – the last time being about ten years ago when somebody had reported a flying saucer passing over the recreation ground.

It is difficult to set down my own first reactions to the extraordinary article. At first I was fearful lest my own name and home were advertised, for I led a quiet life and disliked publicity of any sort. But Colin had tactfully avoided this, and referred to me throughout as 'my old friend' and my house as 'the quiet and peaceful Manor'.

When I had finished the article I sat for some while in uneasy and uncertain thought.

I saw now, of course, why Colin had been so insistent in keeping secret his visit and miraculous cure.

Had he allowed me to tell my friends on the Town Council, then the news would almost certainly have reached our local newspaper and appeared in garbled form. It might have aroused some interest with the London papers, but it would have trickled out and gone off at half-cock. It would have had nothing like the impact of Colin's own statement, and knowing what would have happened, he had taken this deliberate course to repay St Mary's in a big way. Also, no doubt, to herald his return to public life with that flair for melodrama for which he was renowned.

But how could it affect St Mary's? It was impossible to say. I don't suppose even Colin would have hazarded a guess. I only knew that something was bound to happen and I did not have long to wait.

I had scarcely finished reading the article when the phone began to ring, and Amy came hurrying out to say that the Town Clerk wanted to speak to me on the telephone.

The Town Clerk was breathless and almost incoherent. Had I read the *Daily Gazette*? He had guessed that the 'old friend' referred to by Lord Colindale was me, because rumour had gone round the town that an important person had been staying at the Manor House, and he knew, of course, that the well was mine.

He called up to say that the Mayor had demanded an urgent meeting of the Town Council. Could I come at once?

Looking back upon that morning, with the knowledge of everything that has since happened, I suppose I replied rather stupidly to the excited Town Clerk. But in the quiet routine of country life we move at a leisured pace: I dislike panic and excitement: a meeting of the Town Council would obviously be needed to consider means of taking advantage of the tremendous advertisement that Colin had given to the town, but it seemed to me most undesirable to plunge into hysterical discussions at a moment's notice.

I began to put this to the Town Clerk. I endeavoured to calm him, suggesting that a meeting at the usual time of eight in the evening would be quite soon enough, and allow us all a few hours to consider things.

But the Town Clerk's voice rose almost to a shout. 'It's the cars!' he cried. 'It's about the cars!'

I had, of course, entirely underestimated the impact of Colin's article. I didn't know what the Town Clerk was talking about. Vaguely I thought he was referring to plans for running cars from the town to take visitors to the well, but I was soon to discover the alarming facts.

My shortest way to the town was along the road that passed the well. It is not the main road and is usually deserted except for an occasional farm wagon or tradesman's van. But that morning I had barely turned out of my drive before I found myself in the traffic. At first the cars were travelling fifty or a hundred yards apart, but after about a mile they began to close up, and long before I reached the by-lane leading to the well I found myself in a solid, hopeless block.

It seemed incredible that Colin's article could bring such quick results, but it was a Saturday, and a fine morning for a run, and it appeared as if everybody owning a car within twenty miles of St Mary's had decided to drive out to see for themselves the miraculous well that had cured the famous Lord Colindale.

I was completely stuck. I could neither go on nor turn back because the road was too narrow for my unwieldy station wagon to swing round. The only thing to do was to drive on to the grass verge and walk on to investigate.

The chaos was indescribable. Hundreds of people had evidently driven into St Mary's to ask the way to the well and had approached from the opposite direction, meeting the incoming traffic more or less head on, and making a solid block for about two miles.

The centre of the chaos was around the by-lane that led to the well house. Some drivers, believing this lane was a way out, had driven down it, only to find themselves in a blind alley from which there was no escape.

Sergeant Allen and two constables of the St Mary's police were doing what they could, but the mess was far beyond them. Impatient drivers, trying to overtake, had found themselves blocked by other impatient drivers overtaking from the opposite direction.

Allen was a good level-headed officer who remained extraordinarily calm in a situation that I'm sure he had never had to cope with before. In an attempt to relieve the pressure he had opened a gate into a stubble field, hoping to get some of the cars into a temporary park, but a big Daimler had stuck in the mud with one wheel in a ditch, completely blocking the entrance.

Most of the visitors had abandoned their cars and were streaming down the by-lane to the well. What it was like down there I dared not think. You could not get more than twenty people at a time into the well house, and they were advancing upon it in hundreds, from all directions. They were all good natured, enjoying the excitement, but that was little comfort to the police.

'The only way out of it,' said Allen, 'is to get right back to where the block begins, and loosen things up by getting the back cars to turn round. But I need half a dozen more men for that.'

Leaving Allen and his two men to work things out as best they could, I set out to walk the rest of my journey into St Mary's. The road was impossible even for a pedestrian, so I took a short cut across country, along the field paths and through the woods. The morning was so lovely and the woods so peaceful that the chaos I had left behind seemed like a disordered dream, but when I arrived in St Mary's I found conditions in the narrow streets worse than those in the country lanes around the well house. Saturday was market day, and distracted farmers were trying to drive sheep and cattle through the mass of cars that continued to converge upon the town from all directions. Some special constables had been called out but it was impossible to organize any kind of oneway traffic at short notice. Motorists had run their cars into side streets and left them to make further blocks while they wandered aimlessly about, asking the best way to the well. The townspeople themselves had made things worse, because everybody with time to spare had come down to the Market Place to watch.

# Chapter Five

Most of the Councillors had arrived when I got to the Town Hall, but anything like a normal meeting was impossible. The windows of the Council Chamber opened directly on to the Market Place, and we could scarcely make ourselves heard above the bellowing of frightened cattle, the shouting of the drivers and the incessant hooting of motorists trying to get through.

The Town Clerk opened the proceedings by reporting what he had already done. Urgent calls had gone out to neighbouring towns for police reinforcements, and Major Digby, the Chief Constable, had telephoned to the Automobile Associations for expert assistance in arranging road diversions and a one-way plan to keep the traffic moving.

The Mayor of St Mary's was Jim Blundell, proprietor of The Coach and Horses, our principal hotel. The Blundells had owned The Coach and Horses for generations and had always played a leading part in town affairs. In the old days when the main road from London to Norwich ran through St Mary's the hotel had been a famous coaching hostelry, but the advent of motoring and the new by-pass had robbed it of its old importance and reduced it to a rather seedy bed-and-breakfast establishment for commercial travellers. But it still remained the centre for local meetings and club dinners, and the bar was always crowded because Jim was a popular host. His father and grandfather had been Mayors of the town before him, and Jim was now in office for his fourth consecutive year.

I can't say I liked Jim Blundell as much as other people did. He was a big fat red-faced man who always looked as if he were bursting through his waistcoat. He was too obviously jovial: too self-assertive and self-assured for my liking. Nature had given him the appearance of a traditional country innkeeper and he played the part with relish.

He annoyed me that morning by suggesting that I had persuaded Lord Colindale to write his sensational article for my own personal advantage: to bring money into my pocket by boosting the waters of the well. I could only reply that the article was as big a surprise to me as it was to him, but I don't think he believed me. He laughed it off, and that was the nearest we ever came to a quarrel, for as time went on my prejudice gave way to admiration for him. He certainly rose to the occasion on that turbulent morning and proved himself as a leader. He was the only man on the Council who grasped the significance of what had happened, and once he had grasped it he never let go.

Most of the Councillors were inclined to think that the whole affair was a seven days' wonder, possibly no more than a weekend wonder. A 'stunt article', they said, in a popular newspaper notorious for its stunts was bound to stir up public curiosity: specially on a fine Saturday morning when everybody with a car would be out for a run. It would no doubt happen again on Sunday if the weather held, but on Monday, when people went back to work, the whole thing would fizzle out and be forgotten. 'A shower of rain or a thunderstorm,' said Mr Sweetman the chemist, 'and the motors will be gone – and all we shall have to do is to clear up the mess they leave behind.' The majority agreed and offered their own reasons for believing that a few days would see the end of it. Tom Cookson the coal merchant reminded the Council of the flying saucer reported over the recreation ground in the summer of 1952. Several journalists had come down and a party of motorists from Colchester had sat up all night watching for it, but in a couple of days the whole thing was dead and forgotten. Another Councillor spoke of the pageant organized by the near-by town of Holcaster to celebrate the ninth centenary of its founding. He mentioned, significantly, that this pageant was also the subject of a 'stunt article' in a popular newspaper. It had brought a considerable crowd to the first performance, but the audience had dwindled to a handful before the week was out, and the town had lost £500.

To all this Jim Blundell scarcely listened. He was far more interested in the noise and excitement outside than he was in the opinions of his fellow Councillors. It was sweet music to his ears and in his ponderous way he was already groping into the future. 'Whether it lasts or not,' he said, 'depends on us. And if I have my way it's damn well *going* to last.'

Jim Blundell had his way, and it did last, but on that first morning I doubt whether he had a glimmering of the things that were going to happen.

Something happened, in fact, very quickly, and it went a long way to discredit those who believed it was only a flash in the pan. We had not been long at our meeting before a secretary came in to tell the Town Clerk that the London representative of an important American Press agency was on the telephone, seeking further information for readers across the Atlantic.

Jim Blundell was delighted. 'If it gets around America,' he said, 'we're made! – The Americans have got the rheumatism *and* the money.'

There was nothing we could do that morning by sitting round a table, so the meeting was adjourned until the following afternoon, and after a cup of coffee the Mayor, the Town Clerk and some of the more active members of the Council set off with me to see what was going on at the well.

It was now almost midday and the chaos was worse than ever. With the roads completely blocked by traffic, people were climbing gates, breaking through hedges, trampling down young crops in their efforts to find a short cut to the well. The more difficult it was to approach the centre of interest, the more they wanted to get there, but when they finally reached the well house they found a long queue waiting to go in, stretching up the by-lane and down the main road. When we tried to force our way through we were assailed by angry shouts to take our places at the end of the queue, so to avoid an unpleasant scene we withdrew into a field and stood watching – helpless to do anything. There was a man selling ice-cream, a gypsy trying to sell baskets, and some enterprising local boys offering what they described as 'St Mary's Water' in old lemonade bottles which they later admitted filling from a near-by duckpond.

Some extra police who had now arrived had managed to drag the ditched Daimler away from the entrance to the stubble field. They had laid down straw from a nearby rick to cover the churned-up mud and were getting some of the cars into the field as a makeshift park. But as fast as they got cars off the road, other cars closed up behind, and nothing was really achieved beyond imprisoning the cars in the field for the rest of the day.

At about one o'clock a television recording-van managed to get through, creating a diversion for the sightseers, who crowded round the interviewer, eager to appear before the camera. A man who had managed to get into the well house for a glass of the water declared that he felt magnificent; absolutely a different person, and an old local woman whom I knew as a cleaner at the school said that the people of St Mary's had always known the waters of the well to be miraculous, which of course was a downright lie considering that the majority didn't even know that it existed.

I saw a man whispering to the interviewer, pointing to us on the fringe of the crowd. He was apparently telling him that the Mayor and the Town Clerk and the owner of the well were on the spot, for he brushed aside the people trying to be interviewed – pushed his way across to us and asked us to come before the camera.

I held back because I didn't feel in a condition to make a public appearance, but Jim Blundell and the Town Clerk were pleased and flattered by the invitation, and I heard Jim booming into the microphone about the ambitious plans that the Council already had in hand.

I was not, however, allowed to escape. Feeling no doubt that the owner of the well was the most interesting person present, the interviewer urged me, almost forced me, to appear. He was an alert young man who knew his job, and by a few adroit questions got from me the whole story of Lord Colindale's visit and the astonishing cure that I had witnessed with my own eyes.

He asked me whether I had previously known of the miraculous properties of the water, and I hesitated before I answered. I didn't want to appear stupid by confessing that the whole thing was a complete surprise to me, so I compromised by telling him about the Roman coins discovered in the well: thank offerings, I suggested, that proved the renown of the waters in ancient times.

'Well, Colonel,' he said, 'it seems as if you've got a gold mine on your hands! What are you going to do with it now?'

It was then that I said what I have lived to regret so bitterly.

'I am going to give it,' I answered, 'to the people of St Mary's.'

It is easy to be wise after the event. I know now that had I kept the well in my own possession, the appalling things that have since happened might have been avoided, but at the time it seemed the only right and proper thing to give it to the town.

My generosity has since been vaunted to the skies, but I've got to be honest about it and put the thing in its proper light.

If I had had a son to succeed me at the Manor House, then of course it would have been my duty to keep the well as part of his inheritance. But I had no heir, and nobody with any claim upon my property.

In my will I had in fact left the Nunnery ruins to the National Trust, but that was merely because of their historic interest.

There was also a good practical reason. If the well was to be a 'gold mine' it would have to be exploited. Money would be needed to develop the property if it was to attract visitors in a big way, and although I had enough to rub along with, I had no cash to spare. It would have meant forming a company and raising money from other people. I am not a business man: far less a company promoter, and I should have got mixed up in things I didn't understand.

It seemed to me at the time a simple and happy solution. I was getting the best of it both ways. I was giving the people of St Mary's a handsome present for which I received a shower of thanks, and was hoping to preserve for myself the quiet, peaceful life that was all that mattered to me. I little knew that it was to bring upon my head a thousand times more trouble and anxiety than I ever dreamed of.

But at least it provided the television people with one of those unexpected, spontaneously dramatic scenes that they always hope for and so rarely get. My announcement was greeted with cheers from the onlookers; somebody threw his hat in the air; the Town Clerk pushed forward and shook my hand in gratitude, and Jim Blundell gave me such a boisterous thump on the back that I barely saved my upper teeth from falling out. As millions of viewers saw the episode on their screens that night I was very thankful that it did not include such a humiliating mishap.

From that moment, however, my name was made. I might almost say that I became famous – at least for a few days. Had I wanted to declare my gift to the world I could not have chosen a more spectacular way than through the television camera, but I did it without thinking, on the spur of the moment on account of an unexpected question from the interviewer. If I had known the embarrassment it would cause me I would have kept the announcement for the privacy of the Council Chamber. As it was, I was immediately surrounded by newspaper men asking innumerable questions about the history of the well and my family's association with it. I found myself the centre of an informal Press conference with dozens of eager listeners from the public, craning forward to hear what I had to say. I was photographed with my hands upon the shoulders of two small boys to show what a kind man I was.

During the afternoon the crowds grew even thicker. A helicopter arrived overhead, sent down by the Automobile Association to investigate the traffic problem. More police arrived, and profiteers began to appear on the scene.

A local newsagent turned up with a packet of old picture postcards of the well that he had unearthed from some forgotten cupboard in his shop. They were crude coloured photographs taken years ago, but he was selling them at a shilling each, and for an extra sixpence offered to post them off for visitors who wanted a record of the noteworthy occasion – with the St Mary's postmark on them.

Towards sunset the crowds gradually dispersed, but it was almost dark before the road was sufficiently clear to get my station wagon off the grass verge and drive home.

I was completely exhausted. I had had no lunch and felt fit for nothing but a light supper and early bed. But I had to stay up to see the television news at ten o'clock when I had been told that the pictures taken at the well would be shown.

I waited with considerable foreboding for my first appearance on the television screen. Fred and Amy came into the library to watch, and I wished that I had not invited them because I was shocked by my appearance. I looked much older and thinner than I realized; almost senile, with dark rings under my eyes and a thin wisp of hair sticking up from the back of my head.

The close-up was almost revolting. It was no doubt a trick of the light, but it looked as if alternate teeth in my lower jaw had been removed and my eyebrows had been shaved off. My only comfort was that the Town Clerk looked even worse. He is a plump little man who invariably wears a bowler hat that seems too small because of the fullness of his face. His small tooth-brush moustache gave him the appearance of a blown-up Charlie Chaplin and his thin high-pitched voice was ludicrous. Fortunately the helicopter overhead drowned most of what he said.

But Jim Blundell more than made up for the shortcomings of the Town Clerk and myself. He played the part of a stalwart English innkeeper and a shrewd country Mayor quite brilliantly. Without saying anything specific he hinted that the Council already had ambitious plans in hand whereby the fine old town of St Mary's would soon be ready to play host to visitors from all parts of the world. The miraculous waters of the well that had cured Roman Emperors and other famous men like Lord Colindale would soon be available to all others who desired the blessings of perfect health. He added that he himself, at the age of fifty-seven, was as fit as a youth of twenty entirely on account of his daily glass of St Mary's water. He was certainly a fine advertisement for it, although I knew quite well that he had never drunk a spoonful of the water in his life.

I turned off the television and went to bed. I had never been so tired, but I barely slept. My brain was seething with vague, indefinable apprehension. Incongruous though it may seem, the thought that kept recurring to me was that of the three boys, selling 'St Mary's waters' out of lemonade bottles, filled at the nearby duckpond. They were local boys: upright, honest youngsters who had never done a disreputable thing in their lives. Yet they had revelled in that bare-faced deception and no doubt made a good thing out of it.

I devoutly hoped that this was not to be the shape of things to come.

# Chapter Six

When Fred brought in my cup of tea at eight o'clock on Sunday morning I was so tired that I told him I would stay in bed until ten in the hope of a little sleep.

But a few minutes later he came back to say that Lord Colindale was on the phone, so I had to put on my dressing-gown and go down to speak to him.

My head was aching, and his loud, booming voice made me wince.

'Well?' he said. 'What d'you think of it?'

My feelings towards Colin at that time were rather mixed.

In his own peculiar way I'm sure he expected me to believe that the sole motive of his sensational article was to express his gratitude by giving the town a unique advertisement. That he had certainly achieved, but I am fairly certain that the people of St Mary's were of small concern to him compared with his own personal motive. He had never hoped to return to public life, but now that it was possible, he wanted to come back with a flourish of trumpets that would echo round the world. If he had returned with the mystery of his long absence unexplained, then questions would have been asked: where had he been and why? Mystery of that sort does a public man no good. Colin knew that very well, and his sensational article had served its double purpose admirably. No town had ever been given such a tremendous free advertisement and no man had ever returned from retirement in such a dramatic way. But I never got over the feeling that if it had suited his purpose better he would have ignored St Mary's and never said a word about his cure.

It rankled, too, that he had kept his intentions secret from me.

He must have known that his completely unexpected article would catch St Mary's unawares: hopelessly unprepared for the avalanche of cars and sightseers that descended upon it. If he had trusted me to warn the Council in advance, we could have made preparations, and overcome the chaos.

But having said these things of Colin, I say no more. His help and generosity were invaluable in the days ahead.

I must have sounded dull and lifeless on the phone. I was too sleepy and exhausted, but Colin was so full of zest that he probably never noticed it. His editors had given him full reports of everything that had happened at the well on Saturday. His vanity was tickled by the excitement he had caused, and he laughed enormously when I described the dilemma of the Council and my own personal embarrassment.

'It's up to the town now, Peter,' he said. 'You've got a gold mine, and what you get out of it depends on you. It's not a flash in the pan, I assure you. The whole thing's headlines in the American papers this morning, and the same, I guess, in most parts of Europe. If you play your cards well, St Mary's will be a boom town from now on.'

He told me to look in at nine o'clock that evening when he was making a personal appearance on the television – 'to catch the odd million or two who didn't read my stuff,' he said. He asked me to ring him up on Monday to give him the latest news and to call on him for any future help or advice that the Town Council might need.

Our newspapers had arrived by the time I was dressed and down to breakfast. Almost the whole front page of the Colindale *Sunday News* was given up to pictures and descriptions of the scenes at the well on the previous day. There was a map of St Mary's district showing the various routes and diversions now in force for motorists, and a leading article suggesting that Britain might well search for other health-giving springs, forgotten or undiscovered, in order to secure a greater share of the valuable Spa business at present monopolized by the Continent of Europe. Even the more sedate

Sunday papers gave prominence to the news, showing clearly that they did not regard it as a 'stunt' on the part of a single group of newspapers. As Colin had said on the telephone, it was definitely not a flash in the pan.

At midday I drove down to the well. I was prepared to park before I reached my destination to avoid becoming blocked again, but vigorous measures had now been taken to keep things under control.

As it was a Sunday and another fine day, the crowds were if anything greater than on Saturday, but thanks to the motoring associations and a full turnout of special constables, the arrangements were much better. Several pieces of common land adjoining the road had been converted into car parks. Signboards 'To the Wells of St Mary's' were at every road junction, and I was told that the 'bottle neck' in the narrow streets of St Mary's had been by-passed by diversions round the town.

As a member of the Council I was allowed to drive straight through to a reserved space close to the well, passing on my way a line of motor coaches that some enterprising firms had hastily mobilized for sight-seeing excursions.

But no amount of organizing could solve the problem of getting people in and out of the well house in an orderly way. It only had one narrow door and as every visitor wanted to see the well and drink the water, a solid queue was moving at snail's pace down the by-lane. The gypsy was still trying to sell baskets; a man and a woman were offering bags of peanuts and slabs of caramel, and a group of boys in outlandish costumes, with small hats held on with elastic bands, were walking about playing banjos. But I was glad to see that the police had stopped our local boys from peddling spurious 'St Mary's Water' in lemonade bottles.

On Saturday it had been impossible to get near the well house, but I thought it my duty as a Town Councillor to see what was going on inside, so I got Sergeant Allen to make way for me.

I wished afterwards that I hadn't. I was shocked by what awaited me, and by the atmosphere inside the building. Even when Colin and I had been there alone the air was damp and stagnant through lack of ventilation. The windows, high up in the walls, had not been opened for years and were impossible to move, and now the fetid odour of damp and decay was horribly intensified by the suffocating press of humanity.

But far worse than the nauseating atmosphere was the appearance and behaviour of Henry the caretaker. I was prepared to find the old man confused and bewildered by what had happened, but instead of a humble old man struggling to overcome his inadequate abilities, Henry had been transformed by his sudden importance into a grotesque figure of conceit and arrogance. The whole thing had completely turned his head.

He had evidently decided that he must dress for the occasion, and was wearing a dreadful old swallow tail coat, green with age and far too big for him, with a dirty celluloid dicky and a wing collar with an enormous maroon coloured cravat.

I could have forgiven his appearance if his antics had not been so appalling. I had been told by Sergeant Allen that the old man had been very drunk in the town on the previous night, obviously from his takings during the day. He had apparently brought a bottle back with him, for he reeked of spirits and his speech was slurred and incoherent.

He was standing on an old box inside the well showing off to his audience in a preposterous way, making a rambling speech about the 'many famous Roman Emperors' who had drunk the water, and how the Nuns of St Mary's had 'washed away the sins of many a crowned head'. What the audience thought I don't know, but I was angry and ashamed that people who had come long distances expecting to see something impressive and almost miraculous, should be inflicted with a ridiculous lecture by an arrogant, drink-sodden old clown.

But there were things still worse and even more humiliating.

Henry had apparently engaged a staff to help him. Seated at the door behind a rickety old marble-topped wash-hand-stand was a revolting youth of the teddy boy type with side whiskers and long greasy black hair who was raking in the entrance money with a gloating leer on his face and a cigarette dangling out of his mouth. He was charging each visitor half a crown, throwing the money into a soup plate which he occasionally emptied into a biscuit tin on the floor beside him and stuffing the notes in his trousers pocket. Beside the stone trough into which the waters of the spring were running stood a blowsy woman, also with a dangling cigarette; her sleeves were rolled to her armpits, and she was serving the water in thick glass tumblers and dirty enamel mugs which she occasionally swabbed round with an unsavoury dishcloth.

It was a sickening sight, and my first impulse was to stop it, but I might as well have tried to stop an avalanche. Impatient people, who had waited hours, were pushing their way through the crowded door, and there was nothing I could do. I pushed my way out, went back to my car and drove home to the Manor House.

I had no appetite for lunch. I went to my library and sat down to face a problem that in the excitement and turmoil of events I had scarcely given thought to.

The problem, of course, was Henry, and the more I thought about it the more difficult and disturbing it became. When I had given the well to the people of St Mary's on the previous afternoon, I had entirely overlooked the fact that, for all practical purposes, my father had given the well to Henry thirty years ago. There was nothing in writing and Henry was not of course its legal owner, but his right to receive all profits from it had been taken for granted. I had accepted without question the arrangement made between Henry and my father all those years ago and if it came to a court of law I could not dispute it. Although no written agreement existed, the court might well uphold a right established, simply by virtue of its long accepted practice.

It was a fantastic situation, but I had got to face it. People were crowding into the well house at half a crown a head. None stayed longer than ten minutes, and with fifty or more in there at a time I reckoned that at least 3000 would pay their half crown on this one day, and Henry and his two friends would be the richer by about £350. The rush would not last, but if the Town made ambitious plans to exploit the well, then it looked as if Henry might be in a position to claim the profits.

I could see no way out of it, and decided to make a statement at the Council meeting in the afternoon. I had given the well to the town in good faith and would have to leave the Council to settle the problem as best they could.

# Chapter Seven

The special Sunday meeting had been called for three o'clock, but when I arrived at the Town Hall a few minutes beforehand I was taken aback to discover the whole Council already assembled round the table. My first thought was that I had mistaken the time and arrived late, but it soon transpired that the Mayor had sent out a private message for all the Councillors to arrive half an hour early in order to pay me the honour of a special reception.

My gift of the well to the people of St Mary's had evidently made an enormous impression, enhanced no doubt by the publicity over television and in the Press. The whole Council was basking in the reflected glory of St Mary's sudden fame. Even the most insignificant members looked puffed with self-esteem. At the previous meeting I had felt a thinly disguised suspicion towards me. Most of them, like the Mayor himself, had had a lurking impression that I had prompted Colin to write his sensational article for my own personal profit, and this had explained their lukewarm attitude towards the whole affair. They had assumed I would reap a golden harvest from the well, and that the Town would get little out of it.

But my gift had changed the atmosphere like magic. From a crafty schemer I had become a hero. The whole Council stood up as I entered the room, and remained standing until I had taken my place at the table. Jim Blundell the Mayor then embarked upon a speech of thanks. My surpassing generosity, he said, had inspired the people of St Mary's and echoed round the world. Jim was fond of speaking and he let himself go. For ten minutes he fairly plastered me with flattery. 'I devoutly hope,' he said, 'that the people of St

Mary's will rise to the occasion and repay your magnificent gesture by working as one man to exploit this golden present, and bring prosperity and greatness to this fine old town.'

I listened with acute discomfort. Flattery at the best of times makes one prickly and uncomfortable, but on this occasion it was almost unbearable. In a few minutes I had got to get up and tell the Council that the whole thing was a mare's nest: the gift I had made to the town in such a blaze of publicity was not mine to give. I would have to explain that by long established right the profits belonged to Henry, and that I had merely handed on to the town a property that was completely mortgaged. I dared not think what the Council would say. It was bound to get into the papers and make a laughing stock of everybody. I would be hopelessly discredited and forced to resign. My name would be mud for the rest of my life.

Jim Blundell sat down to a round of hearty applause, and when I got up to reply there were shouts of 'bravo!' and a thumping on the table never before heard in our placid Council room.

I briefly thanked them for their kindness, and without further preamble plunged into my painful confession. I saw the jovial faces around me become incredulous, astonished and dismayed. The shock was so sudden, so unexpected that my words took time to sink in, but as I stumbled on I began to feel hostility and anger.

'I can only tell you,' I said, 'that I announced this gift in absolute honesty and good faith – but in the heat of the moment – in the excitement of yesterday I entirely overlooked the position concerning this man's right to receive the profits. I give you my humble apologies.'

I sat down and there was a deadly silence. I had never felt so dreadful in my life.

The Town Clerk was the first to speak. I was grateful to him for his calm and matter-of-fact behaviour, because I saw Jim Blundell's face growing purple with fury, and if the Town Clerk had not spoken, the Mayor would undoubtedly have burst into a torrent of abuse.

'May I ask you a few questions?' inquired the Town Clerk.

I replied that I would gladly answer them.

'Was this man in the employ of your father before he was given charge of the well?'

'Ever since he was a boy,' I answered.

'And because he was unsatisfactory as a farm worker your father gave him the well to look after? Instead of the usual weekly wages, he was given a free cottage and anything he could take from visitors?'

'That was the arrangement,' I replied.

'If the well house required repair,' said the Town Clerk, 'was this man required to pay for it out of his takings?'

'Definitely not,' I said. 'I had some tiles put on the roof last year, and I always sent my gardener down to help Henry cut the hedges in the autumn. I never expected him to pay for anything out of his own pocket because it was my property and I was responsible for it.'

The Town Clerk's face began to clear.

'I don't think the position is as difficult as you feared, Colonel,' he said. 'The man was clearly in your employ. He held no lease of the property and was free to leave the job at any time if he wanted to. You were equally free to give him notice, and his right to receive the profits from the well would cease automatically when he left your employment. You were always free to sell the property, and the new owner would have been under no obligation to employ the man.

'The same applies now that you have given the property to St Mary's. The Town Authorities are now responsible for the upkeep of the well and are free to employ whoever they choose to look after it. This man remains technically in your employ and you can find him other work if you wish to. Beyond that, I can't see that you have any obligation towards him.'

There was a murmur of relief around the Council Table; the smiles returned, and Jim Blundell looked so benevolent that for two pins I think he would have got up and made his flowery speech of thanks all over again. The momentary fear that the town had lost its golden harvest had increased its value, now that it was theirs again.

'We all understand your feelings towards an old retainer of your family,' added the Town Clerk. 'But I don't think you should have any thoughts of injustice. He will be disappointed no doubt – but you can console yourself that he will have collected more money in one week-end than he would have got in five years under normal conditions.'

I was enormously relieved at the happy ending to an affair that threatened such embarrassment. I had saved my good name in the eyes of the Council, but could not help feeling I had done so at Henry's expense. If I had kept the well for myself I should have been in honour bound to give the old man a large share at least of the profits. I could not have thrown him out simply because I wanted to snatch the money for myself. Anyway, the problem, so far as it went, was solved. I little knew what lay in store for us.

Having disposed of Henry, the Council turned to the question of how to exploit the well to the best advantage of the people of St Mary's.

The Town Clerk began by springing a surprise. A letter had reached his office by special messenger on Saturday evening from the Managing Director of the 'Avalon Investment Company' with an address in the City of London, who desired to place an important proposition before the Town authorities.

The proposition was that:

We should grant to the Company a lease of the well, including a sufficient area of the surrounding land at a rental of £2000 a year for a minimum of seven years with option of renewal.

The Company would construct at their own expense a spa building or Casino for the purpose of making the waters available to visitors; also to develop the surrounding land as pleasure gardens for public entertainment.

In addition to the fixed rent they offered to pay a yearly royalty of 20 per cent of all profits on condition that the town authorities granted no other exploitation rights to anyone who might seek to take indirect advantage of the work carried out by Avalon.

The offer was subject to confirmation after technical investigations had been completed, and these would begin immediately upon receiving agreement in principle from the town authorities.

The Town Clerk laid the letter on the table and looked over his spectacles at the assembled members. It had evidently made a good impression and it was soon clear that the majority were enthusiastic about it.

Mr Sweetman the chemist opened the debate with a sensible speech that voiced the general feeling. St Mary's, he pointed out, was a poor town with barely 4000 people. To exploit the well in a big way would need a lot of money – far beyond our limited means, and we should have to go elsewhere for the capital. The integrity of the Avalon Investment Company would have to be examined. If it proved satisfactory, then there was much to recommend the offer. £2000 a year would be invaluable, and the 20 per cent royalty might well provide a very big extra profit for us. All this took no account of the benefits that the tradespeople would secure from visitors. Shopkeepers, cafés, apartment houses, hotels, all would prosper at the expense of the Avalon Investment Company, who would obviously have no share in the individual enterprise of the people.

'The project,' said Mr Sweetman, 'will be in the hands of experienced business men who will do everything in their power to make it prosperous, and we stand to gain a rich reward from their exertions.'

There was a chorus of approval. Left to themselves the Council would have accepted the offer by a large majority. Member after member spoke up in support of Mr Sweetman's proposal, bringing forward in turn all manner of additional reasons, and in half an hour the whole thing seemed a foregone conclusion.

But we had reckoned without Jim Blundell, the Mayor. It was a characteristic of Jim Blundell to withhold his own opinion until everybody else had blown off steam. Often before, in matters of dispute, I had seen him swing the whole Council in the opposite direction: sometimes by his shrewd judgement in having the last say, but generally through the sheer force of his personality.

On this occasion he pulled off the most dramatic victory of his career. For half an hour he sat back in his chair with his hands in his pockets, listening patiently, without saying a word – almost as if he didn't care.

It was not until Mr Sweetman said: 'I move that this Council accepts the offer of the Avalon Investment Company,' that Jim Blundell sprang to life – so violently that we all jumped in our chairs.

'No!' he shouted. 'Not on our lives we won't – who are these bloody Londoners who want to suck the gold out of our well and do down the people of St Mary's? A lot of scheming crooks! That's all they are! They offer us £2000 a year when that old drunkard down there can rake in £500 in two days! 20 per cent of the profits they offer us! How much profit d'you suppose there's going to be when they've taken their own fat salaries out of it? Not a brass farthing! Not a bloody sausage! If they didn't see a fortune in it for themselves they wouldn't come near us and you know it! And seeing there *is* a fortune, then the people who're going to get it are *our* people – not a lot of twisting crooks from London!'

Jim was on safe ground when he appealed to local pride and sentiment, specially when it concerned a small impoverished town that had fought such a long losing battle against its more fortunate neighbours. Many years ago when the railways had by-passed St Mary's and left it in a stagnant backwater, our people had seen prosperous factories grow up in the towns beside the railway while their own agricultural industries were dying away. Ten years ago the new by-pass road had increased their isolation; enterprising young men left St Mary's for the towns that offered better opportunities; the brickfields and timber yards were on half-time and good men had no choice between unemployment and emigration.

Jim Blundell knew very well that nothing lay ahead of us but more depression and decline, and he pressed it home with all the force he had.

'Here we are,' he shouted, 'living on a shoe string! The whole lot of us damn nearly on the dole! Somebody drops a gold mine in our laps and you want to throw it down the drain!'

Mr Sweetman tried to answer back. He applauded the Mayor's sturdy patriotism – but was it wise to allow sentiment and patriotism to fly in the face of reality and reason? The Avalon enterprise would be in the hands of experts who would exploit the well to the last penny of profit from which St Mary's would receive a guaranteed share. Wasn't it better to take the bird in the hand instead of gambling upon two from a prickly bush? Where was the money coming from? And if we could get the money, had we the experience to carry through such a big and hazardous enterprise?

By casting doubts on our ability Mr Sweetman lost the day, for he opened himself to a crushing rejoinder from the Mayor.

'If the Council declares that it hasn't the brains or the guts to manage its own affairs,' he shouted, 'then I for one will resign out of shame and humiliation!'

The opposition collapsed, and Jim Blundell had won the day. I had my own misgivings and no doubt others shared them, but we had saved our self-respect and preserved our civic pride by refusing to lease our land to 'foreigners' from London, and we all felt in our different ways the excitement of being at the threshold of a bold and hazardous adventure.

'I put this motion to the meeting,' said Jim Blundell. 'That this Council rejects all outside offers to exploit the well, and resolves to do it themselves for the absolute and exclusive benefit of the people of St Mary's.'

The motion was carried – with three abstentions, and the Town Clerk was instructed to convey our decision to the Avalon Investment Company.

It was easy enough to pass a resolution, but none of us had the remotest idea of how we were going to embark upon it or what it was going to lead to. But the die was cast and we were bound to see it through.

Despite his contempt for what he called 'the scheming City crooks', Jim Blundell was shrewd enough to respect the proposals they had made.

He read from their letter the passage that appealed to him. 'A spa building or Casino for the purpose of making the waters available to visitors: also to develop the surrounding land as pleasure gardens for public entertainment.'

He looked round the table with a knowing smile.

'If these smart City fellows wanted that, then you can bet your boots it's worth having; so that's the idea for us: a Casino and pleasure grounds.'

I told the meeting that Lord Colindale had offered his help and advice in anything we decided to do. Everybody was delighted except Jim Blundell who didn't want any 'foreign influence'. But I reminded him that Lord Colindale was a millionaire, and scarcely likely to want any profit when his one purpose was to repay what he had gained from the waters of our well. Jim accepted this, withdrew his objections, and I was finally instructed to discuss our project with Lord Colindale.

We had come to the end of what we could do for the present, but we had to decide something about the present conditions at the well. Everybody agreed that Henry and his friends couldn't go on raking in the money, and even if the Council put in a staff of its own, the existing arrangements were quite inadequate for the reception of visitors.

It was therefore decided to close the well house to the public until proper arrangements could be made.

Some of the Councillors thought it was a pity to throw away good money while the boom was on, but the Town Clerk pointed out that the present crowds were merely sightseers who would quickly disappear with a change of weather.

'Our job,' he said, 'is to prepare as quickly as we can for the people who want to take the cure, because those are the ones who're going to pay the big money.'

It was a wise move, he said, to close the well at once, and bottle up the interest and curiosity until we were ready to cope with it properly. If we let things go on as they were, the interest would dribble away and be difficult to revive.

To avoid people making a fruitless journey to the closed well house, we decided to announce our decision through the Press and Radio, and the Town Clerk therefore drew up the statement:

'Owing to the overwhelming crowds desirous of visiting St Mary's well and availing themselves of its curative waters, the town authorities have decided, in the best interests of all concerned, that the well house shall be closed to the public at 10 p.m. on Sunday evening until proper facilities can be arranged for the convenience of visitors.

'Plans to this end are in active preparation and will be made public as soon as possible.'

We all agreed that this was excellent propaganda for the future, and the Town Clerk went to his private office to telephone our announcement to a London Press agency.

We then adjourned the meeting until the following night, when discussions about the future would begin in earnest. After a cup of tea we broke up and went home – proud of the momentous decisions we had made, although I for one was hoping that we hadn't bitten off more than we could chew.

# Chapter Eight

We had had a wonderful send-off from Colin's newspapers, but our best advertisement came when Colin himself appeared on television that Sunday night.

For twenty minutes he discussed his wonderful recovery with two well known interviewers. Millions must have seen it, and if any of our Councillors had any lurking fears that the thing was a stunt or a flash in the pan they were set at rest for good and all.

It was Colin's first public appearance for nearly two years, and that in itself made the broadcast memorable. He looked wonderfully fit and was obviously revelling in his dramatic return. One of the interviewers said that it must be the first time in history that a famous statesman had, as it were, 'returned from the dead' to take a leading part in national affairs, and Colin replied that he felt sure it must be.

As he could not discuss his future place in the Government he spent the whole time describing in vivid detail his arrival at the Manor House as a helpless cripple, the chance, but almost providential visit to the well, and the wonder and joy that he had experienced as, day by day, the miraculous waters had restored his health and vigour.

If the broadcast had been on Commercial Television we could have not purchased the time for such a tremendous advertisement with all the money in St Mary's.

In the news at 10 o'clock there were more pictures of the crowds lined up to get into the well house, and the announcer read our statement about its closing for the time being. St Mary's was bigger news than the Summit Conference that week-end.

On Monday morning I called up Colin to congratulate him on his broadcast and tell him what we were going to do.

He was all in favour of us keeping the thing in our own hands – mainly I think because he wanted to keep his own finger in the pie. If the Avalon Investment Company had taken over he would have been frozen out, and he wanted to be a sort of fairy godfather to St Mary's. He had always enjoyed his power and influence, and he wanted to put it to the proof by lifting a small country town out of its obscurity and making it prosperous and famous. Whether it was personal vanity or genuine gratitude scarcely mattered: St Mary's would be the beneficiary in either case.

'I'll tell you what I'll do,' he said. 'I'll drive down tomorrow for lunch, and if you bring along the Mayor and the Town Clerk we can talk the whole thing over. And while we are lunching, my chauffeur can drive down to the well and fill up my empty bottles.'

The luncheon was a complete success. Jim Blundell and the Town Clerk were greatly flattered at meeting the famous Lord Colindale under such intimate conditions and we got through more work in an hour than would have been done at a dozen Council meetings.

Beneath his blunt and forceful manner Colin had a shrewd understanding of human nature. He said nothing that might have injured the civic pride of the Town Clerk and the Mayor. He didn't patronize them or make them feel he was taking things out of their hands. He made it clear that, as a Minister of the Crown, he could take no direct or personal part in our enterprise, but unofficially, behind the scenes, he would do everything he could to make the thing run smoothly.

'About the money,' he said, 'I would float a Company with five shilling shares to give everybody in the town a chance to take a few and have a personal interest. For the rest, the banks would make a loan to the Council on security of the rates.'

'How much do you think we shall need?' asked the Town Clerk.

'You can't tell that,' said Colin, 'Until you've got the plans and estimates. To set the ball rolling I'd like to pay the fees of a good architect and a firm of lawyers who specialize in Company flotations.'

The Town Clerk accepted with gratitude and relief. Our chief worry at the moment was that we had nothing in hand. We couldn't spend public money until we had shown the people what we intended to do, and we couldn't show them anything worth looking at until we had got the plans and estimates.

'You can't do better than Sir Richard Churchman as architect,' said Colin, 'and my own lawyers Fraser, Wainwright & Co for the legal work.'

Sir Richard, he explained, had done outstanding work on the new medical buildings at Cambridge: he was a personal friend, and Colin said he would put him in touch with us at once.

'It's vitally important,' said Colin, 'to keep the whole thing alive in the public mind while the building and preparations are going on. If you let it fade out, then you'll have a tough job working up interest again. You really need a full time man for publicity and public relations, and if you like, I'll lend you one of my own young men to help you.'

For the first time I saw Jim Blundell hesitate. So far he had been enthusiastic about everything that Colin had suggested, but he wanted to be top dog and I knew he wouldn't take kindly to a busy young man who might push him out of the picture.

But we obviously hadn't got anybody qualified to take over the highly technical job of publicity beyond our own small world. 'Lord Colindale's Young Men' were a by-word: renowned for their efficiency. It was one of the secrets of his success to pick out young men, fresh from the schools and universities, and train them intensively for administrative positions. And I knew that with a project so near his heart he would send us the best available.

'I would send him down on trial,' suggested Colin. 'If you like him, and he does what you want, then you can make him Secretary when the Company's floated. If you don't like him, you can send him back.'

66

'Did I tread on their corns?' asked Colin, as I walked with him to his car.

'Not in the least,' I said. 'They were scared of you at first, but they were eating out of your hand by the time you finished.'

'I know these local bigwigs,' said Colin, 'but you've got two good men there, and if they don't mind taking advice on things outside their ken, then you're going to make a big success of it.'

He promised to call me up when he had seen the architect and lawyers, and drove off with the bottles that his chauffeur had refilled at the well.

Jim Blundell and the Town Clerk stayed on for half an hour to talk over what had happened. They were happy about most of it, but Jim was still worried about the young man that Colin was going to send down to help us.

'Lord Colindale made it clear that he's on approval,' I said.

'That's all very fine,' replied Jim. 'But if he tries to boss things and we throw him out – what happens then? Lord Colindale takes offence and walks out on us, and we're left high and dry – without the cash to get started.'

Considering what Colin was offering to do, I thought Jim Blundell was being unreasonable, and told him so. 'I don't think Lord Colindale would send the wrong man,' I said. 'But in any case, he'd have to be a superman to boss *you*!'

Jim was flattered. He laughed and said nobody had ever bossed him yet, so perhaps I was right. 'Anyway, we'll wait and see.'

They had a cup of tea and drove back to St Mary's.

When they had gone I decided to do something that I was bound to do sooner or later, much as I disliked it.

Henry the caretaker had been told on Sunday night that the well house was being closed, but it had been left to me, as his employer, to explain the reasons.

I couldn't help feeling sorry for the old man. He had behaved in a dreadful way over the week-end but it was scarcely his fault. He had proved himself hopelessly inadequate for his unexpected responsibilities but to have his sudden importance and the prospects of enormous wealth snatched from him so quickly was a cruel stroke of fate.

It was no good arguing that things couldn't have gone on in such a ridiculous way – or that Henry had already cashed in most handsomely. The fact remained that if I hadn't given the well to the town I would have been morally bound to keep Henry on the job and give him a big share of the profits.

How he was going to take it I couldn't guess. He had an evil temper and a good deal to be angry about, but I got out my car and drove down to the well to get the thing over and done with.

Some men from the Borough Engineer's department were already at work putting up a stout wire-fence around the well house, and all the approaches had placards announcing: 'No Admittance. Closed until further notice.'

I walked up the lane to Henry's cottage with the relics of the momentous week-end all around me. The fields were littered with paper, ice cream cartons, bottles and picnic boxes; the hedges were broken down and the grass around the well house was scarred and churned as if a herd of cattle had been over it.

The door of the cottage stood half-open, so I knocked and walked in. I was greeted by the usual musty smell of old furniture, shag tobacco and stale food, but that afternoon there was an additional smell that overpowered the others: the smell of spilt gin.

An extraordinary sight awaited me. for Henry was sprawled in his rickety armchair, surrounded by money. The biscuit tin that I had seen in the well house stood on the table among the relics of the meal; there was a half-empty tin of baked beans with a big tin spoon in it – an enamel plate containing some uneaten beans and the remains of a loaf of bread. A big lump of corned beef lay on a chair beside the table and a bottle on the floor. But it was the money that astonished me. The biscuit box was almost full of silver – in half-crowns, shillings and sixpences and coppers. The mantelpiece was strewn with ten-shilling notes and the sideboard was littered with currency of all sorts – from pound notes to coppers. There were coins lying about the floor – even in the fireplace – and another small stack of currency beneath a gin bottle on the window ledge. Henry had apparently been making an attempt to sort it out and count it, and given it up as a bad job.

We had reckoned that something around 4000 people had pushed their way into the well house over the week-end. If they had all paid their half-crowns, then Henry must have collected at least £500. How much his two assistants had got away with goodness knows. They no doubt stuffed their pockets each night, but it hadn't prevented Henry from converting his sitting-room into an Aladdin's Cave.

The old man was soaked in gin. At least half a dozen bottles stood around the room, and there was one on the floor with a pool of gin in the fireplace. His fuddled condition made my task the easier, because I don't think he understood much of what I said, and I was spared the argument and recriminations that I had been expecting.

I told him I had been in duty bound to give the well to the people of St Mary's: that the cottage had been part of the gift and that later on the Council would need to pull it down when the big building scheme began. I assured him that the Council had promised to find him alternative, and better accommodation in the town, and would do something to augment his old age pension in compensation for losing his present job.

'In the meantime,' I said, glancing round at the stacks of money – 'I'm sure you'll have enough to carry on with.'

I suggested that he took the money into St Mary's, and put it into the Post Office Saving Bank.

He stared at me with bleary, bloodshot eyes and mumbled something about 'looking after his own affairs in his own way'. He desperately needed somebody to take care of him. Anybody could walk into the cottage and fill their pockets at leisure, but if I had pressed him to put it in the bank, he would have got suspicious and resentful.

I left as soon as possible. Lying in the passage was the old tail coat and celluloid dicky: pathetic relics of his vain attempt to measure up to his brief period of importance. I could not help feeling sorry for him – and ashamed of myself for getting out of my own responsibilities towards him so easily.

But as things turned out, I need not have wasted my pity.

# Chapter Nine

A few days later Colin rang up to say that Sir Richard Churchman the architect was coming down.

'See him yourself,' said Colin, 'and let him have a free hand until he's got his plans and designs worked out. If you let the Town Council loose on him they'll plaster him with their own ideas and he won't know where he is. He knows what he's doing and you'll get a much better job if you leave him alone.'

Knowing the Council I couldn't agree more. None of them had the remotest idea of what the Casino should look like, but that wouldn't have stopped them from swamping the architect with advice.

'I'll give him some lunch,' I said; 'then take him down to the well and leave him to it.'

I expected Sir Richard to be a formidable autocrat, but he turned out to be a quiet little man in a shabby old tweed suit, with a shock of untidy grey hair and steel spectacles. He asked me a lot of questions and I told him in a general way what we had in mind. He had two young assistants with him, and when lunch was over I drove down with them to the well.

I showed them round, and left them hard at work surveying and measuring and photographing the land around the well house.

Various other people came down during the next few weeks to look at our local quarries and brickfields, then Sir Richard himself returned, this time to meet the Council and show them his plans.

It was a bold and imaginative idea. I had expected one of those stark white ultra-modern affairs: all glass and chromium and ugly angles, but Sir Richard intended to harmonize the building with its historical surroundings. The spa house, or Casino, was to stand on the site of the ancient Nunnery of which nothing now remained, but the surrounding walls, enclosing fifteen acres, still stood in massive grey stone ruin. The spa house was to be faced with similar grey stone and designed to create the illusion that part of the great monastery had risen to life again.

I need not describe it here because it stands today for all to see, and has been hailed by experts as Sir Richard's masterpiece. It has been the subject of articles in architectural journals and many illustrated magazines, and has become, in fact, as great an attraction as the well itself, for people come miles to see it simply for its interest and beauty.

Its outward appearance of mediaeval austerity belies its interior, for nothing could be more modern and practical when you got inside. There was a spacious entrance-hall with offices on one side and a restaurant with a lounge and bar on the other. The upper floor was almost entirely given over to a big assembly room for every kind of purpose: from conferences and dances to public dinners, and there was to be a well-fitted stage for concerts and dramatic entertainments. It was hoped to attract professional conferences at which people could combine discussions of business affairs with a cure for their rheumatic ailments.

It was arranged that the old well house should remain intact in a courtyard at the rear of the Casino. One of the Councillors thought that this old structure should be pulled down so that the well could be displayed in more impressive surroundings, but Sir Richard shrewdly pointed out that there was a strong sentimental and psychological attraction in letting visitors take the water from the ancient stone trough used by countless pilgrims in the past, and more recently by Lord Colindale himself.

Around the courtyard were to be the buildings required for medical purposes: baths; massage; physical therapy and all the rest of it. To avoid the Casino becoming a depressing rendezvous for cripples there was to be a way in at the back for wheel chairs so that bad cases could enter the well house and medical buildings without the embarrassment of passing through the main Casino.

The Council was very impressed and listened to Sir Richard's explanations with awe and admiration, even although I could see that some of the members were looking at the plans upside down. Sir Richard was such an important architect that nobody dared criticize his work, but some of them were no doubt sharing my alarm about its size. It was a far more ambitious affair than I had expected, and I couldn't conceive how a small town like St Mary's would ever find the money, but it was no good quibbling about that until we knew the price.

'I am only asking this afternoon,' said Sir Richard, 'for comment and criticism of my designs. If you disapprove of anything, then I shall do my best to meet your wishes. If you approve in principle, I will go ahead with the specifications and estimates.'

The hesitant members kept silent because they didn't know how to begin, and allowed themselves as usual to be dominated by Jim Blundell, who as Mayor was in the Chair. He was enthusiastic about the whole thing because it was big and ambitious, and that was what he was after. 'If you want to make big money,' he said, 'you've got to do things in a big way. I move that this Council approves everything Sir Richard has done, and thanks him for the fine job he's made of it.'

And that was that. The motion was carried, and after a glass of sherry and compliments all round, Sir Richard left us to get ahead with the complicated business of costing and estimates.

We heard nothing more for several weeks and Jim Blundell began to get impatient. Then the Town Clerk got a letter from Colin's lawyers Fraser, Wainwright & Co, who were going to help us with the Company flotation. They said that estimates had now come in, and invited us to send a small deputation to London to discuss them, and to hear from the lawyers their proposals for the financial arrangements.

The Council appointed the Mayor, the Town Clerk and Mr

Lawton the Borough Treasurer to form the deputation with myself as the fourth member, and we went up to the offices of Colin's lawyers in Lincoln's Inn.

Mr Hardy the senior partner met us and took us into a sort of conference room where a long table was laid out with the plans and estimates and a lot of papers.

It was all very formal and impressive. There was a girl secretary to take notes and a dictaphone for anybody who wanted to record what they had to say. Mr Hardy told a clerk that he was not to be disturbed for the next hour and that any calls for him were to be taken by another partner. The clerk went away and shut the door and Mr Hardy got down to business.

I was prepared for a shock and I soon got it. We were told that three contractors had been invited to submit estimates. There was not much difference between them and Mr Hardy gave each of us a copy of the one most favourable.

In round figures the Casino building would cost £120,000; furnishings and fittings £30,000; services and layout £20,000: a total of £170,000.

'You would need, we estimate, another £20,000 for publicity, exploitation, running costs and salaries payable before profits began to come in,' said Mr Hardy. 'An emergency reserve of £10,000 would be advisable, so, in all, the Company should be floated with a capital of £200,000.'

I don't know what the others thought about it, but my own first reaction was relief: relief that the whole thing was so far and away beyond our means that it was scarcely worth considering. Ever since the architect had laid his plans before us my conviction had been growing day by day that we were plunging into a reckless adventure. There was nothing wrong with the enterprise itself: for a wealthy, progressive town it would no doubt be admirable, but for St Mary's it was impossible, simply because we hadn't got the money.

I had had no idea what the estimates would be. I had never been a wealthy man. All my life I had had to count the pennies, and these vast sums belonged to another world. Once people began talking in terms of thousands I was lost. £10,000 was more or less the same as £50,000 – or a million for that matter – but the figures on the estimate before me gave the relief I hoped for. We could reject the whole thing without loss of dignity and turn to a more modest project that we could reasonably afford.

But once again I had reckoned without Jim Blundell. He never turned a hair. He took the figures in his stride and began discussing them as if they were the accounts of the Brewery Company that supplied The Coach and Horses with its beer.

'If we give these people the job,' he asked, 'would they employ local labour?'

'Certainly,' said Mr Hardy. 'It's far cheaper than bringing men from a distance and finding them accommodation. And materials, too. The architect has gone into that question very carefully. You have your own brickfields: and the Clanton quarries just outside the town. Sir Richard has examined the stone and thinks it probable that the original stone used for the Nunnery was brought from there. It would suit him admirably because he wants the structure to blend with the ancient walls that still survive.'

Jim Blundell beamed with satisfaction. He knew of course that it would fall upon him to sell the project to the Council. He also knew that we had more than 200 unemployed: many of them skilled workmen. The brickfields were on half-time and the quarry had been disused for years. If he could promise an industrial revival he would have a hand of trumps to play with.

The Town Clerk and the Borough Treasurer also brightened up, but it was cold comfort to me. However much was spent on local labour, we still had to find the money for it.

I began to see that it was useless to suggest we scrapped the thing and went for something smaller. Jim Blundell had set his heart on it. If it came to a showdown the Town Clerk and the Treasurer would back the Mayor and I would be alone. I might raise an opposition party in the town, but that would lead to hostility and bitter feelings and endless trouble. I wanted peace and quiet, and I took the easy way.

The lawyer explained his proposals for the Company. Most of it was technical and above my head, but in simple terms it was what Colin had suggested. £200,000 would be raised in 5s. shares. One half would be taken by the town through loans from the banks, and the other half would be offered to the people of St Mary's for personal investment.

'You are in a better position than I am to judge whether your own people can invest as much as £100,000,' said Mr Hardy. 'If there is any difficulty I think the balance could be raised from outside investors . . .'

'We don't *want* any outside investors!' broke in Jim Blundell. 'It's our property and we're going to keep it ours! If we let outsiders in they'll want to start running it. We'll raise every penny of it from our own people! I give you my word on that! I'd sooner not do it at all than let a bunch of outsiders get hold of it!'

It had become an obsession with Jim Blundell to keep the 'foreigners' out. I'm sure he was right in principle, but I still couldn't see where our people were going to get £100,000 from. But there was no point in meeting trouble half-way and it was decided to lay the whole thing before the people at a public meeting in the town. If they supported it in sufficient numbers, the lawyers would go ahead with the Company and work would begin.

In the train going home Jim Blundell was exuberant. He was bursting with ideas. His enthusiasm was so infectious that I began to feel ashamed of my own cold feet and admire him for his courage and determination.

For ten years I had sat with him at the Council table. He had always been energetic and domineering but he had never suggested anything original or imaginative. I had never thought of him as anything but a rough and ready innkeeper who had pushed himself into the office of Mayor for the sake of the local importance it provided.

But the affair of the well had transformed him: he had become a man with a mission: Churchillian; Napoleonic; determined that nothing should stand in the way of absolute, complete success. Difficulties existed merely to be swept aside; money existed merely to be raised and spent.

In the train he let himself go and gave us a full picture of the enterprise as he now envisaged it. The well itself was merely to be the focal point of a new playground for London and the big towns surrounding us. He was inspired by the success of the Duke of Bedford's enterprise at Woburn Abbey. Townspeople, he said, were no longer content with a conventional day at the seaside, they wanted variety, excitement, and that's what we would give them. The big meadow adjoining the Nunnery ruins would be a full scale amusement park with every conceivable entertainment: dancing and fireworks on summer evenings.

All this would be apart from the money to be got from people who came to take the cure. 'Seaside resorts have their off-seasons,' he said. 'But there's no off-season for rheumatism.' Everybody in St Mary's with a spare room must clean it up and prepare it for wealthy visitors; new teashops must be opened; tradesmen must lay in a wider variety of goods; souvenirs must be manufactured. By the time we got home, Jim Blundell had turned every citizen of St Mary's into a millionaire.

# Chapter Ten

The councillors were shocked by the estimates and certain that the money could never be raised, but they had to agree that it was something for the people themselves to decide at a public meeting.

Jim Blundell was taking no chances about this public meeting. He wanted time to prepare for it. 'You've got to give people something to look at and think about before you sail in for the cash,' he said. 'If we throw it at them tomorrow, it'd fizzle out and go down the drain.'

The local printers were called in. An attractive brochure was prepared, setting out the whole project in a clear, simple way for everybody to understand. There were illustrations from the architect's drawings and an estimate of the expected profits. Into each copy went an application form for shares and the brochure was distributed to every householder in St Mary's a week before the meeting.

But the 'piéce de résistance' was a scale model of the Casino specially made by the architect and set up for display in the entrance lobby of the Town Hall. The model did more to sell the project to the people than a thousand brochures because they could see with their own eyes what they were being asked to buy. There were crowds round it all day, and on the Saturday market day you could scarcely get into the lobby for the crush. All the surrounding farmers came in and had a look at it; some of them substantial men whose support would count.

The meeting was better advertised than anything that had ever happened in St Mary's. There were posters everywhere: a slide on the screen of the cinema, and on market days when the town was crowded, a car went round with a loudspeaker urging everybody to come.

It was held on the first of July. Every seat was taken half an hour before the advertised time, and when the Council came on to the platform at eight o'clock people were standing two deep around the walls and the double doors had been thrown open so that those who couldn't get in were able to listen from the entrance lobby. It was an historic occasion; the biggest meeting ever held in St Mary's, and the most fateful.

The Town Clerk made a few introductory remarks, then called upon the Mayor who stood up amidst a round of applause.

Jim Blundell made a masterly speech and he struck the right note with his opening words.

'Thanks to the generosity of Colonel Joyce,' he said, 'this well is yours; the property of the people of St Mary's. It's for you, and for you alone, to say what shall be done with it. We've worked out a plan that we hope will appeal to you; a plan to work this gold mine to bring the last ounce of treasure from it. But we are only your servants. You're the bosses – and if you don't like what we've done, you've only got to say so. I don't want to persuade you one way or another. I'll put the thing to you fair and square without any ornaments to it. I'll give you the plain facts and leave you to decide with a show of hands.'

He put it squarely, and reasonably fairly – but certainly not without ornaments, for, as he warmed up to it, his enthusiasm took command and he painted the whole thing in colours so dazzling that at times he was in a world of fantasy.

'The cost of a three weeks' cure,' he said, 'will be £60 – or £20 a week. We shall be able to give the cure to a hundred people at a time, and after the world-wide publicity we've had, it's a safe bet that we shall be full up from the word "go". Inquiries from America are already coming in, and when we begin our advertising campaign we shall find ourselves with a waiting list as long as your arm!

'A hundred people at £20 each is £2000 a week: more than

£100,000 a year. Half must go on running expenses, but the remainder will be profit for the Company, and after the tax is paid, we estimate a clear profit of £30,000 a year. If we put £10,000 to reserve there'll still be a 10 per cent dividend to shareholders: 6d for every 5s share!'

But the dividends to shareholders, he declared, would be a mere fraction of what would come to the town itself: to every citizen, rich or poor, who had the imagination and enterprise to seize his chance. At week-ends through the holiday season thousands would flock to the pleasure grounds and amusement park. Every job would go to a citizen of St Mary's. No 'foreigners' would be employed; everybody would benefit: man, woman, and child.

He made much of the fact that local labour would be employed for constructing the Casino and laying out the grounds, and that local materials would be used where such were available. He had a tempting bait for everybody.

But he had kept his highest trump for the end: a piece of news that had only reached us a few hours before the meeting.

'You all know,' he said, 'how much we owe to Lord Colindale for the tremendous publicity he has given us, but you may not know the measure of this great man's gratitude for his miraculous cure. This he has expressed this evening in a telegram to the Town Clerk which I will read to you.'

He picked up the telegram and adjusted his spectacles amidst a profound and expectant silence that he nursed for as long as possible.

'This,' he said, 'is Lord Colindale's magnificent gesture.'

'MY THOUGHTS ARE WITH THE PEOPLE OF ST MARY'S TO-NIGHT AT THE MEETING WHICH I TRUST WILL HERALD A GOLDEN ERA OF PROSPERITY FOR THEIR TOWN.

IN TOKEN OF GRATITUDE I WISH THEM TO ACCEPT A GIFT OF £10,000 TO LAY OUT THE GROUNDS SURROUNDING THE WELL AS MEMORIAL GARDENS.'
COLINDALE

It was indeed a magnificent gift and it would be ungrateful to belittle it, but how much of it was genuinely inspired by gratitude, and how much by Colin's personal vanity and ambition, I would not like to say.

He was not mean or miserly, but he had never to my knowledge established anything as a permanent token of his wealth. Mainly I suppose because he had been too wrapped up in his own affairs to think of it, but when suddenly his chance had come, he had leapt at it with enthusiasm. He wanted to see a princely new spa town rise from the touch of his magic wand and was determined that nothing should happen to prevent it. His solicitors had no doubt reported our meeting with them, and that everything now rested with the people of the town. He had timed his telegram for its utmost effect, to turn the scale if the fate of the venture hung in the balance, and it succeeded triumphantly.

I think Jim Blundell's speech would have won the people without the telegram, but if anyone had harboured any doubts or misgivings they were swept away for ever by that final dramatic message. It was received with a roar of applause and cheers. If the famous Lord Colindale could express his confidence in the enterprise so bounteously, then nothing remained to be said. It was a gilt-edged investment, backed by one of the wealthiest and shrewdest business men in England.

Perspiration was dripping off Jim Blundell when he sat down. It was a hot sultry evening and during his speech thunder had been muttering and rumbling in the distance like a Wagnerian accompaniment. There was a loud, excited buzz of conversation from the audience. Everybody in the hall felt as if they had come into a fortune, and were no doubt deciding what to do with it. The Town Clerk called the meeting to order and the Borough Treasurer got up to explain the terms of the proposed Company. It was precise and factual: rather an anticlimax after the fiery oratory of the Mayor, but it was listened to with interest because he gave some figures prepared by experts who had carefully analysed the project and estimated that the profits could be reasonably assessed at 10 per cent of the capital.

'I don't want to press you unduly,' he said, 'but the sooner we have your applications for shares, the sooner the work can begin, and we want to open the Casino a year from now: on the first of July next summer. The banks have already guaranteed one half of the capital: the other half is free to be taken up by the people of St Mary's. If you fill in the application forms enclosed with the brochure, they can be left here this evening. Spare forms are available in the lobby.'

There was laughter when the Town Clerk got up and said: 'We haven't yet asked the meeting whether they *want* the Company. We should have done this before the Treasurer spoke. I now put it to the meeting: those in favour?'

A forest of hands went up.

'Those against?'

One hand went up – from the local wit who got the biggest laugh of his career when he said: 'I ain't got no money.'

'The motion is carried,' announced the Town Clerk.

A long trestle table had been put up in the lobby for people to fill in their applications for shares. Crowds wanted to say afterwards that they had been among the first to subscribe and a long queue was still waiting when I left the hall.

Jim Blundell said goodbye to me at the door: wreathed in smiles; his eyes bright with excitement. 'How was it?' he asked. 'Okay?'

'Okay,' I answered. 'If you had wanted to, I believe you could have sold them the moon.'

I went out into the hot, still night, got in my car and drove home.

The thing had succeeded beyond my wildest expectations. The people of St Mary's were behind it to a man, but as events turned out it would have been better if Jim Blundell had in fact persuaded them to buy the moon instead.

# Chapter Eleven

Colin rang me up next morning to ask how the meeting had gone. Some reporters had sent short accounts to the morning papers, but he wanted a first-hand report from me.

I told him it was a great success. 'The Mayor made a good speech,' I said – 'and that wonderful gift of yours settled it. They'll probably put up a statue of you in the gardens.'

He laughed. 'Keep the statue for the Market Square,' he said. 'As for the gardens – you must do something really good. Not just lawns and flower beds. You told me there were fifteen acres inside those old Nunnery walls. You'll have room for tennis courts and a bowling green: miniature golf, putting, and all the rest of it. I remember there was an old duckpond that you could clean out and make into a children's boating lake.'

'I'll get the whole thing laid out and send you the plans,' I said. 'With all that money we can do a first-class job. It was a splendid idea of yours and we're very grateful.'

'I rang up about something else,' said Colin. 'Now that you're all set to go ahead, you'll need that fellow I promised to lend you for publicity and public relations. I think I've got just the right chap for you: a boy named Paul Brooks. He's been with me five years and one of my best: lots of push and full of ideas. I'll send him down tomorrow.'

I awaited the arrival of Paul Brooks with some anxiety. I wondered how a young man 'with lots of push' would fit in with Jim Blundell who had a full measure of push and ideas of his own. Jim was ready to listen to Colin because he was a famous man, but how he would react to a pushful youth with ideas of his own remained to be seen. I could only hope for the best.

My anxiety increased when I saw the young man's car swing in my gate and come racing up the drive, because it was an open, small red noisy vehicle that I instinctively associated with self-assertive, noisy young men.

But Paul Brooks was not like that at all I should have known that Colin would pick our man with care, and Paul was a complete success from the day he arrived.

He was a likeable lad of about 25, with a freckled face and a disarming modesty. He told me at once that he knew nothing about the business ahead beyond a few bare details that Lord Colindale had given him, and what he had read in the papers, but during lunch he asked me all manner of searching questions about the town, the well, and the people he would be working with. He was quick and intelligent, and full of enthusiasm. 'It's tremendously exciting,' he said. 'I'm lucky to get the chance of being in it with you.' His confidence was infectious and he did more to strengthen my own faith in the enterprise than all the bull-headed optimism of Jim Blundell had done. If he worked smoothly with Jim Blundell, then I felt sure that success lay ahead.

After lunch I took him down to meet Jim Blundell at The Coach and Horses. Jim took to him at once. He was a young man after his own heart: direct and forceful, but with plenty of tact and charm. He flattered Jim by calling him 'Sir'. Jim beamed all over his big fat face and said: 'Call me Jim like everybody else does and I'll call you Paul.'

I had offered the boy a room at the Manor House, but he wanted to be in the town, at the heart of things, so Jim gave him a large bed-sitting-room at The Coach and Horses, with an adjoining room as a temporary office, and I left them in a vigorous discussion about the design and supply of souvenir ashtrays.

The success of the public meeting let loose a flood of activity and enthusiasm that I would not have believed possible in a town that had been asleep for so many years. But it seemed as if those long years of stagnation had pent up the energies of the people so that when at last their luck had turned, they sprang to their chances with the greater eagerness. Everybody was caught by the spirit of adventure and the lure of wealth ahead. People with spare rooms began preparing them for visitors, shopkeepers rearranged their windows and cleared out old cupboards to lay in bigger stocks; bakers and confectioners pulled down dusty partitions to enlarge their tea and dining-rooms, and the cinema had new seats put in. There was scarcely a soul in St Mary's who did not prepare in his own way to grasp his share of the coming prosperity.

With so many people spending money on improvements I wondered how they would have anything left to buy shares in the Company. But I suppose the people of an impoverished town save more than those in more prosperous communities, and the lure of good profits revealed many unsuspected nest eggs.

At our next meeting the Treasurer reported that more than a hundred people had filled in application forms for shares before leaving the Town Hall after the big public meeting on the 1st July. They were mostly for small amounts of ten or twenty shares, but they all added up. Then the big ones began coming in. Mr Parsons the miller, reputed to be our wealthiest citizen, came in for £5000 and Major Digby the Chief Constable for the same amount. I was not a wealthy man myself: apart from my Army pension I only had some Government Securities inherited from my father, but it was my duty to set an example, so I sold the stock and put £4000 into the Company.

To encourage subscribers a big chart in the shape of a barometer was put up outside the Town Hall and marked up every morning. As the end of the second week it showed that a little over £18,000 of the £100,000 expected from the people had been subscribed. A fair start, but a long way to go.

When the articles of the Company arrived from London the solicitors told us that a Board of Directors would have to be appointed. As the shares were to be held equally between the town itself and private individuals the Directors were to be drawn to represent both sides.

Eight Directors were appointed, with a Chairman, and as these unhappy people were to bear the brunt of the awful business that lay ahead I must say a word about them here.

The town was represented by Jim Blundell the Mayor, Dr Stagg the Medical Officer, the Town Clerk and the Borough Engineer. The people's representatives were Major Digby the Chief Constable, Mr Potter our leading solicitor, Miss Fanshawe, Headmistress of the Girls' High School, and the Vicar.

At first sight an odd collection, but in practice it worked well. Mr Jackson the Vicar was a quiet studious old man who professed no business ability, but he had been Vicar for thirty years and everybody loved and trusted him. He was devoted to the town, and cautious people who might otherwise have held back came forward to buy shares with the certainty that their interests would be in safe hands with old Mr Jackson on the Board.

Miss Fanshawe the Headmistress was an institution – almost a legend in St Mary's. She had a first class Oxford degree, and with her genius for administration could have risen to a high place in her profession. But she had chosen to stay in St Mary's and had given herself to it heart and soul. She was now in her sixties and near to retirement, but her vigour was unquenchable. She was the mainspring of everything that concerned the women and children: she produced the best school plays I have ever seen, and was an indefatigable bicyclist. She was downright and outspoken, with nothing of the blue stocking about her; respected rather than loved, and a scourge to the lazy and half-hearted. Like the Vicar she came on to the Board from no desire to be a business executive: only to do another duty to the people, and to see that their interests were served.

It may seem strange that Jim Blundell was the man who proposed the Vicar and the Headmistress, and persuaded them to join the Board, for no two people in the town were more different from him in background and temperament, but the shrewd Jim Blundell well knew their influence with the type of people who disapproved of him as a vulgarian and upstart, and might have hesitated to buy shares if people they trusted were not on the Board to reassure them.

Of Mr Potter the solicitor and Major Digby the Chief Constable, I need only say that they were sound, dependable men, whom everybody knew and respected. The Borough Treasurer and our newcomer Paul Brooks were not Directors, but came to all meetings as Treasurer and Secretary of the Company.

I had taken it for granted that Jim Blundell, as Mayor, would be Chairman of the Board, but to my surprise he proposed that I should be the Chairman. 'If it hadn't been for you,' he said, 'there wouldn't be any Company or any Casino, so you're the man for the Chair.'

I accepted the honour as in duty bound, bitterly as I have since regretted it, but I think Jim Blundell's real reason for proposing me was to give him the freedom to speak his mind and push his own ideas more vigorously than if he had been restricted by the impartial duties of the Chair.

So there we were: eleven of us, with the fate of the big enterprise in our hands, and with it the fate of the town and all its people. I no longer thought of it as a hazardous enterprise. With such heartening enthusiasm behind it I could not conceive that it could possibly go wrong.

# Chapter Twelve

The day came when a convoy of lorries arrived and the work began. The land around the well house was soon a honeycomb of trenches, swarming with surveyors and engineers with theodolites and coloured sighting poles and measuring tapes. Cranes and scaffolding and cement mixers arrived and the boys went down after school to watch the big rotating machines spewing the liquid into the trenches.

The town soon felt the benefits. Except for specialists and foremen the whole labour force was recruited from St Mary's and within a month we had no workers unemployed. The brickfields came to life again and took back men who had long been idle; the quarries were opened up; weeds and undergrowth were burnt, and masons who had almost forgotten their craft were busy shaping the blocks of stone for the Casino. Our local plumbers and decorators were flooded with work on the houses that were being got ready for visitors, and nearly every shop had a new coat of paint. St Mary's became a boom town. There was money to spend – even although it was our money – and everybody was happy.

In October Colin came down to lay the foundation stone, and the Town Council made a big occasion of it. There was a luncheon in the Town Hall, with champagne and Michaelmas goose and Colin made an inspiring speech. He looked tremendously fit: a fine advertisement for the waters of the well, if advertisement was still needed. 'I am proud,' he said, 'to be with you on this memorable occasion. It is indeed a matter of pride for any Englishman to witness the rebirth of an ancient town after years of frustration and depression, to see that the magnificent spirit of adventure and enterprise of its people remains undaunted.'

The Town Clerk, in his speech, took a somewhat more practical approach. He reminded the people that, while many had subscribed well for the shares in the Company, more than half those allotted to the people had not yet been taken up. 'I am sure,' he said, 'that we could sell these remaining shares many times over if we offered them to the public at large, but we want, if possible, to keep the whole enterprise in the hands of our own people.'

The laying of the foundation stone had been well advertised in the Press. Lord Colindale's presence was an extra attraction and as it was a Saturday, and a fine day, a big crowd of visitors joined the townspeople to witness the ceremony. It reminded me of that hectic first week-end. The television people were there, and the newsreel cameras, and Colin made another lively speech. It brought us right back into the news again.

The occasion touched off another boom in share buying. Some cautious people had held back from doubts whether the thing would ever go through, but now that work had begun, and they could see the fine buildings rising higher day by day, their doubts were finally removed. It was a big strain on their resources and it needed every ounce of faith. My bank manager told me that many of his customers, especially elderly ladies, were selling gilt-edged securities that they depended upon for their sole income in order to buy shares in the Company. It troubled him because these people would lose their immediate income and have to bridge the gap as best they could until the Company began to pay. But he had complete faith in it himself and had put his own savings into the shares. His wife had done the same, and he had bought some for his children.

At Christmas there was a 'Shares Week' in the town. All manner of devices were employed. There were raffles with shares as prizes. The Dramatic Society produced a Pantomime for which 5s tickets were sold with numbered counterfoils. The counterfoils were collected at the door and put in a bag, and in the interval Jim

Blundell came on to the stage and drew ten counterfoils that won for the lucky ticket holders a prize of 50 shares each in the Company. The pantomime itself wasn't very good, because too much obvious propaganda was inserted. They had chosen 'Aladdin' who of course found several sacks of Casino Company shares in the treasure cave. People laughed, but I thought it cheapened the thing. In his speech on this occasion, Jim Blundell brought in a new incentive. He reminded the audience that when all the shares were sold there would be no more, which meant that as the Company grew and prospered the shares would be worth much more than their present value, probably double or even treble their purchase price of 5s.

This appealed to the gambling instinct in everybody, and another small boom resulted. People mortgaged their houses; raised money on insurance policies; some even sold their bicycles.

All these plans and devices may suggest that the citizens of St Mary's were half-hearted about the enterprise and had to be enticed into it, but that was far from true. Everybody was enthusiastic and convinced of its success; it was only that sufficient spare money for investment simply wasn't there, and the people had to scrape the bottom of the barrel to find it.

But find it they did. Early in the New Year the Town Clerk announced that £89,000 of the people's shares had been taken up:£11,000 only remained to be raised. A few of our wealthier citizens made a final effort. They dug deeper into their resources so that one day the last blank space on the chart outside the Town Hall was filled in, and the enterprise was proudly and triumphantly declared the exclusive property of the people of St Mary's. Not a penny of 'foreign money' had been called for – except possibly the £10,000 from Lord Colindale, and that was a free gift.

Colin frequently rang up to ask how things were going and how the young man he had lent us was getting on.

I assured him that Paul Brooks was a complete success. He had used all manner of means to publicize the Casino and the travel agencies were working in every part of the world from which visitors could be expected. Mr Philpot the Town Librarian had been told to dig up everything he could find about the ancient history of the well, and Paul had rewritten it as an attractive booklet to capture the interest of visitors from abroad. On the front was a coloured picture of the Casino and inside an even more highly coloured story of the well itself. It described how the Romans had valued it so much that they threw thanksgivings of silver coins into it, how pilgrims in the Middle Ages had flocked to it, carrying sick friends from remote parts of the island to drink the healing waters: how, with the destruction of the Nunnery, the wells themselves had all but been destroyed and forgotten until the miraculous cure of the famous English statesman Lord Colindale had restored its fame, and the benefits of its curative waters were soon to be available to suffering mankind throughout the world.

It was embellished with a great deal of imaginary detail, but it was very effective and produced results. The back page contained a tariff of charges. It explained that the normal £60 cure was set at three weeks because that was the period in which Lord Colindale himself was cured. There would be accommodation to suit all pockets and inquiries were to be addressed to the Town Hall.

Ten thousand of the booklets were distributed through the big international Travel Agencies and inquiries began coming in from America even before the walls of the Casino had risen from their trenches.

I soon found out that Jim Blundell's enthusiasm for the project was not entirely inspired by his devotion to the town. He was working on an ambitious project of his own, and he put into it everything he had got.

The Coach and Horses inn was a big rambling old place famous in the past as a coaching hostelry, but it had fallen upon bad times and most of its bedrooms had long been disused, a few only being kept for occasional commercial travellers. But Jim saw his chance and was determined to make the inn an exclusive centre for the best and wealthiest visitors from abroad. All through the winter and spring the place was swarming with decorators, plumbers, carpenters and electricians. New plumbing was installed; bathrooms put in, lavatory basins with hot and cold in every room and telephones in the best of them. A big dining-room was built out at the back, with an elaborate cocktail bar, and the stables were converted into garages.

Jim showed me round when it was nearly finished. He was tremendously proud of it, and I have to admit that he had made a wonderful job. He told me it had cost him £6000. I could quite believe it, but where he had got the money from I don't know, I don't imagine he had any in hand, but the inn was an old family property and no doubt he raised a mortgage from the bank.

The hard frosts of that winter delayed work on the Casino, but we were determined to open on the advertised date of 1st July, and through the spring they worked double shifts with arc lamps lighting the scene far into the night.

Paul Brooks saw to it that the project was never allowed to fade out of the public mind. Everything of interest was relayed to the Press and Colin's own papers gave generous space to it. We had sightseers at every week-end. As the fine Casino building neared completion it became a centre of interest on its own account, and when the flags went out along the streets of St Mary's we began to look like a carnival town.

At last the day arrived when the building was sufficiently advanced for the Directors to hold their first meeting in the Council Room of the Casino. It was the second week in May: six weeks before the official opening: a red letter day, worthy of celebration, that was fated to be the most dreadful day that any of us had ever experienced.

# Chapter Thirteen

Nothing could have been more auspicious for that first meeting of ours in the impressive Council Room of the new Casino. It was a lovely afternoon in early summer, the banks beside the road were bright with primroses as I drove from the Manor House and parked my car for the first time in the courtyard. The hardest part of our work was over, and I remember thinking how well this bright blue sky and bracing air symbolized the happy and successful days that lay ahead.

The others had already arrived, and before we began our meeting we made a leisurely tour of inspection. The entrance hall containing the reception office and inquiry bureau was already fitted with desks and chairs upholstered in blue leather. Blue and cream were the motivating colours throughout: blue leather; blue curtains and cream walls in every room. We walked through the big restaurant where the walls were decorated with frescoes illustrating the history of the well. We inspected the kitchens with their ultra-modern fittings that all of us would have liked in our own homes. We went up the broad staircase to the fine assembly room still waiting for its furnishings. Even the smell of paint and varnish gave one a stimulating sense of things achieved. It was strange to see the old well house standing unaltered in the inner courtyard, surrounded by the bright new range of medical buildings. It looked like an ancient tree surrounded by young saplings, but the architect had planned things so well that there was nothing out of place or incongruous, and we all agreed how right he had been in keeping it exactly as it was when Lord Colindale had made the fateful visit that was destined to restore its fame. The interior of the well house had been cleaned up and fitted with wrought-iron light brackets, but the old well remained untouched, almost as if it were a holy relic: even the lichen in its grey stone walls remained. We watched the precious spring water running through the old stone trough, as clear and fresh, said the Town Clerk, as it had been when the Romans drank it two thousand years ago. But the overflow no longer ran away into a culvert outside: it had been piped into large tanks to supply the hot medical baths that would be a feature of the cure.

Much still remained to be done. The Colindale gardens could not be laid out until the workmen had cleared the ground of the final scaffolding and débris, but the plans had been carefully made, and young ornamental trees had already been planted so that they would take hold and be flourishing on the Opening Day.

We sat down to our meeting at three o'clock; happy and content at what we had seen. Everything had gone well: far beyond our expectations, and the contractors had assured us that their work would be completed in a month: with two weeks in hand.

Our principal business that afternoon was to discuss arrangements for the sumptuous gala luncheon that was to mark the Official Opening. The assembly hall would seat 300 guests who were to be chosen with great care: with an eye, of course, upon their respective publicity value.

The General Election returning the Conservatives to power had brought with it the news of Lord Colindale's appointment to the new Ministry. He now had a seat in the Cabinet and the announcement of his appointment had given us another good advertisement because the newspapers had reminded everybody of the miraculous cure that had enabled him to return in such splendid health and vigour.

Colin would of course be among our principal guests, and Paul Brooks had been working with such effect that he was able to report that the Prime Minister, and even a member of the Royal Family, might honour us that day.

It was after all by way of being a national event. No new spa

94

had been opened in England in living memory, and we were determined to make the most of it. Famous men and women in all walks of life were upon our list for invitations, and a number of foreign Ambassadors.

To entertain such a brilliant galaxy of guests would be a nerve-racking ordeal for inexperienced people like ourselves, but the thing that worried us at the moment was the cost of it. When £20,000 had been earmarked for preliminary expenses it had seemed to me a fabulous amount out of all proportion to what we should need, but as things were working out it wasn't going to be a penny too much. Publicity had run us into a small fortune. Printing and distributing the elaborate booklet had cost £500 alone, and Paul was pressing for a new supply. A big advertising campaign had been launched, with posters on the railway stations and buses, while salaries of the Casino staff, including highly paid medical attendants, were due to begin a week before the opening. A grand display of fireworks was to be the climax of the celebrations with all manner of attractions for the general public – so it couldn't be wondered at that most of us were alarmed at the cost of entertaining 300 important people who would expect the best that money could buy.

Jim Blundell was all out to make it an occasion that even the most exalted guests would remember. Champagne was essential, but at a previous meeting he had declared that we must also have caviare. A well-known firm of suppliers had quoted 15s an ounce for the finest Beluga caviare. They said that a half-ounce portion should be allowed each guest, and quoted a special price of £120 for ten large jars.

At this we put our foot down, and for the first time Jim found himself outvoted. He blustered and protested that it was spoiling the ship for a ha'porth of tar, but in the end he reluctantly agreed to smoked salmon, although he warned us that as smoked salmon was usually very salty, it would simply mean that everybody would want more to drink.

Except for this brief interlude it was a pleasant harmonious meeting.

The Town Clerk reported that negotiations with a firm who wanted to bottle and sell the water were going well – promising substantial royalities for the Company. More than a hundred bookings for accommodation had been confirmed, and as all these people wanted to take the cure a waiting list was now in operation. Jim Blundell said that every room in The Coach and Horses was booked right through to September and he was already considering building an annexe.

'This only accounts for visitors from abroad,' said the Town Clerk. 'People from all over England are writing in, and it looks as if we shall be packed – right through the summer.'

Paul Brooks said that several motor coach companies were preparing daily excursions for sightseers. 'They won't take a course of the waters,' he said, 'but they'll fill the amusement park and teashops.'

With these gratifying reports our formal meeting ended, and Jim Blundell, who never missed a chance of making a speech, wound up the occasion with one that fairly swamped his fellow Directors with praise and flattery.

He began by thanking me once again for my 'surpassing generosity' – (he always linked these two words together when he referred to me in his speeches) – and went on to thank the others in turn for their individual contributions to the success of our venture. 'I have worked,' he said, 'with many committees – but never before have I had the pleasure and privilege to work with a group of people like those who are sitting around me this afternoon. Such harmony and understanding is a joy to experience and I hope and trust that we shall carry on working together as a team – with the same fine spirit and energy for many years to come.'

It was a bit too effusive and rather embarrassing – but it was well meant and I am sure that everybody deserved it.

I replied, from the Chair, that for my own part, the past six months had been the happiest of my life. And I sincerely meant it, because once my early doubts and forebodings had gone, I had entered into the excitement and adventure of it with a zest that I had not enjoyed since I was a boy.

The others spoke briefly in a similar spirit, declaring their pleasure in working with such inspiring companions and expressing their determination to continue so long as their services remained useful to the Company.

We were in truth a happy band of comrades that afternoon. Our worst problems were over: success seemed assured and we all looked forward to the strenuous, fascinating work ahead.

Jim Blundell then rounded off the memorable first meeting in the Casino by opening a bag he had brought with him and producing three bottles of champagne to celebrate the occasion.

Glasses were brought up from the Casino bar: corks popped and we toasted Jim Blundell; the new Company; Lord Colindale, the architect, the people of St Mary's and everybody else we could think of. The Vicar, who rarely drank, said that if the champagne upset him, he hoped the waters of the well would put him right.

We stood round laughing and talking for half an hour, and were on the point of leaving when a girl who had been working in the office downstairs came up to say that Henry, the old caretaker of the well, had just come in and was asking to see us.

'He went to the Town Hall, thinking you'd be meeting there,' she said, 'but when they told him you were in the new Casino he walked here because he says it's very important.'

The news threw a damper on our informal festivity because most of us guessed what the 'importance' of his visit was.

We all had a conscience about Henry. We felt that he deserved some compensation for losing his job at the well and had discussed it occasionally at our meetings. But in the pressure of more important business we had put it off, and we now felt that it was a pity that we had not done something about it ourselves instead of leaving him to come to us.

The old man had behaved very well considering the disappointment and inconvenience he had suffered. The Council had found him a small cottage on the other side of the town when the old one had been pulled down. It was no light thing to be uprooted at his age from a home of so many years, but he had moved without a word of protest or complaint. He might well have been resentful and envious at the new prosperity growing up around him in which he had no share, but on occasions when I had met him in the town he had asked me how things were going and seemed genuinely happy to hear that everything was working out so well. I had told him that the Directors had not forgotten him, and hinted that they would soon have pleasant news for him, but he had waved it aside and said: 'Don't worry about me, sir. All I want now is to see the people rich and happy.'

I had gained a new respect for him, and regretted the more that we had delayed so long over his promised compensation that he had been obliged to come to us about it.

'The fact that he made a lot of money on that first week-end is beside the point,' said Mr Potter the lawyer, 'and it's no business of ours if he squandered it away. I think we all agree that some compensation is justly due to him and I'm sure the shareholders would support it. I propose that we give him a small pension of, say, £3 a week.'

The champagne had made us all feel generous and, when the Vicar suggested making it £5 a week with a hint of an additional small present at Christmas, everybody agreed.

'Then let's have him in and give him the good news,' said Jim Blundell. 'And maybe a drop of champagne to celebrate it.'

'If there's any left!' put in the Borough Engineer.

'There's just enough for a small glass,' replied Jim Blundell, holding up a bottle. 'I don't expect he's ever tasted champagne, so it'll be quite an event for the old boy!'

Word was sent down, and Henry came in. He was a poor, shabby old figure in the smart surroundings of the new Council Room, but he had done his best to clean himself up, and I felt a pang of pity for him. His family had worked for mine for generations, and he was the last of them: the sole remaining link with the past. As a boy he had worked for my grandfather, as a young man for my father, as an old man for me. He had never been much use: lazy and dirty, and drunken when he had the chance, but that was all forgotten now: only the old memories and sentiments for the past remained, and I was glad that we were going to make his last years easier for him.

We sat round informally and invited the old man to take a seat, but he was shy and nervous, and asked to be allowed to stand.

I left Jim Blundell to break the news to him, and Jim could not resist another speech, even when it was only to a humble, pathetic old man.

He told him that it had been essential to pull the old cottage down. 'You can see the reason why,' he said – with a wave to indicate the magnificent new buildings. He explained that owing to Henry's advanced age it had been impossible to find him a place on the new staff.

'But it's not our way in St Mary's to forget the old people,' he said – 'and owing to your good work looking after the well in the past we've decided to give you a nice little pension of £5 a week. All you'll have to do is to walk round to the bank each Friday and pick it up – then round to the Post Office for your old age pension – so from now on you won't have anything to worry about. You'll keep the free cottage and be nicely off for the rest of your life – and we all hope you'll live long to enjoy it.'

Everybody said: 'Hear, hear,' and half-expected to see tears of gratitude in Henry's eyes. But Henry behaved very oddly. The news made no impression upon him at all. He stood looking at the Mayor as if what was being said had nothing to do with him. He fidgeted, twisted his grimy old cap in his gnarled old hands, and waited patiently for the Mayor to get it over. And when Jim Blundell finished, Henry peered round at us and said:

'It wasn't that. It was something else I come about: something that's been on my mind these many years – and it's time I come to tell you.'

He hesitated, and seemed lost to know how to go on. He was a strange old man: shiftless and dishonest, yet with an occasional twist of disarming frankness about some small misdeed that had happened long ago, and was gnawing at his conscience. He had once come to me about an old pair of my hedging shears that he had sold, in a weak moment, to a friend – always meaning to buy them back. The friend, he said, had left the neighbourhood, the shears with him, and they had gone for ever. It had worried him for months, he said, and kept him awake at night, and now he had come to make a clean breast of it, and repay me, or work off their cost in overtime.

They had been very old shears and I had never missed them, but Henry was so humble and penitent that I gladly forgave him, and he went away mumbling his gratitude.

As I watched him now, standing before us so nervous and confused, I remembered the hedging shears, and expected him to confess to something of the same kind: some tools, perhaps, or cleaning materials belonging to the well that he had got away with and couldn't return.

I tried to set him at his ease: 'Come along, Henry!' I said. 'Whatever it is, I'm sure we can soon put it right.'

He pulled himself together, cleared his throat and began to speak slowly and haltingly, as if he were repeating something he had many times rehearsed.

'It was away back in the summer of 1954,' he said, 'getting along for seven years ago . . . I can't say exactly when I first noticed it, but as time went on I saw that the water in the well was going down. It wasn't nothing sudden, you understand: just gradual, but the time come when it didn't flow into the trough no more. I 'ad to tie a bit of rope on a bucket and let it down the well when people come in for a glass of the water. Then I 'ad to tie a bit more rope on. It's a deep well: best part of a hundred foot deep, but when the next summer come round I was scraping the bottom to get the water. It used to come up muddy, and I 'ad to keep it in cans to let it settle before I give it to visitors.'

He paused for breath, and peered round at his silent, bewildered listeners.

'You understand,' he went on – 'the water in that well was my livelihood. I 'ad to live by what I got from giving it to them visitors. It used to be as much as £5 or £6 a week in a good summer, but it was all I 'ad – and I was facing ruin, because the Colonel 'ad told me 'e didn't want me in the farm no more. So that autumn I went down to see Wilf Parsons, the plumber in the town. We was old friends, and I told 'im if I didn't get water in that well by next summer, I was finished.

'Wilf come down and 'ad a look and said there wasn't a doubt the well had dried up. 'E said things did happen like that sometimes: a shift in the rock underneath, or something.

'But in the corner of the field about eighty yards off there was the old duckpond. Wilf measured things up and said the pond was just about the same level as the top of the well, and if I liked, he could lay pipes that would fill the well up to where it used to be.

'We 'ad a good look at the pond. It's got the bulrushes all round and there's the frogs there in the season, but it was clean water and it never dried up – not even in a dry summer because the field drains go into it.

'So when the winter came we got to work. There wasn't no visitors and nobody ever came that way, and Wilf made a fine job of it. We took out a narrow trench, but 'ad to go down six feet to get a proper flow and bring the pipe into the well below where people would notice it. We 'ad to burrow under the wall of the well house and take up some flagstones inside, and Wilf laid a good three-inch galvanized pipe the whole way from the pond to the well. He cemented it into the side of the wall and rebuilt the surrounds and when 'e unplugged the end in the pond the water come through beautifully – all nice and clean – and poured down the well. We put the flooring back and filled in the trench and turfed it over so as nobody would ever notice a thing.

'It took the best part of a week for the well to fill right up again. The level of the pond fell quite a bit, but once the well was full, there was a pressure backwards, so it just flowed quietly through the trough like it used to, and the pond soon filled again.

'That was seven years ago this winter, and we ain't 'ad no trouble ever since. I used to give Wilf 'arf the takings every week to make up for what he spent on the pipes, and if'e 'adn't died last year

I'd 'ave given 'im 'arf of what I took when the rush come because if it 'adn't been for Wilf there wouldn't 'ave been no water to sell.'

I have only a blurred impression of what my fellow Directors did when the old man had finished. The shock had sent the champagne to my head and the whole thing became hazed and unreal.

Slowly I became aware of the Town Clerk speaking: his voice sounded hollow and strident. 'If this is true – then why didn't you tell us before?'

I saw the change come into the old man's face. He was no longer the decrepit, mumbling old creature that had shambled into the room. He had seen the astonishment and dismay in the faces of his listeners and he knew that he had got them where he wanted. There was a cunning leer on his wrinkled face when he answered.

'If I'd told you before, there wouldn't 'ave been nothing for nobody, would there? I wasn't going to let down the people of the town when there was a mint of money in it for 'em – and for you too, for that matter.

'I've 'ad the best part of a year to think this over and I know where I stand. If I was to speak out now and say what I know, there'd be ruin for everybody and this 'ere palace you've built wouldn't be worth a pile of potaters.

'But I ain't going to ruin nobody. I ain't going to say a word. If the Lord Chief Justice 'imself was to ask me, I'd say that well's as good as it ever was, that it ain't been tampered with by a soul ... and nobody on God's earth is ever going to know about it unless I tell 'em ...'

He peered round at us with a hideous grin of triumph and repeated his last words as if he were tasting their delicious flavour. 'Unless I tell 'em ... and whether I let it out or not depends on you. I won't say a word so long as I get what's due to me, see? I want half of all the takings; half of every penny that comes in to this 'ere Company of yours – paid over to me in 'ard cash every Friday morning. And I want it in writing, see? Fair and square on paper. I'll come along round tomorrow morning at twelve o'clock, and if it ain't ready for me, you've got to take the consequences for what 'appens.'

I remember little else of that dreadful afternoon. As if in a dream I saw from the window the old man shambling along the road on his way back to the town. I heard the Town Clerk saying: 'We had better meet tomorrow: tomorrow morning at eleven o'clock.' I don't remember that any of us said 'Goodbye' or that anybody said a word except the Town Clerk. Down in the courtyard some men were whistling and singing as they unloaded a lorry full of turves for the Colindale memorial garden.

# Chapter Fourteen

We met again next morning at eleven.

I suppose the primroses were still in bloom on the banks beside the road, that the birds were singing, and the young corn was shining in the sun, but I saw nothing and felt nothing as I drove to our fateful meeting. The catastrophe that had befallen us had numbed my powers of thought and reason. If a tornado had wrecked St Mary's, then at least the surrounding towns would have come to our rescue. There would have been a relief fund: everything would have been done to help the people and repair the ruins. But nobody would come forward to help us in the disaster that faced us now. A town that had wrecked itself on the waters of a duckpond would be more of a laughing stock than the object of charity, yet the misery ahead of our people was unthinkable.

Through a sleepless night I had groped for some possible way of salvaging a little from the wreck. Could we let or sell the Casino as a factory or offices to a business firm? It was barely worth considering. The Casino was buried in the country, ten miles from the railway, away off the main roads, and the design of the buildings was obviously unsuited for anything beyond what it was built for. It would be a hopeless white elephant, as the hideous old Henry had truly said: it wasn't worth a sack of potatoes.

We barely exchanged a word as we sat down at the Council table. I glanced at the gaunt faces and haunted eyes around me. It was hard to believe that these were the happy, enthusiastic people who had drunk so confidently to our success on the previous afternoon. The empty bottles and glasses still stood on the side table where we had left them. Nobody had thought to clear them away.

The Borough Engineer began the miserable proceedings by confirming what all of us in our hearts had expected. There had been a thin shred of hope that Henry's story might have been the crazy invention of a senile brain: a malicious attempt to frighten us into giving him some money. But I knew the old man too well to believe that he had the capacity to invent such a detailed story. There had been a deadly flavour of truth in it from the moment he had begun.

The Engineer had investigated things as far as conditions allowed, and everything confirmed the old man's story. He had discovered the inlet pipe from the pond. It lay about two feet below the surface and the job had been well done. The opening of the pipe was enclosed in a smallbrick catchment pit from which one brick was missing to allow the water to pass through, and the inlet was covered with wire mesh to prevent weeds or rubbish from entering to choke the pipe.

The course of the buried pipe to the well house could be traced by a slight depression where the soil had sunk, but nobody would notice it unless they were looking for it, and the flagstones in the well house had been skilfully returned without a sign of disturbance. He had not been able to see the pipe where it passed into the well because it was at least six feet below the water, but he had probed with a rod and discovered a small projection from the inner wall that was undoubtedly the end of the pipe.

Everything confirmed the old man's story. There were no grounds for doubting it.

Nerves were on edge and tempers flared. There were accusations and recriminations. Major Digby the Chief Constable, who was always blunt and to the point, demanded to know why the Medical Officer had not discovered the imposture. Surely he had had the foresight to analyse the water?

The indignant Dr Stagg replied that of course the water had been analysed. It was his first and most essential duty. Samples had been sent to the County Analyst, but the Analyst was only concerned with harmful bacteria that might render the water unfit for drinking. The report had been satisfactory.

Major Digby then swung round upon the Borough Engineer.

'You held a watching brief for the Council from the day the work began,' he said. 'They dug trenches all over the place! – surely to goodness you must have seen *something*!'

The Engineer hit back with a perfectly good answer.

'You know quite well,' he said, 'the Architect's definite order was to leave the well house undisturbed. Nothing was to be tampered with, not a stone of the old structure was to be removed. It was an essential feature of his plan. Are you blaming me for respecting his orders? D'you suggest I should have dug round for a pipe that nobody had the least reason to suspect?'

'But the trenches!' persisted Major Digby. 'Those new Medical rooms are built right round the well house! They must have dug foundations where this pipe is?'

'The medical range is built in the bungalow style,' said the Engineer, 'with light foundations. They run across the line of the pipe, but it's at least five feet down at that point, so they wouldn't have got near it.'

We were wasting precious time. Arguments and postmortems were fruitless. The thing had happened, and that was the end of it, and now we had the aching problem of Henry on our hands.

As Chairman I called the meeting to order. 'I suggest we settle the most urgent matter first,' I said. 'This man is coming here at twelve o'clock and I think we ought to decide beforehand what we are going to do.'

There was a silence. Nobody seemed anxious to be the first to speak and I couldn't blame them. For my own part I felt so exhausted and helpless that I was thankful for the privilege of the Chairman to make others speak before me.

The Town Clerk was the only one of us who appeared matter of fact and normal. He was an insignificant little man with a slight stammer, but he never lost his head.

'I have taken it for granted,' he said, 'that none of you wished me to prepare the agreement that this man demanded? On that account I have written nothing down, and have no intention of doing so.' He glanced round the table. 'I hope you all agree with me on that?'

We all agreed.

'Apart from every other reason,' he said, 'the Directors have no power to make over any part of the profits of the Company without the approval of the shareholders at a general meeting.'

There was another silence. The Town Clerk had evidently said all he was prepared to say. I looked at the clock. It was nearly a quarter to twelve. 'I hope everybody will give their personal opinion on what we ought to do,' I said.

'Then I'll give you mine,' replied the Borough Treasurer, a tough Scotsman who never minced his words. 'I'd give this old rogue a dose of his own medicine and kick him out. It's blackmail, and the way to treat a blackmailer is to scare the wits out of him.

'I'd tell him straight that he sold that water to those crowds and made a packet of money for himself by false pretences. He sold it at half-a-crown a glass, pretending it was spring water when he knew quite well that it came out of the duckpond. I'd tell him it was a barefaced fraud, and if he's taken to court for it he'll go to prison. You won't have any more trouble if you tell him that. He'll go away shivering in his shoes and keep his mouth shut for the rest of his life!'

It was a plausible idea – in theory. But none of us thought it would work out in practice. Henry had little to lose. The threat of prison wouldn't frighten him when he was gambling for a fortune.

'I doubt whether a court of law would convict him,' said Mr Potter the solicitor, 'but that's beside the point. We must consider this in the light of our own position as Directors of the Company. Whatever we decide to do, however we decide to make this unhappy state of affairs known to the public, the announcement must come from us – not from that old man. Otherwise it may be suggested that we have concealed the facts ourselves. We would stand in danger of an accusation of false pretences.'

'Then let's get down to brass tacks and settle something,' broke in Jim Blundell. Jim had not said a word so far, and I think we were all glad when he took the lead again with something of his old aggressive spirit. He was pale and haggard. There were dark pouches beneath his eyes and his big fat hands were trembling. He looked a haunted, ruined man, for, apart from his responsibilities as Mayor of a shattered town, he was facing his own personal disaster. His magnificent new Coach and Horses inn, upon which he had mortgaged every penny, would now be as useless as the Casino itself – burdened with a debt that he could never repay.

'We must look this thing in the face,' he said. 'If we send this old man away empty handed he'll do what he threatened and the whole bloody story will be round the town in a couple of hours. We've got to stop his mouth, but we ain't going to stop it by frightening him. He wants cash, and we've got to give him cash.'

'Bribery,' muttered the Borough Treasurer.

'Call it what you like,' retorted Jim Blundell. 'I call it plain common-sense. We can't give him what he's asking for. We all know that, and he's got enough wits to know it himself! But we've got to give him something. We'll make it £10 a week: double what we promised yesterday. If he argues and threatens to talk, we'll tell him he'll be charged with fraud and sent to prison for selling duckpond water.

'£10 a week is enough for him to get drunk on every night and, if we make it plain it's that or nothing, it's my bet he'll take it and keep his mouth shut.'

He stopped and glared round the table. 'None of you need worry!' he said. 'To save anybody thinking they're mixed up in bribery I'll make it my own personal responsibility. I'll pay him the first £10 when he comes here today – and £10 every Friday morning if he calls at The Coach and Horses and goes on keeping quiet. I'd like to call on the Chairman to put that to the meeting.'

I put it to the meeting, but Mr Potter wanted to propose an amendment.

'I agree that it's the only common-sense way of meeting the emergency,' he said, 'but I don't think it fair that the Mayor should carry the whole burden himself, and I for one would like to make my own contribution to what this man is paid.'

'We can leave that for later,' said Jim Blundell. 'He'll be here any minute now and the big thing is to be unanimous in what we do. If we start arguing among ourselves when he's in the room, he'll take advantage of it.'

And so it was agreed. It was accepted with the listless resignation of people too stricken and exhausted to seek anything more than a temporary release from a problem beyond their powers to cope with in their present state.

For my own part I wondered how long a bribe would serve to keep the old man silent. The extra money would give him ample drink and I knew what he was like when he was drunk. He became arrogant and boastful. His drinking companions would want to know where his newfound wealth was coming from, and one careless word would release the ghastly secret. The whole thing would hang upon a precarious thread of chance, and I could only hope that he would keep silent long enough to give us time to decide how best to make the disaster known in an official statement that would have at least some semblance of dignity.

It was twelve o'clock, and we began to watch from the window for Henry's appearance on the road.

With a definite plan agreed upon, Jim Blundell was much happier: much more his old confident self.

'What this sort of fellow likes,' he said, 'is something on paper, something in writing that he can lock away in a drawer and take out and read when he wants to buck himself up. So I'll give it him in writing.'

He pulled a writing-block towards him and took out his fountain pen.

'I'd be careful,' said the Town Clerk – 'careful what you say. He'll probably show it to his friends.'

Jim Blundell chuckled. 'Let him show it to his friends!' he said. 'The way I write it won't do no harm.'

When he had finished he read it to us:

'In return for his past services at St Mary's Well, and to compensate him for losing his job as caretaker, I have decided to award Henry Hodder a weekly pension of £10 a week for the rest of his life.

'The pension will be paid by me personally every Friday morning at The Coach and Horses.

Signed: James Arthur Blundell.'

'I don't think there's anything wrong with that,' said the Town Clerk.

'Nothing wrong and a lot that's right,' replied Jim Blundell. 'If the old boy wants any persuading, then I guarantee that something fair and square on paper is the thing to do the trick!'

There was nothing now but to wait for the old man to come.

I felt reasonably sure that he would accept the offer when it was guaranteed in writing by Jim Blundell. We were buying a reprieve and the price was cheap considering the chaos that would come if the old man broke the news himself. We stood about the Council Room, passing the time with aimless scraps of talk, watching out of the window for the old man's arrival. Some workmen were clearing the final building débris from the courtyard, loading it in barrows and wheeling it out to a waiting lorry. Another party of workmen were unloading more turves for the lawns of the Colindale gardens. I wondered what Colin would do when he heard the news – and how the whole world would laugh when they were told that his miraculous cure had come from duckpond water.

The Town Clerk stood talking with the Headmistress about some trivial matter of the school. Dr Stagg was telling Major Digby something about a new way to keep blight off rose trees – all were desperately trying to keep away from the appalling problems that we would soon be bound to face.

It was a quarter past twelve, and no sign of Henry. I began to wonder whether the venomous old man had already decided to take his revenge, and was going round the town declaring the awful news. He had never forgotten his brief period of importance at the well. He might well seek to regain his importance by telling the town of its disaster.

It was nearly half past twelve when the telephone began to ring in the lobby outside the Council Room. It was the first time it had rung in the new Casino.

Paul Brooks went out to answer it, and came back to say that Sergeant Longden wanted to speak to Major Digby the Chief Constable.

Through the open door we heard Major Digby talking: 'I see . . . what time was this? . . . Very well, Sergeant. I'll come at once.'

There was a brief silence, then the Major came back.

'It's about Henry,' he said. 'The old man was found in a ditch beside the road – close to his cottage – half an hour ago. He was dead: apparently murdered. Will you come with me, Dr Stagg?'

# Chapter Fifteen

There was a King of France – I believe it was Louis XIII – who had his own special way of dealing with his troubles. When things got into such a mess that he couldn't cope with them, he went to bed and left his troubles to sort themselves out on their own, which they always did: much more quickly than if he had tried to sort them out himself.

After the news of Henry Hodder's murder I never felt more like doing the same thing. If I had driven back to the Manor House and gone to bed for a week, things couldn't have been any worse when I got up. But I doubt whether they would have been any better.

As Chairman of the Company it was my job to take the lead and work out some definite plan for handling the wretched business, but the more I thought about it the more hopeless it became. The news about the well was bad enough, but that was a clear-cut problem compared with Henry's murder and all that it implied.

I wandered about the garden trying to sort things out, but in the end I gave it up and spent the rest of the afternoon planting runner beans. I suppose it was a futile hope, but if I could wipe my brain clear with a hard physical job there might have been a chance of beginning again, and tackling the problem in a new way. It was a relief to get hold of a spade and dig the ground. I tried to think of nothing at all, but as I dibbed in the beans I couldn't help wondering what would have happened by the time they came up, and whether I would still be here to pick the pods in the summer.

I worked until it was dark, and when I returned to the house the telephone was ringing.

It was Digby the Chief Constable.

'I've just got home,' he said. 'I've been at the Police Station all the afternoon. If you're free this evening I'll run over to see you after dinner.'

'Any time you like,' I said. 'I'll be here – waiting for you.'

'Sorry I had to leave the meeting in such a hurry,' said Digby. 'What did you do after I'd gone?'

'Nothing,' I told him. 'I adjourned the meeting, came home and planted my runner beans.'

'Best thing you could do,' said Digby, and rang off.

It was good to know that Digby was going to save me from another interminable evening alone. We had been close friends before we had come together as Directors of the Casino Company, and had a lot of things in common. We were the same age and had served together in the same regiment as young officers in the 1914 war. After his retirement he had taken a fruit farm a few miles from the Manor House, and we often met at each other's houses to compare notes and talk about our various interests in country life. He invariably supported me as Chairman of the Company and was the only Director with the spirit to stand up to Jim Blundell when he used to ride roughshod over everybody else.

He had become Chief Constable more or less as a hobby, having been assured that there would be little to do in such a placid, law-abiding district. As I waited for him that evening I was wondering what he was thinking about it now. I had been so taken up with my own troubles that I had scarcely given a thought to his. As Chief Constable he would be responsible for the investigation of Henry's murder. As a Company Director he shared the burden of our disaster over the well. He was carrying a double load, and all he really wanted in his retirement was to grow his fruit and live in peace.

I went out to meet him when I heard his car outside. He looked dog-tired and I got him a strong dose of whisky and a chair by the library fire. 'It's good of you to come over,' I said, 'after the day you've had.'

'Glad to,' said Digby. 'It's a treat to talk to somebody without having to think twice before every word you say. The worst of this wretched business is the secrecy. After the news yesterday about the well I never slept a wink all night. My wife knew it. She knows there's something wrong. We've never had secrets, but now I've got to cook up a lot of flat-footed explanations that she probably doesn't believe. Same thing at the Police Station. They're all trying to find a motive for this murder. I'm supposed to be leading the investigations – and all the time I've got to pretend I don't know a thing about it.'

He took a drink and lit his pipe.

'You know where this old man lived,' he said. 'There are three small cottages in a side-lane off the old Cambridge road. They belong to the Council. Two are occupied by Council workmen with their families and the other had been lent to Henry. About eleven o'clock this morning a young constable named Martin cycled down the lane to call at one of the cottages about a lost dog. On his way back he happened to see an old cap lying in the grass beside the lane. He got off his bicycle to pick it up, and there was the body lying in the ditch close by. The two Council workmen had both used the lane that morning and had seen nothing – but the grass verge is fairly wide with the ditch at least five yards from the road. They both went by on motor-cycles and the body was out of view in the long grass.

'The old man was lying on his back with his arms stretched out. Martin recognized who it was, and knowing Henry's habits his first thought was that the old man had got drunk on the previous night, blundered into the ditch and was still sleeping it off. It wasn't until he took hold of the body to lift it up that he discovered what had happened. The back of his head had been crushed in by two or three heavy blows – possibly from a jemmy or a crowbar.

'There's not much else to say about it. Martin raced off to the Police Station and Sergeant Longden went down to investigate. There was nothing in the way of a clue. The grass was beaten down, but there were no footprints. The body was taken to the mortuary, and there it is.'

'And that's all you've got?'

'All the *police* have got.'

There was a silence. I picked up his glass and went across to the sideboard to get him another drink.

'Dr Stagg says the blows were terrific,' said Digby. 'There were two or three, but one would have been enough to kill. The man who did it wasn't leaving anything to chance.'

'Was there anything to say what time it happened?'

'Before midnight,' said Digby. 'The clothes were drenched through and that must have been from the rain we had. It came down hard for about an hour but stopped at about twelve o'clock. There wasn't enough water in the ditch to account for the sodden clothes. The cap was drenched through, too – and that wasn't near the ditch; it must have happened on his way home from The Coach and Horses. He was there from nine o'clock until closing time at half past ten.'

'What do the police think about it?'

'Robbery,' said Digby. 'The old man carried a battered old leather wallet in his breast pocket. He had it that night at The Coach and Horses because he took it out to show a man it was empty before he cadged a drink off him. It was gone when the body was found. It wasn't at his cottage, so the assumption is that the murderer took it. The police think it was a tramp or a gypsy.'

'You don't think that's possible?'

'I don't personally,' said Digby. 'And I don't imagine the police will when they've had time to consider it because it doesn't make sense. Henry was a feeble old man well over seventy. If a tramp or a gypsy had wanted to rob him they wouldn't need to attack him – much less murder him. Even if they attacked him, one blow would have knocked him out – but those blows had smashed his head to pulp. It was a deliberate murder if there ever was one.'

'And the wallet was only taken to make it look like robbery?'

'I'd sum it up like this,' said Digby: 'if this had happened when Henry was walking about with his pockets stuffed with money, then there's a possibility that some local man might have been tempted. I don't think it likely because the men of this town just aren't the murdering sort. But it was common knowledge that Henry had blown all his money long ago. He hadn't got the price of a drink on the night he was murdered. He was a lonely old man; he didn't have any friends, but I'm sure he didn't have any enemies. He was just a harmless "local character".

'And that brings us down to what you know as well as I do. The only people in St Mary's with any motive for murdering the old man are the ones who were sitting round the Council table at the Casino yesterday and heard those threats he made.'

'Except for one thing that doesn't make sense,' I said.

Digby looked up with a sudden interest. 'What's that?' he asked.

'We all wanted to keep him quiet,' I said, 'simply because we wanted the news about the well to come from the Company and not from him. We wanted to keep him quiet until we had decided the best way to publish the news ourselves and we agreed that the best way to do that was to bribe him. It would probably have done the trick, but even if it hadn't, it wouldn't have made a great deal of difference if Henry had broken the news first – certainly not enough to make anybody in their senses go to the lengths of murdering him.'

Digby looked disappointed. 'I thought you were coming out with something I hadn't thought of!' he said. 'Obviously, nobody in their senses would have murdered the old man simply to stop him from breaking the news before we did. But if somebody was determined that the truth about the well should never come out at all, then the first essential would be to stop Henry's mouth for ever.'

'Does that make any better sense?' I asked. 'If the only people who'd know the facts were Henry and the man who murdered him, then maybe – but there were eleven people at that meeting. Eleven people know the thing's a fraud. Did anybody seriously think he could stop eleven mouths by murdering that one old man?'

Digby shrugged his shoulders. 'None of us know what goes on in other people's minds,' he said. 'We were all feeling pretty desperate last night – and reason isn't a strong point with desperate people.

But let's stick to one thing at a time. The inquest opens next Tuesday, and the best thing we can do is to sit tight and do nothing about the well until the inquest's over. If we jumped the gun and published the fraud about the well before the inquest, then they're bound to tie the murder up with it and the whole lot of us would be under suspicion.'

'Who'll be the Coroner?' I asked.

Digby sighed. 'That's what makes it such a mess,' he said. 'Old Potter the solicitor is the Coroner, and Potter's a Director of the Company. You know what he's like: the soul of honesty. His family have been the leading solicitors in St Mary's for a hundred years. It's highly irregular, but I went in to see him this afternoon to talk things over. He knows as well as we do where the motive is, and who the murderer probably is, but luckily his job as Coroner is confined to receiving the evidence: he isn't there to give it.'

Digby finished his drink, knocked out his pipe and got up to go.

'As for me,' he said, 'as Chief Constable I've already done enough to get myself dismissed in disgrace, and before it's over I shall probably have to do a good deal more!'

We stood for a moment beside the fire. I think he was sorry to leave the old room where we had spent so many peaceful evenings in the past.

'I've enjoyed this,' he said. 'You're the only person in the town I can really talk to now.'

'That goes for me too,' I answered – 'and seeing we can say what we like to one another without mincing words – who was the man who killed old Henry Hodder?'

He looked at me with a smile.

'We think alike in so many things,' he said, 'that I don't even have to tell you.'

# Chapter Sixteen

There hadn't been a murder in St Mary's within living memory and crowds of people were trying to get into the Town Hall when I arrived for the inquest. The fact that Henry was a well known local character made the interest the greater.

As a Magistrate I was offered a seat near the table where the Coroner sat, but I didn't want to be too prominent and chose an obscure place near the wall. I was so nervous about what might happen that I wanted to be as far out of the public view as possible.

Potter, the Coroner, showed no sign of nerves when he took his seat. As the town's leading solicitor he always dressed for the part and looked like a Dickens character with his side-whiskers and high stiff collar and old-fashioned suit. He was rather pale, but quite impassive and very dignified.

The onlookers were very quiet. If they spoke to one another it was in whispers, as if they were in a church.

The proceedings opened with due formality. The first witness was the young constable, Martin, who found the body. He said nothing that I hadn't already heard from Major Digby, and Dr Stagg followed with a description of the injuries and estimated time of death. Then came Sergeant Longden who related his fruitless search for clues. Braddock, our local Inspector who was in charge of the inquiries, merely repeated what the Sergeant had said, and I began to feel easier in my mind. The police had apparently found nothing to help them.

I began to feel anxious again when the inquiries turned to the movements of the old man on the day of his murder. If it came out that he had been down to see us at the Casino that afternoon it would lead to all manner of complications, but fortunately nobody came forward to say that they had seen him on the road, and I later heard that the girl he had spoken to on his arrival at the Casino was not a local girl who might have known him. She belonged to a London firm who were supplying our office equipment and had now returned to London. If she had heard about the murder she would scarcely associate it with the old man who had walked into the building and asked to see the Directors that afternoon. The inquiry then centred upon the evening in the public bar of The Coach and Horses, where Henry was last seen alive.

A number of men had come forward to help the police, and most of them enjoyed their appearance before a public audience. In all main details their evidence agreed. Henry had come in at his usual time: about nine o'clock, and had sat in his usual seat in a corner against the wall after ordering and paying for half a pint of beer. The barman said he was much the same as usual: he had difficulty in finding the money for his drink – searching his pockets and paying with a threepenny piece and a few odd coppers. In the days when he had had a lot of money from the haul he had collected at the well his visits had been spectacular. He would begin by ordering himself several large gins and having warmed himself up he would flourish his old leather wallet, stuffed with notes, and stand drinks all round. The money, very naturally, had quickly disappeared, and in recent times he had been hard put to it to find the price of a beer. He would brood over his days of opulence and expect others to stand him drinks in return for those he had stood them in his days of wealth.

As each witness described the evening in similar terms, declaring that Henry was 'just like he always was', I began to feel satisfied that nothing significant would emerge.

Then suddenly a few chance words from a young labourer named Wyatt brought us right back to the brink of disaster.

He had come into the bar, he said, about nine-thirty, bought himself a beer, and sat down to drink it beside Henry in his corner.

The old man, he said, was looking gloomily at his empty mug. He had then pulled out his old leather wallet, shown Wyatt that there was no money in it, and asked the young man for the price of a drink, saying as he did so: 'I'll pay you back three times over because I'll be rich again soon. Richer than all you lot put together.'

There was a stir in the hall: people sat up with interest and curiosity, and a cold chill went down my spine. Potter the Coroner, who well knew how near we were to calamity, behaved with commendable self-control. Without any change in his precise formality he said:

'What do you suppose the old man meant by that?'

'I took it to be a bit of his usual boasting, sir,' said Wyatt.

'His boasting?'

'Or bragging, you might call it, sir. You see, he could never forget them days when his pockets was full of money. And when it was all gone he missed the importance it gave him, if you know what I mean.'

'You mean he boasted about becoming rich again in an attempt to regain his importance?'

'Partly that, sir. And partly because maybe it helped him to get a drink out of us.'

'You think it was just an empty boast? He had no grounds for making it?'

'That's what we always reckoned, sir. Sometimes we used to ask him how he was going to get rich again – and then he'd shut up and say, "you wait!", and that was the end of it. Maybe he thought he might get his old job back, looking after the well, and cash in again, like he did in them first days. But of course we all knew he never *would* get it back because he wasn't fit for it.'

'He was in the habit of boasting in that way? It wasn't only on that last night?'

'Oh no, sir. He was always doing it. It was a sort of standing joke with the fellows in the bar. They used to pull his leg about it – and get a bit of fun out of it.'

'What did you do when he boasted in this way on that last evening?'

'I stood him the drink he wanted, sir. Because that's what he was after.'

There was a laugh from the public seats which the Coroner sternly repressed. He thanked the young man for his evidence and told him to stand down. The crisis had passed and I breathed again. I felt that Potter had taken a needless risk in pressing the witness about Henry's 'boasting'. It seemed almost as if he were deliberately trying to expose the whole secret, but he told me afterwards why he had done it.

'If I had passed over Wyatt's statement about the "boasting" without question,' he said, 'or given the impression that I was trying to smother it, then it would have aroused speculation and led to gossip that we wanted to avoid. I felt reasonably sure that the old man had said nothing indiscreet because his whole scheme depended on secrecy, so I took the risk of clearing up that "boasting" business once and for all.'

Nothing further happened at the hearing that afternoon. There was some talk about the possibility of a tramp or a gypsy being the culprit. Since the town had come into the news, several undesirable characters had been seen about, looking for work or anything they could pick up, but as none had been seen in the vicinity during the week of the murder, this line of inquiry soon fizzled out.

The police were obviously anxious for more time, and as soon as possible applied for an adjournment, 'in order to follow up certain investigations'. The hearing had not lasted for much over an hour and the people who had come in the hope of something sensational went home disappointed.

For my own part I drove home to the Manor House with mixed feelings. I had come to the point when I looked upon anything short of disaster as a merciful reprieve, and it was a relief to know that for the time at least the police were in the dark about the murder. But it was clear enough that they were going to hang on to it like bulldogs. If the murderer believed that he had safely disposed of Henry by hitting him over the head he was very much mistaken. Henry dead was going to be a greater menace to us than Henry alive.

# Chapter Seventeen

A few days later we had another Directors' meeting, our first since we got the news of Henry's murder.

We had hoped to delay our final decision until the inquest was over, but time was pressing. A bare five weeks remained before the advertised opening of the Casino and as the inquest had been adjourned for a fortnight we were bound to settle what we were going to do.

The Casino was seething with activity when I arrived. Two big vans were in the courtyard unloading furniture and fittings. Men were carrying in piles of light metal chairs and tables for the restaurant and the handsome blue leather-topped chairs for the assembly hall. A small army of men and women were hanging curtains, fitting lamp shades, and laying carpets. Medical equipment was being wheeled into the rooms around the well house, and in the grounds outside, gardeners were laying turf for the lawns, planting out flower beds, and rolling gravel paths.

The great enterprise was rolling forward according to plan. There was a cheerful whistling and singing and hammering. The fine building was beginning to display its full magnificence. As I walked through the hall I was saluted respectfully by the men in charge of the work. As Chairman of the Company I was a great man: almost a legendary figure as the benefactor whose 'surpassing generosity' had made the achievement possible. I felt like a fraudulent Company promoter whose cardboard empire stood on the brink of collapse and ruin.

I met Digby on the stairs and we had a word before we went

into the Council Room. I asked him if the police had got anything new about the murder.

'I'm keeping out of it as much as I can,' said Digby. 'Inspector Braddock's in charge. I told him to let me know of any developments. He hasn't rung me up so I don't imagine they've tumbled on anything.'

'He said at the inquest they were following up a certain line of inquiry?'

Digby shrugged his shoulders. 'I don't know what it is,' he said. 'I didn't ask him. I'm leaving it to him.' He paused and said: 'How are you going to handle things at this meeting? Are you going to put forward any proposal?'

'You probably think I'm a dud Chairman,' I said. 'But I'm just going to open the meeting for discussion and see what they've got to say.'

'Sensible man,' said Digby.

'They've had a week to think things over. We'll have to make a decision this afternoon.'

'Whatever it is, it's got to be unanimous,' he said. 'A majority vote isn't going to get us anywhere.'

The others had all arrived. Most of them were standing round with a guilty hangdog look about them. At our first meeting in this lavishly furnished Council room everybody had had a proud sense of possession. Now they looked as if they were here on false pretences.

One of the girls in charge of some work downstairs had put an attractive vase of spring flowers on the table. Even the flowers had a pathetic irony about them.

I took the Chair in a strained silence. For obvious reasons no minutes had been kept of our previous meeting so I got straight down to business: 'Our best plan,' I said, 'is to start with a general discussion. I hope everybody will express their views, and then we shall have to decide what we're going to do.'

There was another strained, uneasy silence. It looked as if everybody had decided to play for time and wait for the others to commit themselves first, and it was a relief when Mr Potter the solicitor finally asked leave to put forward a proposal.

He was pompous and precise, as he always was, and talked as if he were addressing a legal conference.

'We owe it to ourselves,' he said, 'to consider and safeguard our personal position as Directors in this unfortunate affair. We must face the fact that, from a legal point of view, we have already compromised ourselves. If information reaches a Board of Directors that seriously affects the fortunes of their Company, then it is their legal and moral duty to place that information before the shareholders immediately. This we have failed to do.'

'For a perfectly good reason,' put in Digby.

'That I fully agree with,' said Mr Potter. 'But the reason would not hold good in a court of law. We are all anxious that the murder of this old man Henry Hodder shall in no way be connected with the imposture of the well. If it was so connected, and the culprit was still undiscovered, then we should all be exposed to serious suspicion – possibly even of conspiracy. None of us would be entirely clear, and the mark would remain against us for the rest of our lives.

'This, then, is what I propose. Unless anything unforeseen occurs I think it probable that the inquest will close with a verdict of murder by a person or persons unknown.'

He glanced furtively around the table. He knew, of course, as we all did, that the 'person unknown', with little doubt, was sitting with us.

'We should then allow a few weeks to pass,' he proceeded, 'and having given time for the murder to become, as it were, a disconnected occurrence, we shall then discover the pipe to the duckpond ourselves, if you see what I mean. We can announce that we had just made a careful inspection of the pond with a view to turning it into a children's boating lake, and by chance had discovered the pipe connecting it with the well.

'By this means the integrity of the Directors will be unquestioned. We shall have made it appear that the murder occurred several weeks *before* we discovered the pipe. Nobody would then suspect that the two things were connected, and by announcing the imposture immediately after we had apparently made the discovery, we shall have fulfilled our duty in the eyes of the law.'

Mr Potter sat back with a smile of satisfaction. He seemed quite pleased at finding such a clever solution to the problem, but it didn't last for long.

'That's all very fine,' said Major Digby. 'No doubt it puts the Directors in the clear, but what happens next? You don't suppose the people of St Mary's are going to take it sitting down! They'll demand a public inquiry. They'll want to know who put the pipe there and when it was done – and the man they're bound to pick on is the man who owned the well before he gave it to the town, and that's Colonel Joyce, our Chairman!'

Mr Potter looked upset. 'I'm sure we can find some means of . . .' he began.

'There aren't any means!' barked out Digby. 'The whole thing's impossible! When the Colonel's asked for an explanation what can he say? If he tells the truth: that Henry Hodder did it, then we're back where we started – in a worse mess than ever. If he says he had the pipe laid himself, then he's open to a charge of fraud and they'd probably send him to prison! You're simply trying to shift the blame from a guilty man to an innocent one!'

It was time for me to say what had been on my mind ever since the wretched affair began.

'I can hardly call myself innocent,' I said. 'If I'd done my job properly that old man would never have dared to do what he did. But I didn't go there for months on end. I never even looked into the well to see whether the water level was normal, and during the winter when he laid the pipe I never went there at all. I can hardly blame Henry for thinking the well was something he could do what he liked with. If you put a man in charge of a job and never supervise him, then you've got to share the blame if he goes wrong. So if you feel that Mr Potter's proposal is the best way out of it, then I'll do my best when the time arrives.'

'If you'll forgive me saying so,' replied Digby, 'it's a lot of bunkum. If the well had been mine I guarantee I shouldn't have gone there any more than you did – especially in the winter when there was nothing doing. If you put a man in charge of a job it's for him to report when anything goes wrong. That's what he's there for. So if you take the rap yourself and say you did it, I tell you here and now that I shan't keep my mouth shut. I shall tell them you're a liar, and I'll tell them who it was!'

That was the end of Potter's proposal. Somebody then suggested that we should postpone the Official Opening on the grounds that we had discovered a fault in the supply of spring water; that we should then disconnect the pipe to the duckpond; drain the well and see whether we could get the original spring to flow again.

It was all right in theory, but the Treasurer said that we just hadn't got the money for such a big undertaking. It would take at least a year and we should go bankrupt, and the Borough Engineer said the chances of bringing a dried-up spring to life were scarcely worth considering.

The suggestion, like Potter's, fizzled out. We were getting nowhere, and the Town Clerk embarked upon a long explanation of the legal aspects. He considered that we should first discuss the matter in confidence with the London solicitors who were responsible for floating the Company: possibly a discussion with Lord Colindale himself. 'The legal aspects,' he said, 'are complicated and involved. We must have them thoroughly examined before we make our announcement.'

Jim Blundell hadn't said a word. He had played the game he always played when he was preparing to launch a plan of his own. He sat back with his thumbs in his waistcoat and listened with apparent interest to everything that was said. He never gave a sign of whether he approved or disapproved. He never nodded or shook his head or showed any impatience. But a man with such a dominating personality can be as formidable in silence as in speech, and Jim knew it. By keeping his eyes fixed on each speaker he was able to disconcert them and make their suggestions sound much lamer and more unconvincing than if he had interrupted and given them a chance to answer back.

For half an hour he allowed every suggestion all the rope it needed to hang itself from its own inadequacy and add more power and conviction to what he had got to say himself.

He allowed the Town Clerk to finish his long and dreary explanation of the 'legal complexities' and having given the Directors time to realize how fruitless it all was he took his thumbs out of his waistcoat, leant forward and looked around the table as if the real meeting was now about to begin.

'It seems to me,' he said, 'that we're all talking about saving our faces as Directors when the only thing that matters is to save the people of this town! Isn't that what we're here for? Isn't that what they trusted us to do? What's it all come to, anyway? If that old crook hadn't come here and told us about that pipe we should never have known a thing about it and nobody else would either! We should be going right ahead with the job of getting this Casino opened, and if we've got any sense that's what we'll do now!'

There was something that sounded like a gasp of astonishment, but from some at least I'm pretty sure it was a sigh of relief: relief that one of us had at last come out into the open and declared himself for something that the rest were too frightened to put into words.

'What's our position?' demanded Jim Blundell. 'What are we sitting round this table for? We're here because the people of St Mary's put their trust in us. They trusted us to make their town as prosperous as any in England, and God knows they deserve it!

'And because they trusted us they put every penny they had into this Company! They gave up their savings and mortgaged their houses and even sold their furniture! Old people sold the investments they'd bought from years of hard work and are going hungry while they wait for their dividends from the Company! Dividends we promised them! Are we going to throw these people into misery worse than death because we haven't got the guts to take a risk?'

'If we only had ourselves to consider,' said Stagg the Medical

Officer, 'then you know quite well that none of us would put our own personal risks before the interests of the people. But there are others to consider, besides ourselves and the people of this town. There are the thousands of visitors who would come here to drink the water . . .'

'The water!' shouted Jim Blundell. 'The water they want is the water that cured Lord Colindale, and that's what we're going to give them! If it cured him it'll cure them, so what's all the fuss about?'

'Whether it cured Lord Colindale or not is a matter of opinion,' replied the doctor. 'The plain fact is that we should be giving them water from a pond that's fed from an open ditch over which we have no control: a ditch that's exposed to every sort of contamination. If it caused an epidemic of typhoid and people died, d'you realize the responsibility we should be facing?'

'*We!*' retorted Jim Blundell: 'It's always *we*! I'm thinking of *them*!' He waved his hand dramatically towards the town. 'Are you going to bring certain ruin to thousands of our own people because a few strangers might pick up a few germs and get sore throats!'

'You must bear in mind,' said Mr Potter the solicitor, 'that we should be exposing ourselves to the gravest possible charge of fraud – including conspiracy. If the imposture were discovered, we could not deny our knowledge of it. There would be criminal proceedings that would certainly lead to imprisonment. If people died from drinking the water that we know to be exposed to contamination, then it would amount to a charge of manslaughter.'

Things were beginning to look dangerous. Stagg was getting very angry and Digby was going red in the face. If Jim Blundell went too far and got too free with his insults, anything might happen. If the Directors who refused to be brow-beaten got up and walked out, the whole board of management might disintegrate and heaven knows what would happen then.

It was time for me to intervene as Chairman. It was no use looking for a compromise. It had got to be all or nothing now, but things had got so heated that anything approaching a calm decision was impossible. The only way to avoid a break-up was to play for time.

'We've still got five weeks before the date fixed for the Opening,' I said. 'It's not long, but long enough to give us a few days to think over what's been said today. We've got to bear in mind that the inquest on Henry Hodder has only been adjourned. When it re-opens next week there's no knowing what the police may have to report. Something may transpire that will decide things for us. I suggest we close our discussion now, and meet again on the day following the inquest. We shall know then more clearly how we stand, and in the meantime we shall all have the opportunity for some careful thought.'

Jim Blundell demurred. He had made up his mind to force a decision that afternoon, but he was shrewd enough to see that he had provoked more opposition than he expected, and when the others grasped thankfully at another short reprieve, he gave in.

We got up from the table with relief. Mr Potter fumbled in his waistcoat-pocket, pulled out a small silver box, and took a tablet. Jim Blundell ran his handkerchief round his neck to remove the perspiration and the Town Clerk blew his nose.

We parted company with a show at least of friendliness.

We were not the 'happy team' we had so smugly called ourselves in the early days, but we hadn't split into two hostile camps that would have led to chaos.

Digby walked with me across the courtyard to where our cars were parked. The vans were still unloading furniture for the Casino and a big green lorry had arrived with a statue of the Goddess of Health.

'Good thing you stepped in when you did,' said Digby. 'Blundell was a fool to smash about like a bull in a china shop.'

'At least he told us one thing,' I answered. 'He told us who the man was who murdered Henry Hodder.'

Digby began to say something, but stopped himself as he glanced over my shoulder towards the Casino.

'You said the other night,' I went on, 'nobody would have gone to the lengths of murder unless he was determined to suppress the truth about the well.'

Digby shook his head and signed to me to be quiet. I looked up to see Blundell coming towards us across the courtyard – to his car that was parked near ours.

'I'll drive over to see you this evening,' said Digby. 'There are one or two things I can tell you about that.'

# Chapter Eighteen

Waiting for Digby that evening I began for the first time to take stock of my own future and what would happen to me when the truth came out and disaster swept the town.

I had put all the money I had into the Company. When the campaign began I had sold out my Government Securities of £4000 to buy Casino shares, and when the final drive was on I had put in another £600 that I always kept by me for emergencies on the farm. It was a reckless thing to do, but as Company Chairman I had to set an example when the appeal went out for the last great effort to raise the money. Like everybody else in St Mary's I had scraped the bottom of the barrel. I had nothing left beyond my small Army pension and the precarious profits from the farm that in bad seasons would amount to very little. By cutting things to the bone I might scrape along if I had nobody to think of beyond myself – but there was far more to it than that. The blow to the people of St Mary's would be appalling, and in their poverty and anger they would cry out for a scapegoat.

They wouldn't have far to look. I had given the town a worthless property and helped to cheat them by what in their eyes would seem like a shameless confidence trick. Would they believe that I knew nothing about the fatal duckpond pipe? – that a man in my employ could possibly have done it without my knowing? Henry was dead. His story, if ever told, would come to them by hearsay. How were they to know that I had not conspired with him to lay the pipe?

There would be some sort of public appeal to relieve their misery. I would be bound to make amends to the utmost. I would have to sell the Manor House and give the proceeds to the fund. I would have to leave the town. I could never face life among people who saw me as the man who had caused their poverty.

What could I do? Retire to some obscure boarding house by the sea? I might even have to change my name. The wretched story would be headlines in the newspapers and the name of Colonel Evelyn Joyce would be written down among the most notorious impostors in history.

I got myself into such a state of gloom and despondency that when I heard Digby's car outside I wished he hadn't come. I couldn't face another hopeless talk about the wretched business. I wanted to go to bed and be left alone.

But you couldn't be despondent for long when Digby was about. However bad things were he always managed to be alert and vigorous, and he brought some unexpected news that quickly stopped me brooding over my own misfortunes.

'There was a message from Inspector Braddock when I got home,' he said, 'asking me to go down to the police station. They were tremendously excited because they think they're on the track of the murderer.'

He saw the look on my face and laughed.

'It isn't what you think,' he said. 'It's something quite different, took me completely by surprise.' He pulled out his pipe and began to fill it. 'D'you know a young man named Sydney Glover?'

I shook my head. The name meant nothing to me.

'He was a fellow that Henry called in to help him collect the cash that first week-end when the crowds turned up.'

'Of course,' I said. 'I remember him well. I never knew his name.'

My mind went back to the unsavoury youth with the side-whiskers and dangling cigarette who had sat at the door of the well house, raking in the money and throwing it into a biscuit tin.

'Apparently he was a nephew of the old man,' said Digby. 'He lived in lodgings at Gateby about five miles off. He came over to help his uncle on the Saturday and Sunday, and when the boom was over, he seems to have developed a grievance. What the old man had promised him I don't know, but Sydney was convinced that he had been cheated out of his rightful share of the cash, and pursued his uncle with demands and threats. The police got word of it from a man who had seen Sydney stop his uncle outside a pub. There had been an angry scene, and Henry had told the man afterwards what it had been about, saying: "He's had what's due to him and he ain't going to get another bloody penny," or words to that effect.'

'Why didn't this come out before?' I asked.

'It's the way people are,' said Digby. 'Some are bursting to come forward; others do all they can to keep out of it. This man only told his story to the police last night. It seemed to them a hot clue: the first thing they'd got, and off they went to Sydney's lodging in Gateby where they were told that he had left with his belongings a week ago and disappeared: no address; nothing. Braddock was so excited that he wanted to put out an appeal and description right away. I suggested he held his hand until they'd made an effort to trace the fellow.'

'You don't think he's the man?'

'Personally I don't,' said Digby. 'Because it doesn't make sense. If Sydney Glover had wanted to rob the old man he'd have done it when there was something to steal. Everybody knew that Henry had blown the lot months ago and was cadging for drinks every night. Sydney would obviously have known it too. I can't believe he'd have waited until there was nothing to steal, then waylaid his uncle and murdered him for an empty pocket-case.'

'What happens if they arrest him and charge him?' I asked.

Digby raised his hands in despair. 'We'll take that hurdle when we get to it,' he said. 'In the meantime it's just another little ghost to haunt us. If they catch the wretched youth, and he has no alibi, if they charge him for want of any other suspect and he gets convicted on circumstantial evidence, are we to stand by and see him hung to save the secret of the well from getting out?'

'You still think it was Jim Blundell?'

Digby didn't answer at once.

'I thought what you did,' he said. 'I'm convinced that the man who murdered Hodder must have been at that meeting when the old man came and threatened us. And when I looked round the Council table I was sure that the only man who was ruthless enough – and strong enough to deal those crushing blows – was Blundell. I couldn't conceive it possible for any of the others to have done it. But I've been making some discreet inquiries and so far as I can see, Jim Blundell's in the clear. He was in and out of the public bar of The Coach and Horses all that evening. He always mixes freely with his customers, and at closing time he went outside with the last of them to see them off. Then he went in and shut and locked the doors. Henry walked off with the others; said good night and went on alone down the road that led to the side-lane where his cottage was. It would have taken him about twenty minutes to get home. He was killed before he got there so it must have happened about ten minutes after he left his friends.

'Soon after closing time young Paul Brooks came back to The Coach and Horses and let himself in at the side-door. He still has his room there, and he'd been for a walk. When he got in the two barmen were still clearing up and turning out the lights and Jim Blundell was in the sitting-room writing up his accounts. He asked Paul in and they sat there talking till midnight – long after the old man was dead in that ditch. So it looks as if we can count Jim Blundell out of it.'

'Could he have hired somebody to do it?'

'I think we can leave the "hired assassin" out of it,' said Digby. 'It would have been an appalling risk. Even Jim Blundell wouldn't have taken it. In any case he would never have found a local man to do it.'

'If we rule out Blundell,' I said, 'then who was it?'

Digby shrugged his shoulders. 'We might be right off the track,' he said. 'It might have been a tramp or a gypsy after all: it might even be Sydney Glover. But I just can't believe it. I can't believe in the thousand to one chance of a passing tramp knocking the old man off on the very night when so many people had an obvious motive for doing it.'

'Assuming it wasn't you or me,' I said, 'we're left with eight other people who were at the Casino meeting.'

'I think we can rule out the Vicar and Miss Fanshawe the Headmistress,' said Digby, 'even though the old lady's got a bicycle for a quick get-away. The doctor isn't likely because he obviously takes the view that danger from poisoning will force us to announce the facts whether Henry was alive or dead.'

'There's Potter the solicitor?'

Digby laughed. 'You mean the Coroner may be presiding over the inquest upon his own victim? It's a good situation, but too good to be true. I think Potter's a humbug. All that talk about announcing that we'd discovered the fraud ourselves. It nearly made me blow up.'

'You don't think it was sincere?'

'Not a word of it,' said Digby. 'He simply wanted to back his chances both ways. He wanted to go on record as an honest man urging the rest of us to tell the truth so that he'd be in the clear if the thing were found out. But all the time he knew he was safe in suggesting it because Jim Blundell was certain to fight it. Nobody's got more to lose than Potter if the Company collapses. He's got £10,000 of his own money in it.'

'So he might have murdered Henry?'

'He might,' said Digby. 'But I don't think he did. I can't imagine him hitching up those starched linen cuffs of his and sailing in with a crowbar. I'd rule out the Town Clerk for the same reason. He just hadn't got the physique for it. It was done by a powerful man and that podgy little Town Clerk of ours could never have dealt three crushing blows that smashed the old man's skull to pulp. We can rule out young Paul Brooks because he's the only one of us who hasn't got a motive. As a stranger he hasn't any money in the Company, and if the Company collapses he simply goes back to his job with the Colindale newspapers.'

'That accounts for everybody except the Borough Engineer and the Borough Treasurer?'

'Both big men,' said Digby; 'physically strong – otherwise no more likely than any of the rest of us. We could talk this thing round in circles for ever and get nowhere. Whoever did it covered his tracks all right. If the police had a ghost of a suspicion that one of the Directors was involved, then they could ask where we all were that night and have a look at our alibis, and I guarantee that the murderer would have a better one than any of us. The best thing we can do is let the murder look after itself. We've got quite enough on our plates without it.'

'If the inquest doesn't decide things for us,' I said, 'what's going to happen at the next meeting?'

Digby shrugged his shoulders. 'Your guess is as good as mine,' he said, 'but one thing's certain. You won't be able to step in and adjourn it again. It'll have to go on next time until there's agreement or a complete blow-up.'

'If I put Jim Blundell's proposal to the meeting – that we hush things up and go ahead – what support will he get?'

'He'll have the majority with him,' said Digby. 'Because when you come down to brass tacks it's the only possible thing to do. We'd be committing a God Almighty fraud and if it were found out we'd probably go to prison for it. Nobody with a free choice would bring disaster to the town because they're frightened to take the risk. But they don't all have a free choice. How can the Vicar, or the Headmistress, lend themselves to a fraud that cries out against everything they stand for? Or how can the Doctor shut his eyes to a wholesale poisoning if the water gets contaminated? If those three dig their heels in and refuse to accept Blundell's proposal – then we're back where we started.'

'And then what?' I asked.

'And then,' said Digby, 'we've had it. We're through. Unless somebody steps in and murders the opposition. But we don't really know at present what any of them mean to do. Some of them hardly said a word this afternoon. Why don't you go round and have a private talk with everybody before the next meeting? You're entitled to do that as Chairman. Make it confidential and find out what they really feel about it. They'll open up and say more in a private talk than they would at the Council table with Blundell riding rough-shod over them. You don't have to persuade them one way or another. It'll show you the way the wind's blowing and prepare you for the meeting. That's what I'd do if I were Chairman.'

Soon after Digby had gone I had another visitor. I was in the hall, turning out the lights on my way to bed when I heard a car draw up. Thinking it was Digby coming back for something I opened the door and found Paul Brooks there.

I have said very little of Paul since the day he arrived on Colin's recommendation to help us with the business of the Company; mainly because his work was so smoothly and efficiently done that we had taken him for granted. He had shown himself to be a first-class organizer and secretary. He never spoke at Board meetings unless asked for his opinion, and when this happened he was sensible and straight to the point.

I had barely given him a thought since we had run into our present troubles because the problems we were up against were scarcely his concern. As a stranger with us in a purely business capacity he stood apart from the rest of us. He had no responsibility for what happened to the town if disaster came, and if I thought of him at all it was to envy him his freedom and independence. If the Company collapsed he would simply return to his job with the Colindale newspapers, with nothing lost and a fine career ahead of him, because I knew how highly Colin rated him as one of his most promising young men.

On this account it was all the more a surprise to see him standing there, pale and agitated – without warning, and close to midnight. He looked so distracted, so different from the calm, restrained young man I had always known that I felt sure he had come with the news that the worst had happened: that our secret was out at last.

He was full of apologies. 'I'm very sorry,' he stammered. 'I hope you'll forgive me. It's very late, but could you spare me a few minutes?'

'Of course,' I said. 'Come in.'

I took him to my library and poured him a drink. His hand was trembling when he took the glass.

'I know how much you've got to worry you,' he said. 'I oughtn't to have come like this. I should have come in the morning – but I couldn't face another night like the ones I've been having. I had to see you – and I do hope you'll forgive me.'

'Whatever it is, Paul – go ahead and tell me everything you want to say.'

He hesitated. 'I'm only the Secretary,' he said. 'I'm here to do my job and not to interfere. I've said nothing at our meetings since this awful business happened, but in all their talks the Directors have scarcely mentioned Lord Colindale. Do they realize what it would mean to him if the truth comes out?'

I breathed again. At least he hadn't come to tell me that the worst had happened.

'I've thought about that, Paul – many times,' I said, 'because Lord Colindale is one of my oldest friends. But to most of the others he's merely a name. They've scarcely met him. They know what he's done to help us, but with so much to worry them you can understand if they haven't given much thought to his personal feelings.'

'It's nothing to do with the help and the money he's given,' said Paul. 'It's what it would do to his whole life and career. You may think I'm being silly about this, that I'm exaggerating. You may say that he's strong enough to withstand anything, but do you realize what a deadly, destroying thing ridicule is? Everybody in England believes he made this wonderful return to public life through the waters of that spring. Because of it he's now one of the leading men in the Government: he may well be Prime Minister in a few years' time. He has declared to millions over television that he owes everything to the miraculous waters of St Mary's – but what will happen if it is announced that all he drank was ditch water out of a muddy duckpond?'

'Men don't rise to the head of affairs from what they eat and drink,' I said. 'Of course I know the power of ridicule in malicious hands, but nobody in their right mind would think any the less of Lord Colindale if this came out.'

But Paul was not to be persuaded. The more I tried to reassure him the more desperate he became.

'People think he's made of iron,' he said; 'they think he can stand up against anything, but I've been his private secretary and I know how different he is from what people think. He's sensitive and introspective: his enemies know that, and they'd glory in this if it were made public. He'd be pursued with ridicule; made a laughing stock; a target for cheap jokes; burlesqued and jeered at; it would go on and on and I'm certain it would wear him down and destroy him. And there's another thing. We know now that the water he drank couldn't possibly have cured him. By chance he was a little better after his first visit to the well, and his cure was built up on faith: nothing but faith in what he believed to be a miraculous spring. But if that faith were broken, I believe the shock would ruin everything and he'd become a helpless cripple again. You see – if his enemies didn't destroy him with ridicule, he would destroy himself.'

I began to wonder why Paul had thought it necessary to come and tell me all this at midnight when he must have known I couldn't do anything about it. I listened with all the sympathy I could manage because he was so earnest, so desperate to save the feelings of a man he was passionately devoted to. But I thought he was exaggerating what it would do to Colin. It would hurt his pride and cause a lot of ridicule, but I was reasonably sure that he was tough enough to take it. In any case the fate of one man, even so illustrious a man as Lord Colindale – was a small thing compared with the fate of a whole town. I didn't tell Paul that; I didn't want to seem indifferent to the fate of a man he was so devoted to.

'I would do anything I could to save Lord Colindale,' I said. 'But you were at the meeting this afternoon, and you know how things stand. It rests entirely with the Directors. There's little I can do personally.'

'But there is!' cried Paul. 'I'm certain you can save Lord Colindale from this humiliation and ridicule! You can save the people of St Mary's too – if you'll do what I've come to ask you!'

I began to sit up. If Paul had a solution to the hopeless mess, then he was a worker of miracles.

'If the Directors decide to suppress what we know about the well,' he said, 'and go right ahead – then everything's all right. But if they refuse, if they say they must publish the news – will you stop them from doing it until you've seen Lord Colindale and asked for his help?'

My hopes of a miracle were gone.

'But what could Lord Colindale do?' I asked him.

'It was suggested at the meeting today,' said Paul, 'that we might postpone the opening on the grounds that the spring was failing and we had got to work on it to restore the supply.'

'That was turned down on account of the expense,' I said.

'I know,' replied Paul. 'But Lord Colindale's a millionaire. The expense to him would be nothing compared with what would happen if the truth comes out.'

'It would still mean telling Lord Colindale what you want to avoid,' I said. 'He would have to be told it was the duckpond water he drank.'

But Paul had got everything worked out.

'He needn't know!' he answered. 'You needn't say a word about that pipe! You only have to say that the spring began to fail after the Company began to build the Casino! He's taken such an interest in the scheme that I'm certain he'd come to the rescue, and he'd be spared from ever knowing what he really drank!'

'You heard what the Engineer said,' I replied. 'Whatever we spent, whatever work we did – the chances of bringing a dried-up spring to life again are remote – barely worth considering.'

'But we *must*!' – the boy was desperate: on the verge of tears – 'we've *got* to find a way of saving Lord Colindale because I'm certain it'll ruin his career if this awful thing comes out! When that old man came and told us what he'd done, I knew that I'd got to do anything on earth to save Lord Colindale. If I took the blame myself, if I promised the Directors that if the pipe was discovered I would say that I had arranged for it to be laid myself – would that help?'

'If the pipe were discovered, Paul – it would make little difference who had laid it.'

'But it would!' said Paul. 'It would make all the difference! I've been here nine months now. Supposing I were to say that when I came here I discovered that the level in the well was falling, and to save things I arranged secretly to lay the pipe from the pond? I've thought of this for days and I'm certain it would work. Nobody could say exactly when the pipe was laid! That old man's dead, so nobody could prove that I didn't do it myself! It would save the Directors from responsibility and it would save Lord Colindale because it would seem as if he had drunk the real spring water before I had tampered with the supply!'

It was ingenious, but hopelessly impractical. I thought of the distracted boy lying in bed through sleepless nights, thinking out his pathetic, fantastic plan.

It was pointless and cruel to argue with him. He had come to me as the only man he could open his heart to. The least I could do was to respect his confidence.

'If it comes to the point,' I said, 'I'll discuss what you've suggested with the Directors. But I still hope it won't be necessary. Everybody wants to save the people and the town. We're all fighting the same battle in our different ways and I hope to goodness we shall find a way.'

He seemed easier when he got up to go. I felt guilty at raising his hopes beyond any that I secretly held myself, but he thanked me again and again for listening so patiently and so understandingly.

'Come along whenever you want to have a talk,' I said. 'I shall always be here in the evenings and always glad to see you.'

I had been on the point of going to bed when Paul had come. It was well past midnight when he left me, but he had taken with him all hopes of any sleep I might have had.

Discussing Henry's murder earlier in the evening Digby had said:

'We can rule out young Paul Brooks because he's the only one of us without a motive. He hasn't any money in the Company or any personal interest in what happens to the town.'

I recalled to mind what an elderly reporter on one of the Colindale newspapers had said to me when he had come down in the early days to interview me. Our talk had turned to 'Lord Colindale's young men', of whom Paul Brooks was one: the young men who were hand-picked by Colin for their ability and enterprise, whom he trained for future office. "They worship him,' the reporter had said; 'they venerate him. He's their hero; their God. They'd do anything for him; anything on earth. If necessary I think they would do murder for him.'

Digby had mentioned that Paul Brooks had been for a walk on the night when Henry died: that he had returned to The Coach and Horses some while after closing time.

# Chapter Nineteen

Next morning I followed up what Digby had suggested and began the business of seeing each Director privately.

I didn't relish the job. I hadn't got much confidence in my diplomacy and if I gave the impression that I was hatching some sort of plot behind the backs of the others I'd probably do more harm than good.

But the decisive meeting in a few days' time was going to be acutely difficult and the more I could find out in advance the better I would be able to handle things. At least I wouldn't be going into it completely in the dark.

I decided to begin with Jim Blundell, so I rang him up after breakfast, got the car, and drove down to the town.

The renovations to The Coach and Horses were now complete and the old inn looked resplendent. Ever since I was a boy its shabby brown brick walls and empty windows had been a forlorn picture of decay: a once prosperous coaching inn sunk to the level of a seedy commercial hotel. But Blundell never did things by halves. He had pushed the boat out and employed the best architect in Colchester who had transformed the place beyond recognition. The gloomy old Georgian frontage now gleamed in its coat of clean white paint, with attractive blue window frames, and window boxes gay with flowers. The name of the inn spanned the frontage in big letters of gold and a brand-new sign swung proudly in the breeze. It showed a stage coach with four horses galloping down a country lane, with a fat coachman, not unlike Jim Blundell himself, blowing a long brass horn.

When I saw this bold symbol of Jim Blundell's enterprise and thought of the money it had cost I could scarcely blame him for fighting so hard to save it from disaster.

Jim Blundell himself was an odd mixture of flamboyant enterprise and shrewd conservatism. He had spent a small fortune on modern conveniences for wealthy visitors from overseas, but he hadn't forgotten old local customers who would have felt like fish out of water among chromium fittings and ultra-modern furnishings. He had accordingly preserved the old saloon and public bars exactly as they had always been, even down to the outmoded handles that the barmen pulled to fill a tankard with draught beer. The old scarred wooden benches and tables were still there, and the old stagnant smell of beer and tobacco that gave the bar its pleasant homely flavour. You entered these old rooms from a narrow lane at the side of the inn, so the ancient locals would never have to mix with the expensive overseas visitors shortly to arrive.

I found Jim Blundell in his dark little sitting-room at the back of the public bar. This too he had kept as it always had been, no doubt through sentiment. It had been his father's and grandfather's den before him. There were some old black metal spikes for bills and receipts, a row of battered account books on the sideboard and a bloated, bulbous-eyed stuffed fish in a glass case on the wall.

The strains of events had made its mark, even on the stolid, massive Blundell. He had got thinner. The buttons on his blue-serge waistcoat no longer strained across his stomach. His cheeks that used to be so plump and shiny had sagged and lost their colour; his eyes were bloodshot with dark hollows round them.

He was wary and suspicious until I assured him that I had come for an informal off-the-record talk to prepare the way for our next and decisive meeting. When I told him I supported his proposal to hush things up he unfroze and got quite affable and offered me a glass of sherry.

'It's the only common-sense thing to do,' I told him. 'Whatever might be said against it, we've no choice unless we want to wreck the town.'

'It's some of the others that make me mad,' he said; 'them that haven't got the guts to take a risk.'

'That's what I've come about,' I said. 'It's possible that some of them won't come in. They might refuse to lend themselves to a fraud. We've got to be ready for anything.'

'They've bloody well got to come in,' said Blundell. 'If they don't, the whole thing's finished. It's that or nothing.'

'If they won't budge,' I said, 'if we're bang up against it, there's another possibility that might keep them quiet and save the worst from happening.'

I told him about the suggestion Paul Brooks had made: to go to Lord Colindale and tell him the whole thing, and get him to pay the expenses of draining the well in an effort to bring the spring to life again.

'He's a millionaire,' I said.' I think he'd pay almost anything to save himself from the ridicule if the real facts came out.'

Jim Blundell stared at me in blank astonishment.

'When did Brooks put this to you?' he asked.

'He came to see me last night.'

'Has he talked about it to the others?'

'Not so far as I know.'

'Then the first thing you do is to tell him to keep his interfering mouth shut. If you don't, I will. He must be off his head. It's a crazy, cock-eyed idea.'

'It's a last resort,' I said,' if the others refuse to accept things as they are.'

'A last resort!' he shouted.' I'd say it is! It'd be the end of the whole bloody thing! Suppose Colindale *did* put up the cash – how long would it take to do the job? I guarantee they'd muck about for a year. Who's going to pay compensation to the people who've spent all they've got on their shops and houses getting ready for the boom? And all the shareholders who've sunk their savings expecting quick dividends? And what happens if they don't get the spring going? The Engineer said himself it's a hundred to one against it! – and suppose they *did* get the old spring working? Nobody's going to believe it's the same water that cured Lord

Colindale! Once you start mucking about you kill their confidence. If you let the whole thing rot for a year you're never going to warm it up again! And what about all the people who've got their rooms booked up from the day we open in four weeks' time? What about all these visitors who've booked for The Coach and Horses?'

He picked up a bundle of letters and spread them out on the table.

'Here's Mr and Mrs Joseph Hanna: he's a cattle millionaire from Chicago – booked my best suite for two months at £80 a week; Senator Steve Fletcher from Melbourne: booked in with his wife for six weeks; Parker Willis: oil millionaire from Los Angeles; Martin Buhler: big car manufacturer from Detroit.'

It was an impressive list. All the most important and wealthiest applicants had been handed to Jim Blundell from the inquiry centre at the Town Hall because he had the best accommodation to offer.

'I'm booked solid for nine months,' said Jim. 'There's three thousand quids' worth of customers here – and there's letters coming in every day. D'you suppose I'm going to sit down and write letters putting 'em all off because a few white-livered skunks haven't got the guts to take a risk?'

'It was only in case some of the Directors refused. . .' I began.

'They aren't *going* to refuse!' said Jim Blundell with a grim finality. 'You leave it to me.'

There was no more to be said. Jim Blundell was determined to force things through: to hush up the truth and go ahead. I saw his point and sympathized with him, but how he was going to persuade the Doctor and the Vicar, the Headmistress and Potter the solicitor to become conspirators in a monstrous fraud I couldn't even guess at.

He offered me another glass of sherry and began talking about plans for the Official Opening as if it were a foregone conclusion. He even came back to his proposal to serve the guests with caviare at the ceremonial banquet. 'We've got to do everything in slap-up style,' he said. 'I ain't going to stand for smoked salmon.' I couldn't help admiring his superb confidence. Having forced the complete surrender of the Directors, he was even planning to cap his victory by reversing his original defeat over the caviare.

As I was leaving he returned again to Paul Brooks.

'Will you tell that young fool to keep his mouth shut, or shall I?'

'I don't think he's likely to talk to the others,' I told him.' He suggested it to me and left it in my hands.'

'All the same, you better tell him. If he puts ideas like that across the Council table, some of 'em will jump at it – anything to save their skins. They'll want to run to Colindale and blow the whole thing up.'

I promised to speak to Paul, but I didn't think it necessary.

At the door of the inn, Jim Blundell laid his hand on my arm and looked around to see that we were alone.

'If you get any trouble from him,' he said in a low voice, 'if he threatens to talk – then tell me. I happen to know a few things to keep him quiet. Did you know he left his room here after dinner on the night old Henry was murdered and didn't get back here till after it had happened? He said he'd "been for a walk". One of his hands was bleeding and he told me he'd "caught it on a thorn bush beside the road". I ain't going to bring that up against him: if he reckoned it would help to save old Colindale by bumping off Henry Hodder then that's okay with me, because it helps us too, but if he threatens to put this damn silly idea to the Council, he'll think better of it when he hears what I got to say.'

I walked away in disgust. I had never liked Jim Blundell. I despised him now as a blackguard. I also knew that he was a desperate man who would stop at nothing to get his way.

After my distasteful interview with Blundell it was a relief to sit down in the quiet office of the Town Clerk who was the next on my list for private talks. He was a sensible, realistic little man who had everything neatly sorted out in his orderly mind.

'I feel quite certain,' he said, 'that we must suppress what we know and go straight ahead as if nothing had happened because the only alternative is unthinkable. We are committing a fraud, but in my opinion it is by far the lesser of the two evils. We are setting the possible risk of infecting a few people by contaminated water against the certain misery of thousands.

'In my opinion the waters of every spa depend mainly upon the faith of those who drink it. If they believe that the water from St Mary's well is going to cure them, then it makes little difference whether it comes from the spring or the duckpond.

'The Doctor, of course, has his professional integrity to consider, and I respect it, but my own first duty is towards the people of St Mary's.

'If you put Mr Blundell's proposal to the meeting, then I shall support it unreservedly.'

In the evening I went to see the Borough Engineer and the Borough Treasurer. They were both family men living in small houses with children running about all over the place, and I wished I had asked them to the Manor House where we would have had the privacy we needed. In both cases the wives mistook my visit for a social call and wanted to make me tea or coffee, and I had to spend time making small talk before I could get down to business with their husbands.

It was clear that both had talked the matter over with the Town Clerk and were in full accord with him. In their opinion the legal crime of hushing up the truth was nothing compared with the moral crime of bringing disaster to a town they had served so faithfully for so many years.

'As for the change in the water supply,' said the Engineer, 'I guarantee that if you could take a hundred people and dose half with the old spring water and half with the water from the duckpond, without letting them know the difference, then the percentage of cures would work out at more or less the same.

'As for contamination: I admit there's a risk – but when my wife and I were in Germany last year we both drank the water at a famous spa and both got violent diarrhoea, so it looks as if it cuts both ways.'

The Engineer's chief worry was the galvanized-iron pipe that connected the duckpond with the well.

'If we go right ahead and accept things as they are, we shall still have that damn pipe to give us nightmares.'

I asked him how long it would last.

He shrugged his shoulders. 'In theory a good, well laid galvanized-iron pipe will last indefinitely,' he said. 'But there are a lot of factors to consider. Corrosive substances in the water is one: certain minerals like iron and lime can lay a gradual coating that'll clog a pipe until it's almost closed, but it's a big pipe with a three-inch diameter, so that's in our favour.

'The laying of the pipe is another thing. Wilf Parsons who did the job with Henry was a good plumber, but it was done secretly: mainly, I suppose, at night. Unless the bottom of the trench was level and packed hard you might get subsidence: distortion in the pipe: possible fracture. The foundations of one of the medical huts run straight across the pipe trench. They're light foundations and the pipe is at least a couple of feet below it, but you can still get a down-thrust that might break the pipe at a connexion.

'I wouldn't worry about any of this if the damn thing wasn't a secret. But you see the problem? If anything goes wrong I can't put a gang on the job without giving the whole thing away. We'd have to do it ourselves without anybody seeing us at it, and how we'd do that, God knows.

'But it's no good taking our hurdles before we get to them. We've got enough to worry about as it is, so we've just got to hope for the best and pray for the damn pipe every night.

'As for what we do now – I'm a hundred per cent with Jim Blundell in hushing it up and going ahead.'

The Borough Treasurer was a hundred per cent in favour, too. Nobody knew better what appalling results would follow the collapse of the Company because he had been in charge of the business of raising the money and knew the sacrifices the people had made: reckless sacrifices in a lot of cases.

'It's too late now,' he said. 'The harm's done and we can't do anything about it, but we should never have given that assurance about a ten per cent return for their money. They took our word for it, and it turned into a sort of fever. They mortgaged their houses and borrowed on insurances, right up to the hilt. If the truth came out and the Company collapsed, there are hundreds of decent, steady-going people who'll be out on the streets; without a home; without a penny; completely ruined.

'And because we encouraged them with golden promises, we've got a moral obligation to save them – no matter what we have to do in terms of fraud and deception.'

I went home with a useful day's work done. The Town Clerk, the Engineer, and the Treasurer were solidly in favour of hushing things up and going ahead. Digby and I were in favour and that, with Jim Blundell, made six. If a majority vote was all we needed, we were home, but it wasn't as simple as that. I still had to see the Vicar, the Headmistress, Potter the solicitor, and Dr Stagg. These four stood apart from the rest of us. They all had compelling moral reasons for refusing to lend themselves to a fraud. It only needed one of them to turn the tables on the rest. If one stood out and demanded the truth to be told, there was nothing we could do about it.

I had made appointments to see them all on the following day, but I wasn't looking forward to it.

# Chapter Twenty

The Vicar was the first on my list. He was anxious for me not to go to the Vicarage. He asked me to meet him at the church: in the vestry.

It was a lovely morning in the first week of June, and with plenty of time on my hands I left the car behind and took the footpath across the fields and through the woods.

The people of St Mary's were leaving nothing to the last moment. Although four weeks remained before the opening of the Casino the decorations were almost complete. As I walked through the quiet streets on the outskirts of the town I saw that even the humblest people had made their contribution. Homemade garlands were strung from the windows: there were flags and little streamers and banners with 'Welcome to St Mary's' on them. Old Coronation and Jubilee decorations had been unearthed from forgotten corners, and some people had strung coloured electric bulbs among the trees in their front gardens.

I hardly recognized the High Street, so drab and dull in former days. The local authorities had organized the decorations here, and strings of coloured flags criss-crossed the street. There were brightly painted wooden shields fixed to the lampposts, bearing the arms of St Mary's, with masses of imitation coloured flowers around them and 'Welcome to St Mary's' everywhere. Every shop was resplendent in a fresh coat of paint and every window had its own special display. Some were already filled with souvenirs. There were china ornaments with the town arms on them, brass ashtrays and paperweights, and silk handkerchiefs bearing a colourful picture of the ancient monastery with the well in the foreground, and nuns handing out the miraculous water to a crowd of pilgrims.

Several people waved to me, or stopped me as I went by, calling out: 'Good luck!' or asking how things were getting along. I had become almost a legendary figure: the man whose 'surpassing generosity' had made it all possible.

Some engineers were busy in the churchyard installing the lamps that were to floodlight the church on the night when the Casino was opened, and throughout the summer. I walked up the path, threading my way between the wires and cables to where the old Vicar was waiting for me at the vestry door.

He apologized for not asking me to the Vicarage. 'My wife would have insisted upon making coffee for you,' he said, 'and joining in our talk because she knows nothing of our troubles. It has been a great trial keeping it from her. In all our years together I have discussed every little problem of my work with her: every difficulty. She has guessed, of course, that there is something on my mind. She knows that I am sleeping badly. I dread the nights because I have always had the misfortune of talking in my sleep and every morning I expect to find that I have given this dreadful secret away.'

I felt more sympathy for the Vicar than for any of the others. The rest of us at least were young enough to face the problem and grapple with it in our own ways. But the Vicar was old and frail: well over seventy, far beyond the age to carry such a burden. He had been Vicar of St Mary's for more than thirty years and his placid life in a sleepy town had totally unfitted him to play a part in our present troubles. He was aware of this himself, but refused to use it as a means to rid himself of his responsibility.

'I know of course,' he said, 'why Mr Blundell, our Mayor, pressed me so hard to join the Board of the Company. I had little talent for business affairs, but he knew that a great many people looked to me for an example and would put their money into the Company if I were on the Board. I was proud to play my part to the best of my ability, but you see the terrible dilemma I am placed in now?

'You mustn't think I am being self-righteous about this. If I were free, then I would gladly support Mr Blundell's proposal to suppress the truth because it is the only way to save our people. But when I became a priest I bound myself to certain principles that I've got to observe. If I break them, then I cease to have the right to carry on my duties. I cannot be Vicar of St Mary's and Director of a Company that I know to be fraudulent. I cannot preach the obligation of truth and honesty from my pulpit if I were conspiring to carry out a fraud and a deception in the Council Room.

'You see what I am bound to do? If I remain a Director of a fraudulent Company I must leave the Church. If I remain Vicar of St Mary's I must resign from the Board of the Company. I feel sure that I am a better priest than business man, so I shall place my resignation from the Board in your hands at the next meeting.

'I shall give an assurance that I shall do nothing to prejudice the work ahead if the others decide to go on with it because I am certain that they are doing the only right and proper thing. My resignation will be of little consequence and I can explain that it is due to my health and advancing years. But I shall be with you heart and soul, and I trust that God will not frown on me if I pray every night that the pipe from the duckpond will produce clean water and will never be discovered.'

Miss Fanshawe's position was very much like the Vicar's and she took the same line. She talked to me in her study at the school she had given the best years of her life to: the school that she had raised from drabness and obscurity to one of the best in the county. She had never aimed at spectacular academic distinctions for her girls. She went for character and common-sense and personal integrity, and because of her success, parents sent their children to her school from miles around.

'You must understand,' she said, 'that I'm not claiming loftier morals than those of the other Directors. As a private individual I'm no better or worse than any of them, and if I were a free agent

I would go the whole way with them. But I can only demand the highest standards of behaviour from my girls so long as I keep rigidly to those standards myself.

'If I demand truth and honour in the schoolroom and conspire to commit fraud and deception at Board meetings I should be a hypocrite and a humbug – no longer fit to be headmistress of a school.'

She would therefore resign, she said, at the next meeting, but gave me an assurance, as the Vicar had done, that she would say nothing or do nothing to prejudice our work if we went ahead. The secret, she said, was safe with her. 'I only hope,' she added, 'that nobody will think I'm running away because I'm frightened. On the contrary I shall always regret missing the excitement ahead. Even if we were discovered, I would have gone to prison with a clear conscience and enjoyed the experience of convict life.'

The next on my list was Mr Potter the solicitor and I went to see him at his office in the High Street where the firm of Hartigan, Blake, and Potter had been established for more than a hundred years.

My talks with the others had been honest and straightforward. They had told me exactly what they felt about the thing: what they intended to do and why. But my interview with Mr Potter was very different. It stank of humbug and hypocrisy and left me feeling sick.

I had never had a great deal to do with him until we had come together as Directors of the Company. I had known him more as a caricature of a country lawyer than as an individual. His clothes were cut in the fashion of a bygone age. He wore a high stove-pipe collar and a large cravat that gave him a Dickensian appearance. He invariably wore black, summer and winter. He had side-whiskers and a mane of untidy, dusty-looking iron-grey hair. He had faded, watery blue eyes and his face was the colour of an old parchment document.

His appearance was no doubt intended to symbolize the unchanging integrity of an old established firm. It certainly had its effect. He was looked up to with awe by the small shopkeepers who went to him occasionally for advice: he was trustee of innumerable wills and every old lady in St Mary's with private means placed her affairs unquestioningly in his hands. He looked and behaved the part of leading solicitor in the town as his father and grandfather had done before him.

His big private office overlooked the Market Square and was furnished to impress his clients with the same unchanging stability that characterized his own appearance. The walls were lined with ponderous leather-bound legal books that looked as if they would fall to pieces if taken down and opened. There were stacks of ancient deed-boxes: piles of documents tied with faded red tape and a few prints of long dead legal celebrities in wigs and gowns.

He lived with his wife in a ponderous old Victorian house on the outskirts of the town with tall iron railings round it and a cheerless garden overgrown with laurels. Although reported to be in good circumstances he lived frugally, had no car, and seldom entertained. My only personal contacts with him had been at occasional bridge parties. He played with a deliberate precision, very slowly, but without inspiration or originality and took particular care in adding up the points.

He greeted me with pompous courtesy: invited me to take the armchair beside his desk and asked me to explain the purpose of my call.

I told him I had simply come to find out, in confidence, what his views were concerning our problem, and the line he proposed to take at our decisive meeting in a few days' time.

'It will be a difficult meeting,' I said, 'and it will help me as Chairman, to know as much as possible in advance.'

He was silent for a little while, and then began to talk as if his answer had been carefully rehearsed.

'You realize, of course,' he said, 'that my position is one of exceptional difficulty. Hartigan, Blake, and Potter has been established as the firm of leading solicitors in St Mary's for generations. The first Mr Hartigan founded the firm in the reign of King William IV, and its reputation for integrity has been unquestioned ever since. Our name in St Mary's has become a byword for absolute trust and security. My grandfather joined the firm in 1863, and since the families of Hartigan and Blake died out, my own family have been heirs to its tradition. Whatever my personal inclinations towards the Casino Company may be in its present difficulties, my first duty is obvious. I am bound to uphold the unblemished reputation of this firm: not only as a duty to those who have done so before me, but also as a duty to my son Leslie who is reading law at Cambridge and will join me in a few years' time. On that account alone it is my binding obligation to keep our great tradition unimpaired.'

'You mean,' I said, 'that you will insist upon the truth about the well being published?'

Mr Potter looked startled. 'By no means,' he replied. 'We must not confuse two entirely separate issues. As a private individual I agree absolutely with those who wish to suppress the truth for the sake of the people of the town. It would be monstrous, inhuman to advocate a deliberate exposure that would bring such misery and disaster.'

'But at our last meeting,' I said, 'you yourself put forward a suggestion for publishing the true facts? You said it would be best if we discovered the fraud ourselves – and announced it in a way to disconnect it with the murder?'

He looked at me with a reassuring smile.

'I did that,' he explained, 'on the assumption that the Directors would unanimously insist upon the truth being published. I merely wanted to suggest a satisfactory means of doing it. But when Mr Blundell put forward his proposal for suppressing the facts, I immediately withdrew.'

'But you disapprove?'

Mr Potter became irritated. He spoke slowly and deliberately as if explaining something to a child.

'I spoke just now of two entirely separate issues,' he said. 'The first is simply whether or not the truth shall be suppressed. As a private individual, as a human being, I am whole-heartedly in favour of suppression for the sake of our town and people. The other issue concerns my professional integrity. You realize, of course, that if the truth were discovered and the Directors were called to account, then the degree of guilt would vary considerably. There would be extenuating reasons for men like the Mayor, yourself, and others whom we might call "laymen". It could be pleaded on your behalf that you were not fully versed in the legal aspects of the case. But for a lawyer like myself there could be no such defence. It would be asserted, and justly asserted, that I had become party to a conspiracy to commit fraud fully understanding the gravity of the crime. In other words I would have entered upon it with my eyes open: wilfully breaking the law that I had bound myself professionally to observe. There would be no mitigation for my offence: no grounds for appeal.'

He paused to allow this to sink in.

'The presence of an experienced lawyer on the Board,' he continued, 'might well make it worse for the other Directors in the event of an exposure.'

'In what way?' I asked.

'It could be argued,' he said, 'that I would have made the legal situation clear to them. Their plea of ignorance would be dismissed.'

He took a sheet of notepaper from a drawer of his desk and handed it to me. 'To save my associates from being compromised in this way,' he said, 'I have put my resignation from the Board in writing, stating that pressure of other business compels me to resign. As Chairman of the Company, you will no doubt read it at the next meeting.'

It was not his resignation that made me angry. It was the humbug that went with it.

'You want the truth to be hushed up,' I said, 'but the others must take the responsibility.' He gave a gesture of impatience.

'I have already explained,' he replied. 'Our positions are totally different. The others are laymen, unversed in the law. Their sentences would no doubt be light: they would suffer no dishonour in view of the circumstances, and could afterwards return to their normal lives with no serious damage done. But for me it would involve total ruin. I would be struck off the roll of solicitors and debarred from practising again. This fine old firm would be damaged beyond repair and my son Leslie would lose the inheritance that I am in honour bound to pass on to him.'

And that was that. There was no more to be said. As soon as possible I got up and went, glad to get out into the fresh air again.

No doubt from the legal point of view his behaviour was perfectly correct. It was the hypocrisy that disgusted me. Nobody stood to. lose more than Potter if the Company collapsed. He was one of the biggest investors. He had put something over £10,000 into it, and Digby, who liked him even less than I did, had hinted that some of that money may not have been his to play with. His firm held all sorts of funds, technically in trust and paying perhaps five per cent to beneficiaries. By borrowing on such money he was hoping to make ten per cent in Company dividends and keep the difference for himself. If such were the case, then disaster to the Company would land him in alarming difficulties, and he was desperate to cover himself as best he could. His purpose at our last meeting was obvious. He had urged the Directors to announce the imposture because he knew in advance that Jim Blundell wouldn't accept it, but he wanted to put on record his proposal to tell the truth. I discovered that his letter of resignation was dated for the day of that meeting. He could therefore declare, if the fraud came to light, that having had his proposal rejected, he had at once tendered his resignation from the Board, thereby clearing himself of all suspicion of guilt. He wanted to run with the hare and hunt with the hounds. He desperately wanted his profits from the Company, but was determined to let the others take the risk.

It was a relief to get clear of Mr Potter for an honest, downright talk with the Medical Officer.

Dr Stagg was a bachelor, and he had invited me to lunch with him in the room above his surgery.

He was a young man: the youngest of our Directors; the most constructive and the most intelligent. In his five years as Medical Officer of St Mary's he had swept away a lot of cobwebs from the old neglected town. He had condemned the swimming baths and had them reconstructed; got rid of the earth closets that still lurked in dark backyards and waged a vigorous war against insanitary dustbins. It spoke well for his tact and common-sense that he had lived down prejudice and become so popular. He played a good game of cricket and coached the local football team.

He didn't waste time lecturing me about his 'professional integrity' and 'moral responsibilities' as Potter had done, and got straight down to the heart of things: the water that now fed the well.

'If that old fool Henry had piped in water from the mains instead of from the duckpond,' he said, 'I wouldn't have lost an hour of sleep over it, because the main water would probably have cured as many people as the spring would have done. It's this duckpond water that gives me nightmares.'

'You think there's a serious danger?'

'There's an appalling danger,' he replied, 'and we can't do a thing about it. The pond is all right. It's deep and clear, and below the silt there's a hard clay bottom. It's probably the original fishpond that supplied the Nunnery.

'If it were a closed pond fed by rainwater I wouldn't worry. There'd be small risk and I'd drink it myself any time.

'But the main supply to that pond comes from an open ditch that runs along beside the road for miles and takes in the drainage water from cottages and farms. A dozen things can pollute and poison that ditch water: dead rats; animal droppings; garbage; old containers with the residue of poisonous weed killers and insecticides. We've no way of stopping it from getting into the pond, or from the pond to the well.'

I suggested that we might fit some sort of filter. 'I've gone into that,' he said, 'but it'd be a major undertaking needing expert labour – and that would give the whole show away.

'The water may be perfectly clean one day and poisonous the next. It was all right when I sent samples to the County Analyst, but how do we know that a farmer won't throw a half empty can of rat killer into the ditch tonight?'

'And yet it cured Lord Colindale?' I said.

Stagg laughed. 'D'you think so?' he asked.

'You might say it was a faith cure,' I replied, 'but he hadn't the least faith in it when he drank it. He had forgotten all about it by the time he went to bed, but next morning he was better.'

'And then he remembered the drink at the well; decided that his improvement was due to it, and faith did the rest.'

'Could faith bring a permanent cure? – to a man so badly crippled?'

Stagg shrugged his shoulders. 'You may think I'm cynical about these things,' he answered, 'but I doubt whether the waters of any of these famous spas really cure anybody. Not the water by itself. Most people take the cure because they're ill from over-eating and over-drinking or overwork. They're put on a strict diet, made to rest, lead a healthy life, and get better. The spa water provides the romantic background; there may be a touch of "faith cure" but the medical attention really does the job. In the case of Lord Colindale, who knows? He had been under good medical treatment for a long time. By coincidence the results may have begun to show themselves on the morning after he drank that water from St Mary's Well and faith came in to help what the doctors had already done.'

He showed me a bulky file of papers.

'I've dozens of letters from medical men about this business – asking all manner of questions. Some wanted samples of the water. Knowing what we now do it's lucky I hadn't the time to send them any – but there's one here that comes from an old German doctor named Stein: a refugee from the Hitler days. He's on research at the hospital where I worked as a student. He's a brilliant man: a specialist in rheumatic diseases with his own original lines of research. Naturally he was excited about what's happened here and wanted a sample of the water. I decided to send him some.'

'But for heaven's sake!' I exclaimed. 'It'll give the whole show away!'

'Not in the way I've done it,' said Stagg. 'Obviously he'll soon discover it didn't come from a spring. I've told him I've found a source that might be feeding the well independent of the spring. That doesn't give anything away. I've asked him in confidence what he thinks of the water and he'll respect my confidence. I don't suppose it'll get us anywhere, but there's no harm in finding out what he says.' We got back to the problem on hand.

'You came to find out what line I'm going to take at the meeting next week,' he said, 'when we've got to decide things one way or the other.'

'It doesn't matter a great deal what the others say,' I told him. 'The final word is with you. As Medical Officer you've got the authority to close the well this afternoon if you want to.'

'I know,' he answered. 'And you see what a tough spot it puts me in. In the ordinary way I'd be bound to condemn for drinking purposes any water that came from an open ditch. That's the first rule in the book from the medical viewpoint. But that would end the whole thing and bring ruin to the town. On the other hand I can't just bury my head in the sand and forget about it. It's not just a simple matter of medical routine. It's what might happen if I did. Supposing it led to an epidemic of typhoid or some other poisoning. There'd be an official inquiry and the source of the water would be discovered. We'd have to admit that we knew about it and deliberately concealed what we knew. The whole Board of Directors would be brought to book and we'd be lucky if fraud was the only charge. Potter was right when he put that to us the other day. If people died from poisoning it would amount to manslaughter. I'm the one with the main responsibility and I'm going to do the only possible thing.'

He took me across to a big cupboard fitted out as a sort of miniature laboratory for his personal use.

'I've got the necessary things here for analysing and testing,' he said, 'and I shall test a sample of that pond water every morning. I shall tell the Directors that so long as I find the water harmless I'll go the whole way with them and accept things as they stand. But if I find any contamination that might cause poisoning, then I shall close the well without a moment's hesitation, because nobody in their right mind would do otherwise.'

I had now seen everybody and things had worked out better than I expected. Nobody was going to dig their heels in and insist that the truth be published. The Vicar, the Headmistress, and Potter would resign from the Board, but all three had promised to keep quiet for the sake of the town.

The doctor, apart from his reservations, would stand by us and the others would go the whole way no matter where it led.

The three who were resigning could easily be spared. There were plenty of good people to fill their places. I decided to have some names ready to put forward. Lewis Watson, the Bank Manager, and Farrell the Estate Agent would fit in well. It would be best to elect another woman in place of the Headmistress. Mrs Patterson who owned our biggest drapery shop was a good member of the Town Council and would be a useful Director. The newcomers would know nothing about the duckpond pipe and would be clear if it were discovered. If the resignations were made with adequate reasons, no harm would be done or suspicions aroused.

With things settled more happily than I expected, I had a good night's sleep, little knowing of the storm that was to burst over our heads at the fateful meeting in a few days' time.

# Chapter Twenty-one

A few days later the inquest on Henry Hodder was re-opened and fizzled out in half an hour, much to the disappointment of the onlookers.

Sydney Glover, the youth who had threatened the old man and brought suspicion on himself, was never mentioned. Digby told me afterwards that Sydney had been traced to an amusement arcade in London. He had been able to prove that he was working there on the night of the murder, and that was that.

The police had nothing else to offer. They had drawn a blank, and after a few formalities the inquest closed with a verdict of murder 'by a person or persons unknown'.

With the inquest out of the way and Henry buried with his fatal secret, we met the next afternoon for our decisive Board meeting.

Knowing what everybody intended to do I took the Chair with a good deal more confidence than I had expected, and set the ball rolling by taking things up from where we had left off the week before.

'At our previous meeting,' I said, 'Mr Blundell put forward a certain proposal. After some discussion we decided to adjourn for a few days to give everybody time to think it over and to wait for the results of the inquest.

'The inquest is over. We've had time to think, and I suggest we now go straight ahead.

'Mr Blundell proposed that to save the people of St Mary's it was our duty to suppress what we knew about the well and carry right on with our plans to open the Casino.' I turned to Jim Blundell. 'Is that correct?' I asked.

'That is correct,' said Jim. He was sitting squarely in his chair, his big fat hands palms downward on the table: formidable and defiant: ready for anything.

'Then I'll put it as a simple motion,' I said. 'I'll ask you to vote for or against – then open the meeting for a free discussion of any matters arising.' I looked round the table and took the plunge. 'Those in favour?'

The members who had told me they had no reservations raised their hands immediately; the others hesitated, then raised theirs. Every hand around the table was raised in acceptance.

'Mr Blundell's motion is carried unanimously,' I announced.

Jim Blundell stared round in astonishment at the upraised hands. He had obviously expected the conscientious objectors to vote against him and I flattered myself that I had pulled off a small diplomatic triumph. By putting the motion as a vote involving the fate of the people of St Mary's nobody with personal objections could disagree. Having got unanimity on that, it would be easier to deal with individuals one by one.

Jim Blundell's astonishment melted into a benevolent smile. 'I'm very glad,' he said. 'Very glad. And I'm sure that none of us will ever have cause to regret it.'

'The meeting is now open to discussion,' I said.

Then came the resignations. The Vicar spoke first. He explained his position with dignity and humility. 'I don't want to appear self-righteous,' he said, 'or claim any moral superiority because I am heart and soul in favour of any measures to save our people from calamity. On that account I gladly vote in support of the Mayor's proposal because I would sooner break the law than break our people.' He then explained why it was impossible to combine a Directorship of the Company with his duties to the Church.

Miss Fanshawe the Headmistress spoke in the same terms although she was more practical and businesslike about it. 'In three years' time,' she said, 'I reach the age limit and they'll make me retire from the school. In those three years I've got to finish the work I began when I first came here, and there's a lot to be done. I can't preach truth and virtue to my girls in the mornings and conspire to a fraud in this Council room in the afternoons. The two things just don't go together, so I've got to choose between being one thing or the other. I'm a better schoolmistress than Company Director, so I'll do the common-sense thing and stick to the job I'm best at, but you can trust me to keep my mouth shut because I'm a hundred per cent on your side if you go ahead and open the Casino.'

Mr Potter the solicitor then embarked upon a long and pompous explanation of why a seat on the Board of Directors, in the existing circumstances, was incompatible with his binding obligations to the legal profession. He repeated what he had told me about the exemplary reputation of his firm; its unswerving honesty and integrity to the highest principles; his own binding obligation to uphold a tradition of honour established through a century of devotion from his ancestors. He piled it on and embroidered it to leave no doubt in anybody's mind about the correctness of his decision to resign.

He was still talking when Jim Blundell blew up. I had expected him to protest against the resignations, but felt reasonably sure he would accept when they promised to keep quiet about the duckpond. He would probably have agreed to the resignations of the Vicar and Miss Fanshawe because they were honest and understandable, but the oily humbug of Mr Potter was too much for him and his outburst was shattering.

It began with a piece of melodrama that would have been comic in other circumstances.

He picked up a bundle of official papers, clutched them in his big hairy fists – tore them into fragments and flung them on the floor.

'Then that's that!' he shouted. 'It's all over and done with! All we do now is to ring the newspapers and give them the biggest headlines for years, and misery for the poor God-forsaken people of St Mary's.'

There was a stunned silence, except for Jim Blundell's laboured breathing that was almost more alarming than what he had said. His face was purple; his eyes were bulging. I thought he was going to have a stroke.

Mr Potter began to stammer something. He looked ghastly: 'But ... but Mr Mayor ...' he began, and was drowned by a bellow from Jim Blundell.

'Don't Mr Mayor me! I've done and finished with it! I resign here and now! D'you think I'm going to preside over a wrecked town of desperate ruined people?' He glared at the trembling Mr Potter. 'All they're going to need from now on is *you*, Mr Coroner! You'll have enough suicides in the next few months to make you think of suicide yourself!'

I tried to assert myself as Chairman. I rapped on the table to call for order and began to explain that the resignations, if tactfully announced, wouldn't have the devastating effect that the Mayor believed. But the word 'resignation' added fuel to Jim Blundell's anger.

'Resignations!' he bellowed. 'If a bunch of Directors resign from this Company a few weeks before the Casino opens, is anybody but a half-wit going to swallow their flat footed excuses! You can take my word they'll know there's something bloody wrong and they won't stop asking till they find out what it is! It'll be news in the London papers. We'll have a bunch of reporters down here and they won't go away till they've got the truth! I tell you straight: here and now – with these resignations the whole thing's done with, and the sooner we get it over the better!'

Jim Blundell had remarkable powers of oratory when he was roused. He went on to paint a terrifying picture of the town and its people when the calamity overwhelmed them: of ruined homes; bankrupt shopkeepers; elderly, respectable people destitute and penniless; bitter, disillusioned unemployed forced into crime; the Vicar preaching heaven from the pulpit after he had thrown his flock into a living hell; Potter the lawyer preferring to ruin his clients than damage his 'legal conscience'; Miss Fanshawe the Headmistress preferring to see old pupils, wives and mothers, struggling against poverty in order that she could go on preaching 'truth and honour' with a clear mind. He spared none of them, and all were too overwhelmed by the devastating truth of it to answer back.

He finished as melodramatically as he began. Pushing back his chair, he rose with a superb gesture of disgust.

'How d'you want to do it?' he demanded. 'We better ring the Town Hall and get the loud-speaker van to go round calling a general meeting for tonight,' he looked at his watch. 'It's three o'clock now. We'll have the meeting at seven. We'll tell the people, then ring the London Press to give 'em time to get their headlines in tomorrow's papers.'

He walked across the room towards the telephone in the lobby. What would have happened if everybody had sat firm and let him use the phone I don't know, but before he was out of the room Mr Potter was on his feet, calling him back.

'Mr Mayor! Just a minute, please!'

Potter was a pitiful sight. He was ghastly pale with beads of perspiration trickling down his cheeks. He swayed as if he were going to faint and gripped the table for support. All his pomposity and self-righteousness had left him: in his high starched collar and protruding starched cuffs he was grotesque as well as tragic.

'You . . . you misunderstand me,' he stammered. 'I have lived my whole life in St Mary's. No one feels more keenly for the people; no one realizes more clearly the extent of the calamity if this Company collapses. I offered my resignation just now, firmly believing that it would have no damaging results. But I willingly withdraw it if you think it would do harm. I would far sooner sacrifice my professional scruples than endanger the welfare of our people. . . .'

With the surrender of Potter, Jim Blundell's battle was won. With more dignity and less humbug the Vicar and Miss Fanshawe both said that they would remain on the Board on condition that they would be free to retire after the Casino was opened, when their resignations would cause less comment.

Jim Blundell's rage cooled down as quickly as it had built up. He pushed back his tie that had jerked loose from his waistcoat, returned to the Council table and paid a generous tribute to the Vicar and the Headmistress.

'We all understand the pain and distress of their present situation,' he said, 'and we're very grateful to both of them for so generously supporting us in our present difficulty. Once the Casino's opened and the main job's done – then it's right and proper for them to retire, but until then we've got to stick together.'

He ignored Mr Potter and never looked at him, but he turned to me with an expansive smile and said: 'My apologies, Mr Chairman, for leaving my seat without permission.'

I suspected all along that Jim Blundell's performance had been a gigantic bluff, and when the meeting was over he had admitted it. I had asked him what he would have done if Mr Potter hadn't intervened and stopped him from going to the phone. 'I never bothered to think what I'd have done,' he said, 'because I knew damn well the old bastard *would* stop me. He couldn't afford not to. He's invested money in the Company that doesn't rightly belong to him, so as to get the rake-off from the bigger profits. He wanted his profits, but he wanted to wriggle out of the risks. I gambled on that and pulled it off.'

'Do you honestly think it would have wrecked things if we'd had those resignations?' I asked.

He shrugged his shoulders. 'Maybe so; maybe not – but we're walking on a knife edge and we can't afford to slip an inch.'

With the storm over, we got back to business. Mr Potter still looked sick and ill, and I saw him take one of his little white tablets, but Jim Blundell was back in his old boisterous, buccaneering form again. 'With your permission, Mr Chairman,' he said, 'I propose we now take up our work at the point we had got to when that old man Henry Hodder came in and interrupted us three weeks ago!'

This raised the first laugh I had heard at the Council table since our troubles began. It loosened things up, and with the nerve-racking uncertainties over at last we plunged into our business with a carefree enthusiasm that would have shocked a dispassionate onlooker, if he had known that the whole thing was based upon a colossal fraud that might blow up at any time and send us all to prison.

I still wonder how we managed to do it. Mainly I suppose because no crisis can drag on beyond the limits of human endurance. Something is bound to happen one way or another. You go down or rise above it. You accept defeat or claim a victory, and in our own way we had been victorious. Our victory amounted to an agreement to commit a crime for the sake of the people of St Mary's. You can take that in whatever way you like, but there's no doubt most of us felt the better for it.

It also made us more reckless. There was no more haggling over details. When the estimate for the fireworks had first been presented the cost of almost every squib and rocket had been questioned, and the Directors had almost come to blows over an item described as 'fighting cats' in which two illuminated cats were to appear on an illuminated wall, hump their backs, and spit and squeal at one another. Somebody had protested that it was beyond reason to pay £25 for such a piece and the thing had been put back for further debate. When, however, the estimate was now presented, it was passed without a murmur: 'fighting cats' and all.

Even Jim Blundell's renewed demand for caviare at the banquet was accepted. Paul Brooks displayed a sample of the posters that were to appear on the railway stations and buses when our big advertising campaign began in two weeks' time. The list of guests for the banquet was approved, and orders given for the invitations to be sent out forthwith. The twenty-strong staff for running the Casino was confirmed and the programme for the Opening ceremony passed for the printers. It included a short service in which the

Vicar was to bless the waters of the well. In view of the circumstances the Vicar suggested that this might be omitted, but he gave in when Jim Blundell pointed out that seeing where the water came from it would need all the blessing that the Vicar could give it.

In two hours we got through more work than we did in two weeks in the early days. The green light was given for everything to go ahead, and thanks to the way Paul Brooks had organized things it was as if the whole machine went roaring into life again by the press of a button.

The relief at getting back into our stride had made us like children playing in a fairyland, and it came as a douche of cold water when the Town Clerk brought us back to earth by asking what steps we were going to take about the duckpond.

'Leave the damn thing alone,' said Jim Blundell. 'The less we muck about with it the better.'

'I'm not suggesting that we muck about with it,' the Town Clerk retorted. 'But we've got to make sure that other people don't muck about. In the old days nobody went near this duckpond, but since the Casino was built there's always a crowd of sightseers wandering about. There's only a hedge between the pond and the road, and anybody can climb through. When I came by this afternoon I saw some boys playing about round the pond. If they found the brick catchment round the inlet pipe anything might happen. They wouldn't know the purpose of the pipe, but they might push sticks down it and block the supply.'

The Town Clerk reminded us that the two enterprising boys who had sold 'St Mary's Water' in lemonade bottles to the people who came to the well on the first week-end had admitted to filling the bottles from the duckpond. He had scolded them for their dishonesty: somewhat unjustly as it now turned out because the people who bought the bottles got exactly the same water as those who had queued for hours to get into the well house – on better terms, in fact, because the boys only charged *6d* a bottle whereas those in the well house paid *2s 6d* for a drink out of a dirty glass.

But something had got to be done to keep the boys away from

the pond in future. The problem was how to do it without attracting attention to the pond and arousing curiosity.

A small sub-committee was appointed to do whatever was necessary. It consisted of the Medical Officer, the Borough Engineer, Jim Blundell, and myself, and as soon as the Board meeting ended the four of us walked over to the pond.

We were none too soon, for when we arrived we found three boys with their shoes and stockings off, wading about in the rushes at the water's edge. They said they were looking for dabchicks' nests, but they were prodding about with sticks perilously near to the catchment pit that covered the opening to the pipe.

I told them it was private property and sent them about their business, but they stood watching us from a distance, wondering what we were doing, which made it necessary for us to turn our backs on the pond and pretend we were talking about something else until the boys at last walked off. It was a foretaste of what we were going to be up against in the months to come.

I hadn't been able to bring myself to go near the wretched pond since the trouble began and as I had never had reason to come to it in the past, I was examining it now for the first time in years.

It was almost round in shape: obviously hand-made and no doubt dug originally as the fish pond for the Nunnery. At one time it would have been about a hundred feet across, but the bulrushes now encroached so thickly round its edges that it was barely half its original size. There were no overhanging trees and the water in the middle looked deep and clear.

Stagg showed us the ditch that provided the pond with its main supply of water. It ran along the side of the adjoining lane and passed under a hedge through a roughly made culvert, but years of neglect and accumulations of silt had turned the ditch into a sort of bog before it reached the pond, and the water had to find its way into the pond through a lot of small channels, like a delta.

'You see the problem,' said Stagg. 'If there was a clear-cut channel we could put some clinker down, but as it is we can't do a thing about it. To make a channel would need labourers, and labourers would want to know what we were doing it for.'

'Let sleeping dogs lie,' said Jim Blundell.

'You might fill the catchment pit with filtering material,' I suggested. 'To clean the water that goes down the pipe.'

'The sort of filter I could make myself wouldn't be much good,' said Stagg. 'It would only catch the débris. It wouldn't stop the microscopic bacteria or chemical poisons that do the harm.'

The only comfort we could find was in the quantity of the water. Despite a long dry season it ran briskly down the ditch and gurgled through the culvert as if we had had weeks of rain. Apparently a small natural stream came into the ditch at some point in its course, so there was little to worry about on the score of supply. Henry had told us himself that there had never been any trouble, and the pipe was laid eight years ago.

The Borough Engineer reminded us that the pond had been earmarked as a children's boating lake in the plans for the Colindale gardens. Luckily no work had started, but it gave us a reasonable excuse for fencing in the pond to keep the boys away.

'We can say that we're fencing it in as a preliminary measure,' he said. 'Later we can announce that it isn't suitable for a boating lake. We can invent some technical reason – and nobody's going to be suspicious if we leave the fence up.'

And that was as much as we could do. The Engineer promised to send a foreman from his department first thing in the morning with three good men to put up a six-foot wire-mesh fence all round the pond, with a gate to be kept padlocked. To be on the safe side he said he would supervise the work himself and put up a notice: 'Proposed site for Children's Boating Lake. Trespassers will be prosecuted.'

I went home fairly satisfied with the day's work. I hadn't expected such a stormy meeting, but Jim Blundell's show of bluff had carried us safely through. If the Directors stuck together until the Casino was open it wouldn't matter who resigned when the main work was done.

A bare four weeks now remained before the Grand Opening on the first of July. There was a lot to do, but providing the duckpond pipe behaved itself and the water kept clean I saw no reason why we couldn't settle down to the remaining preparations in reasonable peace.

I had a good night's sleep, blissfully unaware of the new and unexpected shock awaiting us.

# Chapter Twenty-two

Those of us who thought the inquest had settled the business of Henry's murder were quickly disillusioned.

The Editor of our local paper the *St Mary's Gazette* was a fussy little man named Dobson. He wasn't popular with the leading people in the town, partly because he wasn't a local man, but mainly because he considered it his duty to make his paper a sort of watch-dog over local affairs. He was fond of attacking the Town Council for their 'lethargy' and 'incompetence'. He liked to unearth small scandals and criticize the running of public functions. On the whole it did no harm and probably a certain amount of good, but on account of his quarrelsome disposition he had not been invited to join the Board of the Casino Company, as a man in his position normally would have been.

It was a pity we hadn't swallowed our prejudices and made him a Director. If he had been in the know about things he would have played down the murder and let it rest when the inquest was over, but on the following Saturday the *Gazette* came out with sensational headlines attacking the police for the incompetent handling of the affair and demanding further action. It was clear, said the *Gazette*, that a homicidal maniac was at large in the town. The murder had been brutal, senseless, and destitute of motive. At any moment the maniac would strike again. Mothers were afraid to allow their children alone in the streets; people feared to go out after dark; there was a reign of terror, and no stone must be left unturned to run the maniac to earth. The local police, it said, were worthy, conscientious men, but totally inexperienced in handling a crime of this grave nature. It finished up by demanding that Scotland Yard be called in without delay.

The paper arrived when I was having breakfast and it took my appetite away. Soon afterwards Digby rang me up and said he was coming over to see me. He looked tired and worried, but he was philosophical about it.

'Dobson's got the right to air his opinion,' he said. 'I expected something like this, but he needn't have been so violent about it. He needn't have attacked our police because they've handled the thing as well as anybody could. I didn't want Scotland Yard down here for obvious reasons and I wish Dobson hadn't raised the dust about it.'

'Are you bound to call them in?' I asked.

Digby hesitated. 'Honestly, I don't think they could have done more than our own police,' he said. 'And if they come now, I can't see what they can do. It's not as if our own men had concealed anything that Scotland Yard would discover. They had a straight run and did their best. But Dobson won't let things rest as they are. There's no doubt people are worried and Dobson knows it. We're not bound to call in Scotland Yard even now – but if we don't it'll make people suspicious. They'll think there's something we want to hush up. So after a talk with our Superintendent we got in touch with Whitehall and they're sending somebody down tomorrow.'

It was a shock, but I was getting used to shocks by now. One more or less didn't make much difference.

'What happens when they take over?' I asked.

Digby shrugged his shoulders. 'We've never had Scotland Yard in St Mary's before,' he said. 'So I don't know much about it. Apparently there's no formality or routine. You give them a copy of the inquest proceedings and the records of your own police inquiries. You answer any questions they ask and leave them to it. They have a free hand and they go about the job in their own way.'

'And you don't think they'll find out any more than our own police did?'

Digby looked at me sharply. 'You're worrying about the thing that worries me?' he said.

'They might find out that Henry came to see us at the Casino a few hours before he was murdered?'

Digby nodded. 'We were lucky about that at the inquest,' he said. 'I was afraid somebody'd come forward to say they saw him on the road to the Casino that afternoon. Fortunately the only people round the Casino were the contractors' men who wouldn't have known who he was. But these Scotland Yard fellows are going to ferret out all they can, and we've got to be prepared for it.'

'If they do find out that the old man came,' I said, 'what happens? If they interview the Directors and they all tell different stories . . .?'

'The best thing we can do is to talk it over at tomorrow's meeting,' said Digby. 'If it comes to the point we've all got to say the same thing. But it's an outside chance of it happening. There's nothing in the evidence to connect the Directors with the murder, so I hope they won't be questioned. But they'll probably want to see you as Henry's previous employer and that's what I really came to see you about.'

I didn't like the sound of this. I had never been questioned by the police in my life, and all manner of disturbing possibilities loomed ahead.

'I don't see that there's anything to worry about,' said Digby. 'All you've got to do is to forget that one afternoon at the Casino when the old man came and threatened us. Apart from that, when was the last time you saw him?'

'About a week before. In the town. I asked him how he was getting along and he said he was doing a few odd gardening jobs.'

'Then get it clear in your mind that that was the last time you ever saw him. Tell the Scotland Yard people everything you know about the old man. There's nothing to conceal on that score. Tell them his life history if they want it.'

We had a drink and I began to feel better. It didn't look as if my part was going to be so difficult after all: the elderly, respectable country gentleman talking to the police about an old retainer of his family. Forget the one affair at the Casino, and there wasn't a thing about Henry I needn't talk about. There'd be just sufficient spice of danger to keep me on the alert. I was almost looking forward to it. But I caught a glance of Digby's face as he looked up at the clock and realized how he had changed in the past few weeks: deep furrows in his cheeks and hollowed eyes; his hair was greyer; there was a nervous movement: a jerky shake of his head that I hadn't seen before. As Chief Constable he had born the brunt of the murder investigations in the midst of his anxieties as a Director of the Company. The strain must have been well nigh intolerable for a man of his integrity. I asked him what line he would take himself with the men from Scotland Yard.

'Depends what they ask me,' he replied. 'It's an odd thing, but once you've swallowed your conscience and got over the first wrench of it, the rest comes quite easily. If I see these Scotland Yard men getting on to the scent I shall lie right and left to put them off it and I don't think I shall feel any the worse. It's a case of in for a penny, in for a pound. I suppose that's what happens to the little cashier who is tortured by guilt and shame when he pinches the first few shillings out of the till and finds easy excuses for himself when he finally steals the whole payroll.

'But honestly, I don't feel any conscience about concealing what we suspect about this murder. If I knew for certain who did it – then that might be different. But supposing I were free to tell Scotland Yard about Henry's visit to the Casino and the threats he made a few hours before he was murdered? I don't see that it would get them anywhere. Eleven people heard those threats and every one of them had a motive for silencing him. I'd simply be throwing suspicion on ten innocent people: they'd all be grilled by the police and the ordeal might injure some of them for the rest of their lives. Even if I were free to do it, I doubt whether I would.' He looked at me apologetically, as if he had said too much. 'Does that sound like a lot of eyewash and humbug?'

I told him it was plain common-sense, and on that we parted. Digby got in his car and drove back to the police station to get things ready for Scotland Yard.

# Chapter Twenty-three

When I got to the Casino for our meeting next afternoon Digby was waiting outside in the courtyard.

'Well,' he said, 'Scotland Yard's arrived. Fellow named Morris: Detective Inspector Morris.'

'Only one?' I asked.

Digby nodded. 'Seems fairly usual to send a man on his own to begin with. If he wants more help he calls for it. He's a North England man: quite young – pleasant fellow: easy to talk to, but he's all there, obviously. He wouldn't have the job if he wasn't. I was with him most of the morning.'

'Everything all right?'

'So far. But he hasn't begun yet. We gave him an outline of the whole thing and all the papers. It'll take him most of today to read them.'

'Where's he staying?'

'He's got a room at The Coach and Horses,' said Digby. 'Funny if he's staying with the murderer.'

Everybody at the meeting had heard of the Inspector's arrival, and as most of them were anxious about it, I decided to bring it up before the normal business.

'If he discovered that Henry came to see us here a few hours before he was murdered,' I said, 'then he's bound to want to know what the old man came for, and if we're questioned about it, then obviously it'll be much better if we can agree beforehand what we're going to say.'

Jim Blundell immediately took command. He was jovial and

quite happy about it. Having the Inspector staying at his hotel seemed to have given him a proprietary interest in it.

'It's easy,' he said. 'We simply say that the old man came to see us about the pension we'd promised him, and that's the truth, more or less. If you look back in the minute-book you'll find we discussed giving him something – weeks before.'

'That's all very well,' said Mr Potter, 'but we shall be asked why we didn't disclose this at the inquest. Why didn't we come forward and report the old man's visit when the police were asking for information about his movements that day?'

'Because it wasn't material,' retorted Jim Blundell. 'We say that the old man's pension hadn't got any connexion with his murder and that's the end of it. Nobody was likely to murder him for a pension that he hadn't even started to collect.'

It sounded rather thin, and I devoutly hoped it wouldn't be put to the test. But we'd got to say something, and the pension idea was as plausible as any. It was accepted by everybody because, as Jim Blundell said, it was the truth, more or less: we had in fact discussed the pension with the old man when he had arrived that afternoon.

Digby said that if the Scotland Yard man did find out about Henry's visit to the Casino he was scarcely likely to question the whole Board of Directors about it. 'As I was at the meeting myself,' said Digby, 'he'll no doubt ask me about it and I'll do my best to satisfy him – so I hope he won't worry the rest of you.'

'We all have faith in our Chief Constable,' said Jim Blundell, with an elaborate bow to Digby.

'I hope the Inspector has, too,' retorted Digby.


We then passed on to other business, and something so unexpected happened that the Inspector was practically forgotten for the rest of the afternoon.

Dr Stagg had arrived at the meeting with a bulky registered envelope and he asked leave to make a statement.

I mentioned earlier that Stagg had sent a sample of the water to Professor Stein, the elderly German specialist in rheumatic diseases whom Stagg had worked under as a student. He had asked for a confidential analysis of the water and the envelope containing the Professor's report had arrived that morning.

It was written in highly technical, scientific jargon, most of which was above our heads but Stagg translated it into layman's terms as he went along.

I will set it down in my own way, and the gist of it was this. The mineral content of the water was not unusual. There was a trace of iron and certain salts. It was slightly radioactive, and that also was normal, but what interested and excited the Professor was the presence of two substances in 'harmonic solution' which he had never previously encountered in this condition.

Stagg used the term 'harmonic solution' as the simplest way of describing a complicated chemical phenomenon by which two otherwise unrelated substances blended together in a solution to release something that couldn't be extracted from either substance in its normal state.

Many of these combinations were well known, but the thing that excited the Professor was that in the sample of the water sent to him by Stagg he had discovered frog spawn in harmonic solution with the decomposed seed of Scirpus Lacustris, in other words, the bulrush.

The news brought a loud laugh from Jim Blundell. In the spawning season the pond was a well-known haunt for frogs for miles around, and bulrushes, that grew nowhere else in the district, choked its marshy verges. 'It didn't need a big-shot Professor to tell us that!' he said.

Stagg went on reading the report. At first it sounded so wildly silly that I wondered why Stagg was at such pains to explain it to us. It sounded like the wanderings of a senile crank until its meaning began to dawn upon us.

The Professor said he had long believed that a potent factor in rheumatism was a deficiency of certain proteins that were notoriously difficult to release from normal foods in sufficient quantity. The high protein value of spawn had often engaged his attention, but he had sought in vain for a substance that would act in 'harmonic solution' to release this protein and make it available to the body. It now seemed as if, by miraculous chance, the solution had been discovered.

He could not, he said, accept Lord Colindale's remarkable cure as proof positive of his theory, but he had always doubted whether the mineral properties of any spring could have achieved such a cure by themselves.

He blamed himself for never suspecting the properties of the bulrush seed when evidence lay practically beneath his nose. It was a known fact, he said, that the Ancient Greeks had valued the bulrush for its medicinal properties although no records existed to explain how it was applied. The Egyptians too had apparently endowed it with some obscure significance, for a plant very like the bulrush was shown in sculptures and paintings connected with priestly ceremonial.

To sum things up, it was Professor Stein's opinion – given with the cautious reservations and qualifications of a scientist – that the frog spawn and the bulrush seed, having lain together in water at a certain temperature for a period of time, dissolved and combined to release the proteins so potent in the treatment of rheumatism.

He could not understand, he said, how frog spawn and bulrush seed had got into the well, but as Dr Stagg had hinted that the well was receiving a supply independent of the spring, then that would no doubt account for it. He concluded by urging Stagg to do nothing to obstruct or alter the present conditions. 'I firmly believe,' he said, 'that a lucky accident, a miraculous chance, has brought us within sight of a tremendous discovery that may have profound and far reaching results.'

'I shall of course respect the conditions you laid upon me, and keep this report in the strictest confidence, but I beg you to allow me to press forward with my own investigations and would be glad to have another bottle of the water.'

Jim Blundell was jubilant. From his point of view the Professor's report had cleared us of all conceivable grounds of fraud. It had, in fact, transformed us from potential criminals into shining benefactors of mankind. 'I said all along that the water in that pond would do people as much good as the stuff that used to come from that old spring,' he declared. 'Now we know it's going to do 'em a damn sight *more* good! And what's more they're going to get their money's worth! Something they're going to bless us for!'

I could see that he was already envisaging the possibilities of putting up the price.

Dr Stagg was more reserved about it. 'Professor Stein is a great man,' he said. 'He has built up his reputation upon original research: by unconventional methods that a lot of people ridiculed until he proved himself right. He usually has been right and he may be right this time. But he made these optimistic predictions without knowing the full story. This precious "harmonic solution" won't be so effective if it happens to include the putrid entrails of a dead rat poisoned with arsenic. It's an interesting report, but it doesn't solve our problem of keeping the water clean.'

Jim Blundell scoffed at him for a pessimist. 'People bathe in ponds and rivers every day,' he said. 'Thousands of 'em swallow the water but they don't all die of poison. And what's the matter with frog spawn anyway? It's the same thing as caviare, and we're feeding the whole damn crowd on that at the gala lunch at 15*s* an ounce!'

The meeting closed with a vote of thanks to Dr Stagg, proposed by Jim Blundell. 'I reckon we owe a lot to the doctor,' he said, 'for getting that Professor to look at the water and find out what's in it. If it cures our customers like it cured Lord Colindale we'll all be millionaires in five years' time.'

'And if it kills them,' said Stagg, 'we'll all be doing five years in Dartmoor.'

# Chapter Twenty-four

There was so much to do in the final weeks that we had a meeting every afternoon. Paul Brooks had moved into the secretary's office in the Casino and the key members of the staff had arrived. There was a smart young doctor: a masseur and a masseuse to take care of people needing treatment and two attractive young ladies for serving the water to all who wanted it. There was a restaurant manager and two bartenders, and a dozen waiters and waitresses were to arrive on the day before the opening. All except the specialists were local people, and all were picked for their youth and alertness to give the whole thing a cheerful attractive atmosphere.

The big entertainment park in the meadow behind the Casino was a hive of industry. It was advertised as 'the finest and most up to date in Britain' and I'm sure it was. Every conceivable entertainment had been provided for young and old: from the traditional swings and roundabouts to clock golf and archery. It was shut off from the Casino by a screen of trees and precautions had been taken to subdue the noise to avoid upsetting elderly patients who had come to take the cure.

The response to our invitation to the Gala lunch exceeded all expectations. Attracted no doubt by the wide publicity, the novelty of the occasion, and a pleasant day in the country, more than 300 acceptances arrived within a week of sending out the invitations. There were famous people from all walks of life: a bishop, two Cabinet Ministers besides Lord Colindale; the Lord Mayor of London, and the champion jockey. When I looked at the imposing list of names my heart sank at the thought that I, an obscure retired soldier, unknown beyond St Mary's until a few months ago, was to preside at the lunch as Chairman of the Company.

Fate stepped in to compensate us for the miseries and anxieties that we had suffered, and gave us a magnificent summer. The flower-beds around the Casino were a blaze of colour and the flags and decorations in the town were a sight to see. The barometer was set fair and the people were on tiptoe with excitement and anticipation. The ancient silver belonging to the town was brought up from the vaults and polished, and Jim Blundell had his Mayor's chain of office regilded and enamelled.

Jim was in tremendous form, spending tireless hours supervising everybody and everything. When he showed us his Mayor's chain, resplendent in its bright new colours with the enamelled medallion engraved with the arms of the town, he said that the arms should be altered, and replaced with an emblem of two spawning frogs in a nest of bulrushes.

We were so busy that Inspector Morris of Scotland Yard was practically forgotten. Digby had told me from time to time what was going on. The Inspector had studied all the reports, discussed them with the local police, and begun his own investigations, visiting the scene of the crime, searching Henry's cottage and interviewing the various witnesses who had appeared at the inquest. In Digby's opinion he was getting nowhere. He was merely finding out for himself what our own police already knew, and he seemed to have no line of approach of his own. Even the town had lost interest in the murder. The coming events at the Casino had overshadowed everything. The fate of a seedy old man was of small account compared with the golden harvest soon to enrich them all. 'It's my bet that the Inspector will draw a blank and pack up in a few days,' said Digby. 'There just isn't a thing for him to go on, and you probably won't hear any more about it.'

I confess I was rather disappointed when Digby told me this. I had rehearsed so carefully what I was going to say and felt so sure that I would carry it off successfully that it was an anticlimax to be told that I should probably not be needed.

It was therefore a surprise when Amy came in while I was having breakfast one morning to say that Inspector Morris was on the telephone, wanting to speak to me.

The broad north country voice was polite: almost apologetic. 'Is that Colonel Joyce? This is Inspector Morris of Scotland Yard. Good morning, sir. I know you're very busy, but I'm wondering whether I might come over and see you this morning? Would that be convenient?'

'Certainly,' I said. 'Any time that suits you. In half an hour? That'll be quite all right.'

Now that it had happened so suddenly and unexpectedly, I found that I wasn't quite so calm and confident after all. I had always had a sneaking, shamefaced fear of the police. I imagine it dated back to my childhood: to the days when an old nurse used to say: 'I'll send a policeman after you,' whenever I misbehaved. The fact remained that I could never pass a policeman in the street without taking on a different sort of walk: a kind of indifferent swagger to show that I was completely unconcerned. It was very silly, but there it was.

I had never been questioned by a police Inspector before: let alone a Scotland Yard man, and when I returned to the breakfast-room I found that I no longer wanted the excellent grilled herring that Amy had prepared for me. I went to my library and wandered about, tidying my papers, putting things straight, but I couldn't keep my eyes from the window, from watching the gate for the arrival of the car. I had often seen people interviewed by the police in television plays and I tried to recall the formalities and details. The Inspector usually wore a raincoat and a trilby hat. He would open with some conversation about the weather, or some entirely irrelevant remarks to put his victim at his ease. He would be friendly and informal. The victim would relax and drop his guard. Then suddenly, out of the blue, would come the terrifying question that would reduce the victim to a trembling panic-stricken creature, stammering out lies and contradictions that merely drew the net more firmly around him.

I was letting my nerves get hold of me. There was nothing to be afraid of. I only had to forget that Henry ever came and threatened us at the Casino, and everything would be well. I was a fool to worry. I had to be calm, friendly, and helpful, and nothing could conceivably go wrong. But the half-hour that I waited was interminable. A lifetime seemed to pass before I saw the small black car turn through the gates and come up the drive.

Inspector Morris didn't look in the least like an Inspector on television. He didn't wear a raincoat or a trilby hat, but that was hardly to be expected, seeing that it was a fine summer morning. He was a pleasant, ordinary looking young man with alert grey eyes, a snub nose, and freckles. He was wearing a grey flannel suit and a striped coloured tie that might have been his football or cricket club. If he had dressed himself deliberately to set me at my ease he could not have done it better. There was nothing about him that remotely suggested the police.

'I know you're a busy man,' he said, 'and I shan't keep you any longer than I can help.' He didn't even open with the inconsequential stuff that Inspectors did on television. He got straight down to business. 'You know why I came to see you, of course. This old man Henry Hodder who was murdered the other day. I understand he was employed by you at one time?'

I was glad he had cut formalities, and once it had begun I felt much easier and more relaxed than I had expected. I felt instinctively that everything was going to be all right.

'I might say,' I said, 'that Henry Hodder was with my family from the day he was born. His father and grandfather were in our employ. His family had been with us for generations.'

I offered him a glass of sherry and we sat in armchairs by the open French windows that looked across the gardens. The rhododendrons and azaleas were splendid in the warm June sunlight.

'You've a lovely place here,' said Morris. 'And you have your own farm?'

His family, he said, were farmers: somewhere up on the Yorkshire moors. He had worked there until he was seventeen: bleak country in the winter, when a lot of time was spent in digging their sheep out of snowdrifts. His father hadn't liked it when his son had gone to Birmingham to join the police. 'Maybe I was wrong,' he said, 'but I just wanted to. I wanted to get to London and I was transferred last year.'

He was so pleasant and interesting to talk to that I felt quite sorry when he got back to the business of his call. But even then it remained quite informal and conversational. He didn't pull out a notebook to write down what I said.

'This old man: you might call him an "old retainer" of your family?'

'In a way,' I said. 'His father lived in the Bailiff's house. He had several children and they all had various jobs on the farm. But two of the boys went abroad and the girls got married – and when the old man and his wife died, Henry was the only one left.

'By that time we had been forced to sell a good deal of our land and reduce our staff. Henry had never taken to farming. He wasn't a skilled man, but my father didn't want to sack him after all those years, so he put him in charge of the old well house.'

'Was he paid for that?'

'He didn't get a weekly salary. He was given a free cottage near the well and was allowed to keep anything he could pick up in tips from showing visitors round.'

The Inspector seemed to be interested in this. 'How much would that have been worth to him?' he asked.

'It varied with the season and the weather,' I said. 'The well and the Nunnery ruins were mentioned in guide books, and that brought quite a number of tourists in the summer. He probably collected £5 a week, and for the last few years he had his old age pension as well.'

'So it wasn't very much?'

'Sufficient for his needs,' I said. 'He was on his own and lived in a simple way. He never complained.'

I went on to tell the Inspector of the fabulous week-end when Henry had collected a small fortune.

'I gather that was a matter of easy come, easy go,' said the Inspector.

'I wouldn't call him a spendthrift,' I said. 'It was simply that he had never had such money in his life and didn't know how to handle it. I tried to persuade him to put it in the Post Office Savings Bank, but you know what these old country people are. He didn't trust the banks. He wanted to feel it in his own hands.'

I told him about the day when I went to see Henry at his cottage and found him literally surrounded by money.

'It had all gone before he died?'

'I'm fairly sure of that,' I said. 'According to reports he was glad to get anybody to stand him a drink in the end. I don't think he would have done that if he hadn't been broke because he was generous with his money when he had it, and proud to display it.'

The Inspector nodded, and there was a silence. He didn't seem much interested in Henry's sudden wealth and spending spree. His mind was apparently on something else.

'Going back to the time when he was simply looking after the well on your behalf,' he said, 'was he responsible for its upkeep – paying for repairs?'

'Definitely not,' I answered. 'The property was mine and I was responsible. If any repairs were needed, I paid for them. In any case he could never have paid for repairs out of the small sums he collected.'

'You're quite certain he never paid for anything himself?'

I looked at the Inspector in surprise. For the first time I had the feeling that things were not quite so informal as I had believed. I was under examination, but I hadn't an inkling of where it was to lead.

'I've just told you,' I answered. 'It was clearly understood that I was to pay for anything that was needed. On one occasion when the branch of a tree broke in a storm and damaged the well house roof, Henry came and reported it next morning and I had the tiles replaced and paid the bill. There was no question of him paying, and that was the only occasion when anything special had to be done. He once asked me for some paint for the cottage and I paid for that because it was my job to pay.'

The Inspector nodded, and there was another silence.

'Beyond looking after the well,' he asked, 'did he do any other sort of work?'

'None at all,' I said. 'Beyond keeping his garden and growing a few vegetables. He couldn't very well have taken another job because he had to be on hand for visitors.'

'When the well closed down in the evenings – and in the winter when there weren't any visitors – wouldn't he have been free for other work?'

I was more than uneasy now. My heart was racing and it was all I could do to keep hold of myself. The question had an ominous implication in it.

'He would have been free, of course,' I answered, 'but if he had done any other work I feel sure he would have told me. He might have done a bit of jobbing gardening, but he was a long way from the nearest houses – and frankly, he was rather a lazy old man. All he ever did was to walk into the town in the evening for his drink at The Coach and Horses.'

'Regularly, every night?'

'Year in, year out,' I said. 'They could tell you that at the inn. Every evening he was in his usual seat in the bar and he always stayed until closing time. He was a sort of institution – so I can't see how he could possibly have done any evening work.'

'Was he a trained man in anything? I mean, was he qualified to work in any trade?'

'If he had been, then I should have known,' I answered. 'Because he was in my family's employment from the time he was old enough to work. He never did anything beyond the usual odd jobs round the farm and he must have been close on fifty when he left to be caretaker at the well. He couldn't have learned a skilled craft at that age – even if he had had the ability and the opportunity. In fact, he was given the well simply because he wasn't capable of doing anything else.'

There was another brief silence and then it happened. Without changing his conversational manner or moving in his armchair the Inspector said:

'Did you know a man named Wilfred Parsons, a plumber in the town?'

The shock was so sudden and overwhelming that it dazed me. Wilfred Parsons was the man who had helped Henry to lay the pipe from the pond to the well. In a few casual words the Inspector had revealed that he was not only aware of the fraud, but also the motive for the murder. There was no conceivable link between Wilfred Parsons and Henry Hodder except through that fatal pipe. How he had discovered it I couldn't guess, but in one stroke this deceptively casual, friendly young man had apparently got to the heart of things and nothing could save us from complete disaster.

My first impulse was to confess everything and implore the Inspector, for the sake of the town – for the sake of everybody – to treat what I said in confidence. But the thought was barely in my mind before I knew it was impossible. He was here to solve the murder and nothing on earth would stop him.

I had a fleeting vision of the plays I had seen on television: the police interview: the casual, disarming opening: the sudden devastating, overwhelming question that caught the victim and crushed him. I had sat back smugly in my armchair: cheerful that such a thing could never happen to a man like me. And now it had happened, in all its terrifying reality.

It seemed to matter very little what I said. He had got me, and I could only wait for him to end it in his own way, but an instinct for self-preservation made me fight for time. I looked up at the ceiling as if trying to remember that accursed plumber and bring his appearance back to mind. I tried to answer him as casually as he had spoken himself, but the voice didn't sound like mine.

'Yes,' I said. 'I remember Parsons. I didn't know him well. I think he died about two years ago.'

The Inspector nodded. He showed no sign that he had noticed

anything, but I must have gone ghastly pale. He pulled out his pocket book, took three small pieces of paper from it, and handed them across to me.

'I wonder what you make of these?' he said. 'I made a thorough search of the old man's cottage; your own police never found them, but I don't altogether blame them because these bits of paper were hidden away in an old tobacco tin at the bottom of a cupboard. There was a jumble of odds and ends in it – including these.'

I took them and looked at them. They were three pages, torn from a cheap little account book, soiled and faded and written in a cramped illiterate hand. Two were in ink and one in indelible pencil. They were headed: 'Aug', 'Oct', and 'Feb' without any year or date, and appeared to be monthly statements with several missing. As nearly as I remember they read like this:

| Aug. | Due   | £68 | 12 | 6 |
|------|-------|-----|----|---|
|      | Paid  | 4   | 10 | 0 |
|      | Owing | £64 | 2  | 6 |
|      |       |     |    |   |
| Oct. | Due   | £57 | 15 | 0 |
|      | Paid  | 7   | 10 | 0 |
|      | Owing | £50 | 5  | 0 |
|      |       |     |    |   |
| Feb. | Due   | £48 | 10 | 0 |
|      | Paid  |     | 12 | 6 |
|      | Owing | £47 | 17 | 6 |

Each page was signed 'Henry Hodder' with beneath it: 'Agreed. Wilfred Parsons'.

Their meaning was plain enough. Henry had told us he had promised to repay Parsons for the cost of the pipes by handing over half his takings from visitors. The payments had apparently been made monthly, but only three receipts had survived. They had no doubt been written in duplicate: each man keeping a copy as evidence of the deal.

As I read the tattered pages I began to see a gleam of hope. If this was all the Inspector had to go on, it didn't amount to anything disastrous. Both men were dead. There was nothing to show when the receipts were written; it could have been five years ago, or twenty years.

I read them slowly and pondered over them to give me time to think. The well house roof? I'd told the Inspector I'd once had it repaired. Could I say I'd given the money to Henry to pay over to Parsons for the job? – that the receipts suggested that Henry had used the money himself and was paying it off in instalments? It wasn't a likely story. Obviously I would have paid the bill myself with a cheque. Anyway, Parsons was a plumber. He wouldn't tile a roof. If the Inspector caught me out I'd be worse off than before. It was best to plead total ignorance.

'I don't know,' I said. 'They're obviously receipts for something. What do you think about it yourself?'

I could feel the perspiration trickling down my face. He must have seen it. He must have known there was a great deal I could tell him about those flimsy bits of paper, but he didn't press me. He took them back and returned them to his pocket book.

'I think you told me that you always made yourself responsible for repairs?' he asked.

'Always,' I replied. 'There was never any question of that.'

The Inspector thought about this for a little while. 'Is it possible,' he asked, 'that the old man had had something done that for some reason he didn't want to tell you about?'

He was horribly close to it now. It was a logical question, but I still had a deadly foreboding that he knew the whole story and was deliberately leading me on to see what I would say. I managed to keep up my pretence of ignorance.

'I can't think of any possible reason for him doing that,' I said. 'His job was a perfectly simple one. He just had to keep the place clean: show visitors round and take whatever they chose to give him. If repairs were needed, like the well house roof or the painting of his cottage, he reported it to me and I had it done and paid the bill.'

The Inspector took out the receipts and examined them again.

'The amount due on this first receipt is £68,' he said. 'There may have been earlier statements, so the original amount owing was probably greater. It's a lot of money for a man in Hodder's position.'

I shook my head. 'The whole thing's a complete mystery,' I said. 'Have you any theory about it yourself?'

'Only that the old man, unbeknown to you, was living a sort of double life,' said the Inspector – 'carrying on some kind of business with this man Parsons that had put him into debt with him. You see what concerns me? If we knew what it was, it might have some link with Hodder's murder.'

I began to breathe more easily. It now seemed reasonably certain that the Inspector was genuinely mystified, and I felt it safe to trail a red herring across the track.

'I know that the old man was interested in horse racing,' I said. 'We used to talk about it sometimes when I came to see him. I know nothing about this plumber Parsons, but he might possibly have run a book on the quiet and taken Hodder's bets.'

The Inspector didn't rise to the bait. 'I don't think a smalltime bookmaker would have allowed an impecunious old man like Hodder to run up an account to this extent,' he said.

'Unless he encouraged it deliberately,' I suggested. Parsons was dead, so it wouldn't do any harm to cast doubts upon his character. I wished afterwards I hadn't said it because it apparently gave the Inspector a new line of thought.

'I'll see what I can find out about him,' he said. 'There are bound to be people in the town who knew him.'

He got up to go. 'In the meantime, many thanks for your help, Colonel.'

I went out with him to his car. I hadn't liked the way he had said 'in the meantime' or the way he had said the word 'help'. He was still friendly and courteous, and admired my flowering shrubs, but as I watched his car go down the drive I felt reasonably certain I hadn't seen the last of him by any means. I was also fairly sure that if he kept a record of his interviews he would write 'not what he pretends to be' against my name.

I went back to the house and rang up Digby. I was in such a state that I was prepared for the possibility of my telephone conversation being tapped, so I said as little as possible.

'Will you be at the Board meeting this afternoon?' I asked. 'Could you get there at two o'clock? I'd like to see you beforehand. I'll meet you in the gardens behind the Casino, and we'll have a walk round.'

# Chapter Twenty-five

Men were stringing flags across the road when I got to the Casino, and a gang of carpenters was hammering up a platform in the garden for the Regimental Band that was going to play during the reception on opening day. Another gang was putting up a green-striped marquee for the refreshment buffet and a small army of gardeners was busy planting masses of pink and scarlet geraniums that had arrived in pots, already in flower. Electricians were installing the floodlighting, and over in the adjoining meadow the amusement park was tuning up. It was impossible for Digby and me to find anywhere for a quiet talk, so to get away from it all we climbed a stile and walked along a footpath among some trees.

I told Digby everything that had happened when the Inspector called. He hardly said a word until I had finished and didn't seem as worried as I expected.

'I'm sorry he's pitched on something that brings this plumber Parsons into it,' he said. 'I guess it was a shock when he pulled out those receipts, but you've got to keep the thing in proportion. Morris is down here to investigate Henry Hodder's murder. He isn't here to probe the activities of the Casino Company. If he'd been sent down to find out whether everything concerning the well is above board, then those dealings between Parsons and Henry would give him a hot clue, but from what you say, he hasn't a ghost of a suspicion about that duckpond pipe, and in any case it doesn't concern him. Obviously he'll find out all he can about the plumber if he thinks those dealings with Henry might have some connexion with the murder. . . .'

'That's the whole point,' I said. 'If he examines the plumber's books the whole thing might come out. What happened to Parsons's business when he died?'

'We don't get much luck,' said Digby, 'but I think we're lucky there. Parsons was a widower and ran the business with his son. It was a ramshackle little business: just a small shop with a yard behind it. When the old man died the son packed up and went abroad. The radio shop next door took the place over for a store and workroom and I imagine all the plumber's books and papers were just shovelled together and thrown away. There'd have been no point in keeping them.

'But even if the Inspector did find the books and papers, what's the worst that could happen? When Parsons laid that pipe from the duckpond he knew very well that it was illegal. He was working on your property without your permission. It was a secret deal between him and Henry for their own personal gain, so he isn't likely to have advertised it in his account books. Suppose the Inspector discovered that Parsons ordered some galvanized-iron pipes on a certain occasion? It doesn't mean a thing. Plumbers order pipes for all manner of jobs. There's no earthly reason why it should take the Inspector to the duckpond.'

He looked at his watch. It was time for our meeting and we walked back to the Casino.

'If you want my advice,' said Digby, 'forget the whole damn thing and don't lose any sleep over it.'


There was trouble waiting for us at the Board meeting, but compared with the rest it didn't amount to much.

Paul Brooks produced a copy of the *St Mary's Gazette* containing a violent criticism of the Directors. Dobson the editor had dropped his campaign about the murder since Scotland Yard had been called in and switched his activities to what he called 'the high-handed and insulting treatment of the share-holders of the Casino Company'.

Owing to the large number of guests it was impossible to make room for anyone beyond the Town Council and a few prominent local people at the gala lunch and reception. Dobson saw a chance to advertise himself as the people's champion and demanded to know why the ordinary shareholders, without whom the project would have been impossible, were to be shut out and turned away from the opening ceremonies like undesirable aliens.

As more than a thousand people held shares in the Company the complaint was rather silly, but we didn't want any ill feeling, and as about twenty guests were unable to come we decided to fill their places with the first twenty shareholders who applied for seats at the luncheon. We also announced that shareholders could apply for tickets to the reception in the Casino Gardens, weather permitting, adding a request that our distinguished guests should not be inconvenienced by amateur photographers and autograph hunters.

It was our last formal meeting before the great event and most of the time was taken up with final reports. The Treasurer produced a rather alarming statement about our finances. Everything had cost a bit more than the estimates. The gala lunch was going to cost nearly £750 – close on £2 a head including the wines and the caviare. The Regimental Band had been an expensive afterthought and the fireworks were costing more because of Jim Blundell's demand for costly spectacular pieces and the coloured floodlighting of surrounding woodlands. The long and the short of it was that the whole reserve fund had gone and we had an overdraft at the bank.

But Jim Blundell cheerfully pointed out that it was a game of Pay and Receive. It was a fine ground-bait for the big fish we were going to catch in the summer. He announced that the first overseas visitors had arrived at The Coach and Horses: a party of Americans from Kansas City who had ordered smoked salmon and a bottle of champagne within an hour of their arrival: good for Jim Blundell, but no use to the Company. He also expressed a hope that Inspector Morris would soon pack up and go away because he wanted his bedroom.

Against the gloomy finance report stood the boundless optimism of the people of St Mary's. The Company shares were already exchanging hands at a premium. Shareholders who bought £5 worth were getting £6 from people who had failed to apply originally and now saw their mistake. Property values were rising; some of the big chain stores were making inquiries for suitable sites in the High Street and the Town Council were already planning ambitious building projects. Fair stood the wind for St Mary's. No town in England had finer prospects – if only the duckpond pipe kept clear.

# Chapter Twenty-six

It would have been a fitting end to those final weeks of trial if the Grand Opening day had dawned in a drizzling rain, but when I climbed out of bed at five o'clock and drew back the curtains the sun was rising in a clear summer sky. Our luck had changed at last: at least for this day that we had been preparing and planning so anxiously for more than a full year. Saturday the first of July: the most momentous in the history of St Mary's.

For me too it was to be the most momentous and nerve-racking of my life. I got back to bed to get what final rest I could.

I lay thinking of all the things that had happened since the spring evening that now seemed so long ago, when Colin had hobbled painfully on his crutches down the narrow lane to the old neglected well and drunk that glass of water that was to transform a town, and the lives of all its people.

I would never have believed that the people of St Mary's could have achieved so much. It was a new town today: unrecognizable as the sluggish, spiritless community of the past. The people too had changed. They walked more briskly; thought more clearly; and talked of the future as an exciting thing forgotten and rediscovered. The men had had their suits pressed: dry cleaners did a roaring trade, and every woman had made or purchased bright new clothes for herself and the children. Where the money came from goodness knows: the Casino Company had sucked them dry months ago; they were living upon the promise of a golden future.

Those of us who knew the awful truth had spun for ourselves a web of make-believe and unreality. Without it we could never have carried on. The final days of preparation had been so busy that for hours at a time the duckpond pipe was forgotten. When the fleeting thought of it returned I found myself saying: 'It isn't true. It never happened. It was a nightmare that's over and done with.' But when I woke at night reality returned and ached for hours like a nagging tooth. I tried to overcome these gnawing anxieties on account of the part I had got to play at the Opening Ceremony. I didn't want to appear a nerve-stricken wreck. For the sake of everybody, on this one day, I had got to play the part of a proud contented man, without a care in the world. The struggle to relax and nurse my strength made me impatient of Dr Stagg's morning telephone call to report on the condition of the water. Every night he took a sample from the pond, analysed it, and rang me up to give me the result. I felt like saying: 'For God's sake forget about it! Leave the water alone! At least until we've got the big day over!' I could not bring myself to imagine what we would do if he discovered rat poison in the water on the day before the Opening. But thankfully, all had been clear on the night before.

We were clear, too, of Inspector Morris now. Two days ago he had returned to London: officially to report to Scotland Yard and receive further instructions, but Digby didn't think we should see him again. He had done everything and got nowhere. He had probed into the affairs of Parsons the plumber, even to the extent of examining the dead man's banking accounts, but had apparently found nothing to throw any light on the plumber's dealings with Henry Hodder, and he left the town without troubling me again.

When Fred brought in my early cup of tea he was dressed in his best suit with a pink carnation in his button-hole. He and Amy had invested all their savings in the Company, and as shareholders were going to the reception in the gardens.

'A wonderful day for it,' he said. 'A good omen for everybody. You must be very glad, sir – and very proud.'

It was to be an informal occasion, so I put on my double-breasted grey-flannel suit, and regimental tie. It was my dress for special occasions because I had always believed it to give me a youthful appearance, but when I inspected myself in the mirror it made me realize for the first time how much the past few weeks had aged me. I had grown thinner and the suit hung loosely on me. My collars had become too big, puckering when I drew my tie around them. There were lines in my face that I hadn't seen before. I realized how hard I would have to work that day if people were not to wonder what had happened to me.

The reception was timed to begin at midday, but the Directors were to meet in the Board room at eleven, and soon after breakfast I got out the car, stuck the official badge on the windscreen, and set out for the Casino.

It was a morning to bring back memories of childhood, with the warm sun squeezing long-forgotten scents from the wild flowers in the grass beside the road: with the young corn shining in the fields and the hedgerows alive with birds. But I was soon brought back to the business on hand. As I approached the main road it was clear that our publicity had done its work, for a long stream of vehicles was already converging on to the Casino, and a special constable, whom I recognized as Mr Bodwick from the coal office, gave me a smart salute and held up the traffic to let me swing round and join the stream. I had not expected so much on the road so early and was glad that I had given myself plenty of time. There were parties of cyclists: ice cream vehicles and trade vans commandeered for the occasion and packed with children. There were excursion coaches and every sort of private car that began to close up and move bumper to bumper as we approached the Casino. But extra police had been brought in and everything seemed to be under control. The main stream was drawn off into temporary car parks but my official badge took me straight through to a field set aside for the privileged.

The other Directors had arrived when I got to the Council room. Jim Blundell, resplendent in his Mayoral chain of office, was presiding over an array of bottles on the side table. He was on top of his form: almost over the top by the look of his scarlet face, glistening with perspiration. He pushed a big glass of sherry into my hand with a 'Here you are, Colonel! Swallow that up! No harm in a drop of Dutch courage!'

I hesitated. I never drank before lunch time, and as Chairman I was soon to receive three hundred distinguished guests. I had got to keep my wits about me, but Jim Blundell would have been offended if I refused to drink with him. I didn't want to begin the day on a note of discord, so I took the sherry and drank it.

It was strong and sweet. I had been too strung up to eat my breakfast, and what with the nerve strain and an empty stomach the wine went to my head.

A haze of unreality began to surround me. I looked out of the window at the gathering crowds: I saw them clearly but they seemed detached and far away, as if I were looking at them through the wrong end of a telescope. Jim Blundell handed me another glass of sherry, taking away my empty glass. I tried to warn myself: 'You've had enough; you're the Chairman of this incredible affair: you're the principal person. If it hadn't been for you it would never have happened – for the sake of everybody . . . remember who you are . . . for God's sake, don't get drunk!' But I drank the second big glass of sherry.

Perhaps it was a good thing. When it was all over a lot of people came up and congratulated me on the calm and masterly way in which I carried out my duties. Without those drinks I don't think I could ever have gone through with it.

We opened the windows and went out on to the balcony that overlooked the courtyard. The seething crowd beyond the tall closed gates looked up and raised a cheer. We waved back and I began to think what fun it was.

Everything had been beautifully planned: most of it rehearsed the previous day. The St Mary's Boy Scouts were drawn up along each side of the road: a sort of guard of honour for our guests. I had never seen them so clean and neat, shining with soap and suppressed excitement.

Superintendent Braddock, carrying a pair of white gloves and resplendent in his medals, was supervising the police who continually had to press back the increasing crowds.

There were two or three inopportune incidents of sorts that are bound to crop up on such occasions. A pale, wild eyed man with a bushy black beard suddenly jumped on a pile of stones, unrolled a placard, and began to exhort the waiting people to Prepare for the End. He was moved off, fiercely protesting, by Superintendent Braddock. A little bunch of youths in outlandish hats and side-whiskers began to play banjos and guitars and sing some sort of rock and roll melody. They too were moved off and told to go and provide their entertainment elsewhere.

At twelve o'clock the Superintendent began to look expectantly down the road. Shortly afterwards he looked up at us on the balcony and raised his white gloves as a signal that the first of our distinguished guests were approaching. It was the cue for us to go down to the courtyard to meet them. As we walked through the Council room I discovered that I still had a sherry glass in my hand. It was empty, and I think my third. I put it on the table. I was quite light headed now; I was vaguely aware of what was going on and what it was about, but the whole thing had taken on the illusion of a dream.

The Casino looked like a luxury liner waiting to receive the passengers for its maiden voyage. Medical attendants; restaurant workers; office staff; all stood there in their immaculate white coats, embroidered on the pockets with the emblem of St Mary's well. 'If I am not careful,' I warned myself, 'I shall slip on this polished marble floor.' The dread of making an exhibition of myself no doubt contributed to the dignity that was afterwards so generously praised. I walked with exaggerated care; I smiled slowly for fear of breaking into a vacant alcoholic grin.

We assembled just inside the tall iron gates: myself as Chairman slightly in front to receive the guests; Jim Blundell, as Mayor, next to me.

The first arrivals were the Bishop and his wife. He was jovial and debonair, obviously tuned up for a convivial occasion, but his wife seemed a little put out when told that they were the first to get there. After the formal greetings they were passed on to the Vicar, who took them off to see the gardens.

The guests began to arrive in a steady stream. Some were recognized by the crowd and given a cheer. Lord Colindale, who arrived in a magnificent black Rolls with the Minister of Health, was given the biggest ovation because his face was familiar to everybody through his television appearances. He was bursting with health and vigour and waved his hat in obvious pleasure at his reception. But many of the guests, distinguished lawyers and doctors and men of business, were unrecognized. It all seemed to depend upon whether they had been on television.

Our young secretary Paul Brooks was the key to everything. He appeared to know all the guests; he met them as their cars arrived and brought them in to introduce them. Everything ran smoothly in his capable hands: formalities soon disappeared and the whole thing took on the atmosphere of a cheerful garden party.

By half past twelve most of our guests had arrived. I left the Town Clerk to receive late-comers and went with Jim Blundell into the gardens.

'It's a success!' whispered Jim, taking my arm. 'The whole damn thing: a walloping success.'

'Keep your fingers crossed,' I said – but it hardly seemed necessary. The whole thing blazed with success. The gardens were packed: local people, modest shareholders in the Company, were mixing with our distinguished visitors as if they had known one another for years. The Band played martial music: the flags fluttered and the buffet tent was crowded.

I found Colin, although I had a job to reach him. He was surrounded by an admiring crowd, telling them of his romantic first visit to the well. He was in his element: a television camera was focused on him and half a dozen Press photographers were holding their cameras above their heads, trying to get a shot of him. He broke off when he saw me and pressed through the crowd to shake me by the hand. 'You've done a wonderful job!' he said. 'Wonderful!' And we had to pose for the cameras, shaking hands.

We went across to the colonnade that led to the old well house. Along its walls were cases exhibiting historic relics: a collection of the Roman coins discovered at the bottom of the well a hundred years ago; pieces of sculpture and pottery found on the site of the Nunnery during excavations for the Casino and an ancient manuscript, in Latin, referring to miraculous cures that took place in the Middle Ages. Our Town Librarian was on duty here, explaining the exhibits to interested visitors.

The well house was naturally the centre of interest: so crowded with distinguished guests that we could scarcely get in. Two smart, attractive girls, immaculate in white uniforms, were serving the water to all who wished to sample it, and it seemed that everybody did. There was unanimous approval of its soft, elusive flavour. The Bishop was saying that it was somewhat like the waters of Bad-Nauheim, but his wife considered it to be more akin to that of Karlsbad. In one corner Dr Stagg was in conversation with the Minister of Health. I had a fleeting glimpse of Stagg's tired face and haunted eyes.

Although the architect had made no alteration to the structure of the well house, the interior now bore little resemblance to the dark and musty place that Colin had first seen. Attractive wrought-iron brackets were fitted with amber lamps that gave the room a warm, romantic atmosphere, and the dusty broken windows had been replaced by panels of stained glass illustrating the history of the ancient Nunnery. The contrast between this cool, mystic shrine and the noisy sunlit gardens was so great that all who entered it instinctively dropped their voices and the men removed their hats. They stood watching the stream as it flowed from the well into the ancient trough, fascinated and privileged to see with their own eyes the miraculous water that had restored so dramatically the health of the famous Lord Colindale. I could not bear to look at it myself for fear that the worst of my nightmares would become a ghastly reality, and the putrid body of a long-dead frog would appear before the eyes of my guests to bring chaos and ruin to our valiant enterprise. But our luck held, and when we left the well house for the dedication ceremony the water was running clear and free.

The ceremony of blessing the water was held outside in the sunlit gardens in order that everybody could take part in it.

A small platform had been built, and when the Vicar had taken his place, an earthenware container filled with the water was brought from the well and placed before him. The Vicar's revulsion at blessing water that he knew to be fraudulent had not been easily overcome. He had told me with tears in his eyes that it was a sacrilege, but the ceremony had already been announced as part of the programme and to omit it would have led to unwelcome comment. As Jim Blundell had rather crudely pointed out, the water needed all the blessing it could get, seeing where it came from. The Vicar had finally admitted this, and I knew that in his heart he was praying for its purity rather than for the continuance of its miraculous powers. He looked frail and worn, and at times his voice could scarcely be heard, but he spoke so simply and sincerely that the big crowd was very silent and impressed.

With the blessing over, Jim Blundell, as Mayor of St Mary's, formally declared the well open to all who desired to partake of its healing waters. A signal was given for the flag to be raised on the Casino roof; the amusement park sprang to life and the great enterprise was born at last. There was hearty applause from the shareholders as we made our way with our distinguished guests to the assembly hall for the gala luncheon.

The hall was magnificent with its long tables shining with silver and decked with scarlet and white carnations. The stage at the far end was admired by everybody: even by famous men and women accustomed to big occasions. It was a brilliant mass of floral decorations arranged by a firm of experts: every sort of colourful plant was there, the pots artfully concealed in fern, and backed with flowering shrubs and trees in wooden tubs. I was told by the man in charge that they were the most travelled plants in England. After they left us they were due to appear in the Royal Enclosure at Ascot, the Royal Tournament at Olympia, then on to Henley and Goodwood before they returned at the end of the season to their winter quarters.

I took my place as Chairman with Lord Colindale to one side and the wife of the Minister of Health to the other. The most important guests were at this long table with the Directors of the Company mixed in here and there. The Bishop said grace and the assembly got down to lunch.

The caviare had already been served, with slices of lemon and brown bread and butter. I thought of the long, heated arguments about the caviare at our Board meetings, of the motion to replace it with smoked salmon and Jim Blundell's ultimate triumph. I didn't think it was worth the cost: a small dab no larger than a pat of butter, but the psychological effect no doubt made up for its small size, for Colin said: 'By jove, old boy, you've done things proud!'

The luncheon was a tremendous success. You could tell by the buzz of talk that filled the room from the moment it began. There was roast chicken and escalops of veal; ice cream with fruit and a savoury. There was hock and claret and champagne; coffee, liqueurs, cigars. I sat through it all in the dream-like haze of unreality that began with the sherry in the Council room.

After the loyal toast there came a ceremony that took me entirely by surprise.

I had not noticed an easel standing behind my chair, with something on it, draped in a dark cloth.

When Jim Blundell rose to make his speech of welcome to the guests, he began by announcing that he had a happy duty to perform. After a fulsome reference to my 'surpassing generosity to St Mary's' he drew aside the cloth to reveal an oil painting of myself, which he presented to me on behalf of the townspeople 'in grateful recognition'.

In the early, happy days I had given some sittings to an artist who had merely asked to paint my portrait for a local exhibition. I had not guessed that it had been commissioned by the Council for this special occasion.

I barely had time to stammer out my thanks before Jim Blundell was on his feet again: this time to announce that by a unanimous vote of the Council, it was his happy duty to pronounce me the first Freeman of St Mary's, and he handed me the scroll in a silver casket.

Even this was not to be the end of the honours I was to receive, for a small Boy Scout appeared from somewhere with a silver inkstand, came up to the table and with a neat little speech and a smart little salute, presented it to me 'from the boys and girls of St Mary's'. It had a disarming simplicity about it that greatly appealed to the guests, and touched off a big round of applause.

Had I been in a normal state, I would no doubt have been very touched by these unexpected tokens of esteem. As it was it merely added to the fantasy and unreality of it all. I smiled and bowed and said: 'Thank you; thank you very much.' I could think of nothing else, and fortunately no more was needed, for Jim Blundell at once launched into his speech of welcome. I was beginning to get worried about Jim by now. He had obviously done justice to the drinks; his face was the colour of a beetroot and several times his loud laugh had made the other directors embarrassed and uncomfortable. I was terrified lest in his excitement he would say something regrettable, but he was commendably brief, and left it to Colin to make the big speech of the day.

Colin was in magnificent form. Everybody said afterwards that he had never spoken so well. It was a real genuine Colindale speech: full of platitudes, no doubt, but delivered with such gusto that it didn't matter. He pulled out all the stops and let himself go. He spoke in moving terms of the 'Rebirth of an Ancient Town'; he congratulated the authorities upon their 'courageous and imaginative handling of a unique opportunity' and once again expressed his eternal gratitude to St Mary's for the return of his health and strength.

The Minister of Health, who followed him, reminded St Mary's of its good fortune in having in its midst a man of such generosity and public spirit as 'our Chairman, Colonel Joyce' who had given to the citizens a priceless gift that many a less selfless man would have kept in his own hands, for his own profit. I had an overwhelming reception when I rose to make a brief reply.

It was past three when we rose from the tables and went back to the sunlit gardens, but we could scarcely move for the great crowds that had now arrived. The Casino had now been thrown open to all comers. The restaurant was packed: the lobby was full of people, pushing and jostling to buy postcards and souvenir booklets, and a long queue was waiting to get into the well house for a drink of the water at a shilling a glass.

By four o'clock most of our distinguished guests had gone. They all seemed anxious to give me a personal goodbye: a warm handshake and thanks for a memorable and happy day. A famous City financier slapped me on the shoulder and said: 'You've got a gold mine, Colonel – and no mistake! I wish it was one of my group of Companies!' and Jim Blundell roared with laughter and said: 'Better make a take-over bid, old boy!'

I walked across to the amusement park with Jim Blundell and the Town Clerk. The big meadow was seething with people. Admission here was half-a-crown and the gatekeeper told us that more than three thousand people had already paid to go in: more than £350 in the first three hours. I was recognized even by strangers, for my photograph had appeared that morning in the papers. A man sent his little boy to get my autograph, and I was immediately surrounded by a crowd.

By now I was deadly tired. A cup of tea in the Council room revived me, but I was in duty bound to stay for the fireworks at ten o'clock and I knew that I couldn't stand the pace for another five hours. So I made the pretext of hunting for some friends, and went quietly to the car park. It was relatively quiet here and my car was parked in a corner beneath the shade of some trees. Glancing round to make sure that I was unobserved I climbed into the back seat, hung a coat across the window, and in the restful twilight went fast asleep.

# Chapter Twenty-seven

I slept for a long time and when I woke up the sun was setting. I could hear the sound of music from the amusement park. Near by, on the road, a stream of people were walking in from the town to see the fireworks. I would have given a great deal to climb into the front seat of the car and drive home to bed, but I had got to see it through. I was stiff in the limbs and my brain was woolly. I had to pull out my crumpled programme to find out what happened next. It said 'buffet supper in Council room: 8 o'clock'. I looked at my watch. It was already half past eight. I climbed out of my seat and walked back to the Casino.

The place was still packed with people trying to get into the restaurant for supper. Overhead, in the assembly hall, the tables had been cleared and a dance was going on.

The Council room was crowded. Besides the Directors, the Town Council and everybody of any note in St Mary's had been invited to the buffet supper. The first person I met was Dobson the Editor of our local paper. For once he had thrown aside his pose as a hostile critic of everything we did. He had a large glass of sherry which no doubt helped, for he took my hand and shook it vigorously and congratulated me upon a wonderful opening day. 'Couldn't have been better!' he said. 'Spendidly organized! Wonderful success! And what's more,' he added, 'it'll last! It's caught the public imagination! It's momentous! Historic!'

Jim Blundell and the Borough Engineer came up. They too were jubilant, and had figures to justify it. By seven o'clock no less than 6239 people had paid to go into the amusement park: the restaurant was running to capacity and the bar was doing a roaring trade. More than 4000 had passed through the well house and drunk the water and the bookstall had completely sold out their large supply of souvenir booklets. 'It's a hit!' said Jim. 'A smash hit!'

At dusk we walked across to see the fireworks. The crowds, if anything, were greater than ever. Apart from the townspeople, thousands of visitors were staying on until the end. The fireworks had been set up in a big meadow adjoining the amusement park and seats had been arranged for the Directors and Town Council. Once more refreshments were served: this time by smart young men in short white jackets. I had a large iced gin and tonic, and felt better.

It was a lovely summer night. Nearby on the Casino lawn boys and girls were dancing to music from a radio that one of them had brought along. People were playing miniature golf beneath the floodlights and the crack of the shooting gallery and the blare of the roundabout went on and on.

And then the lights were dimmed: the music died away and a resounding boom sent a rocket into the sky to announce the opening of the fireworks.

It was a wonderful display, and I had to admit how right Jim Blundell had been to insist upon pushing out the boat and doing it in style. I had been against the cost and tried to cut it down, but I had not realized what a massive crowd would stay to see them. A cheap show would have been an anticlimax and sent people home disappointed. But this lavish spectacle was the fitting end to a great and memorable day. An endless stream of rockets filled the sky: bright little balls of light shot up and came down wriggling and squealing; the Niagara Falls brought a sigh of admiration.

Then came the big set piece in my special honour. I hadn't been told about it because it was planned as a surprise. At first it was a confused pattern as the innumerable little pieces fizzed into flame; then out of it came a large portrait vaguely recognizable as me with 'Thanks to the Colonel' beneath it in golden letters.

A big cheer went up from the spectators. Somebody began to

sing 'For he's a jolly good fellow' and Jim Blundell turned in his seat and gave me a violent thump on the back with a 'bravo, old boy! bravo! marvellous!' He was completely drunk now. His hot whisky-laden breath nearly suffocated me.

My portrait slowly faded; the glittering eyes dropped out, and after a short period of darkness came the most spectacular, certainly the most beautiful effect of all. Slowly and silently the woods beyond the meadow began to glow with coloured light: blue and green and red and gold; elusive shades of violet and tangerine. It grew and spread until the whole countryside became a fairyland.

It was an ironic chance: a sort of poetic justice that turned that moment of beauty into sickening reality. In the far corner of the meadow lay the duckpond, until now hidden mercifully in the darkness, but now, with the glow of light in the woods behind it, the wire-mesh fence around the pond was floodlit. It shone with a ghostly phosphorescence. It seemed to leer and grin at us triumphantly as if it were saying: 'don't forget I'm here! don't forget you're criminals: you've burnt your boats and there's no return!'

Thousands of people had paid that day to drink the water; victims of a barefaced fraud. How could we know that some pestilent, poisonous stuff had not flowed into the well that day? – that out among that seething, happy crowd some were not already feeling strange uneasy pains? In a few days the papers may report a mysterious epidemic: inquiry would show that every victim had drunk from St Mary's well.

It may have been this sudden, deadly plunge back to reality; it may have been the violent thump that Blundell had given me on the back – or just that I was physically worn out. I only know that suddenly I felt desperately sick and ill. I had got to get out of it; at all costs I had got to get away before I collapsed and made an exhibition of myself.

In an undertone I said to Jim Blundell: 'I think I'll go. I'd like to get away before the crowds.'

He stared at me. 'But there's lots more,' he said: 'the sea battle; the big Catherine wheel; the fighting cats . . . you 'aven't seen half! The grand finale of rockets: two hundred at five bob each.'

It was no use making pretences. 'It's been a long day,' I said. 'Exhausting. I'm not as young as I was. I've got to get away.'

Jim was ponderously sympathetic. 'Poor old chap,' he said. 'I'll see you back to your car: got to see a man about a dog meself . . . damn near bursting.'

It wasn't difficult to get away in the darkness with everybody admiring the illuminated woods. A few steps took us to the gates into the Casino gardens, now dark and deserted.

Jim Blundell took my arm. He was unsteady on his feet and his voice was slurred. He leant on me: his body was like a big damp poultice.

I wished that he hadn't come with me: I devoutly wished that I could have been spared that last ordeal.

At first he went rambling on about the events of the day, saying all over again what he had said at the buffet supper: 'Smash hit! Money pouring in! Fun park a riot! Bar sold out of liquor! Safe bursting with cash! Need a lorry to take it to the Bank tomorrow! Whole damn thing a thumping God almighty success!' He squeezed my arm and breathed a hot cloud of whisky over me. 'And all because of you, old boy! *And* me! If I hadn't bumped off that old bastard the whole bloody thing would have gone down the drain, and you and me would be selling matches!'

Whether he had deliberately intended to tell me, or whether it was out of bravado, because he was drunk, I shall never know, but he lowered his voice to a hoarse whisper and went on with a sort of gloating pride. 'Come to me like the voice of providence, it did – standing there at the back of the bar that night, listening to the old bastard cadging drinks – telling 'em 'e'd soon be rich again! One too many drinks: one loose word from Hodder and the whole damn thing would be out! It was him or us, Colonel – and it wasn't going to be us if I could help it!

'Out the back gate there's a straight cut along beside the allotment gardens to the lane where the old crook lived – less than half a mile. I reckoned I could do it in ten minutes: long before 'e'd get there by road.

'Closing time came along and I did me usual stuff: saw the boys off at the door: come in and closed up and told Harry and George the barmen to go ahead with the clearing while I went down the garden to shut the chickens up – same as I did every night.

'Out there in the shed was the old jemmy for opening the cases ... and there was me, off across the allotment gardens as fast as I could go. Got a bit puffed, but things couldn't have been better: dark as an empty 'ouse with a drizzle of rain – and there was me, nicely behind the hedge with time to spare. I 'ad one nasty shock – because the first thing I 'eard was the old man's voice – talking. I reckoned he'd picked up one of the fellers that lives that way – and the whole damn thing was a fizzle.

'But when he came in sight he was all alone – just talking away to 'imself – maybe telling 'imself what 'e was going to say to us when 'e come to the Casino next day for 'is blackmail money.

'After that there was nothing to it: just clear and easy. I let 'im go by – climbed the gate and come up be'ind 'im. I didn't think no more of it than slugging a rat in the chicken run. 'E never made a sound: never knew what 'it 'im; didn't even know 'e was dead. 'E sort of spun round and the second wallop sent 'im clean in the ditch. Didn't 'ave to do another thing but pull that old wallet out of his pocket to make it look like robbery.

'I was back in the garden shutting up the chickens in no time. If the barmen caught me coming in I 'ad it nicely planned to say a couple of the birds had roosted up in a tree – like they do – and I 'ad a job getting 'em down and putting 'em back in the hen-house. But it all worked fine. The boys were just finishing off – turning out the lights, and when Harry come in with the keys, there was me sitting in the little back room, writing up the books – and the old man's wallet in the coke furnace.

'Best job of work I ever done in me life ... saved thousands of people from misery and ruin with a couple of bangs on an old crook's nut.'

I said nothing in return. There was nothing to say. He had only confirmed what I had suspected from the day of the murder, although until now I had wondered how he had managed it. All that I wondered now was why he had told me – but I felt too tired and ill to care.

We had reached the car park. It was dark and deserted, but the sky still glowed above the illuminated woods, and another burst of rockets lit the sky. My brain was so fuddled that I had difficulty in starting the car. I groped on the dark dashboard for the starter button and set the windscreen wipers going – Jim Blundell leant heavily on the ledge of the open window breathing over me a farewell cloud of whisky fumes and cigar smoke. 'Take care of yourself, old boy. You've done a great job. It's been terrific: two thousand quid in the safe – and 'arf of it clear profit.'

He belched, and walked away. I fumbled for my lights and switched them on. As the lights swung round when I turned, I had a last fleeting glimpse of Jim Blundell easing himself against the back of the Town Clerk's car.

# Chapter Twenty-eight

A year has passed since I began this chronicle on the night when I got home from the gala Opening. I am ending it on the night of another memorable occasion. At a general meeting in the Casino assembly hall this afternoon I read from the Chair a report on the first year's working of the Company, and once again there was resounding applause and fulsome speeches of congratulation.

I need not quote the report in detail, for copies will no doubt exist even if, as I devoutly hope, this chronicle will not be opened and read for many years to come.

It may be recalled that at our inaugural meeting Jim Blundell declared that our annual profit would be £30,000 a year. To my mind it was a wildly extravagant estimate, put forward as a bait for gullible people when we were desperately trying to raise the money. I considered it reckless and dishonest, and that it should never have been made.

But this afternoon I was able to announce that our first year's profit had worked out at £48,729: nearly 25 per cent of the invested capital and far above Jim Blundell's bombastic forecast. After setting aside £10,000 for extensions and improvements, we declared a dividend of 15 per cent. No wonder the shareholders threw their caps in the air.

There were two reasons for these remarkable results. One was that the thing caught on from the word go. The big publicity, the sensational case of Lord Colindale, and the romantic attraction of a modern health centre rising from the ruins of an ancient Nunnery, all combined to capture people's imagination and establish St Mary's as the place to come to for a day's outing in the country.

They come in their thousands: week in week out; they arrive in private cars and excursion coaches; they lunch in the Casino restaurant; crowd into the amusement park or enjoy themselves more quietly in the Colindale gardens. They buy souvenirs, take a drink of water in the well house and dance in the assembly hall. Whatever they do, they all spend money.

The other reason has been the astonishing success of the water itself.

I am naturally suspicious of anything that smells of quackery. When Professor Stein had put forward the idea that a 'harmonic solution' of frog spawn and disintegrated bulrush seed would release proteins vital to the treatment of rheumatism I just couldn't swallow it. It was too much like the nostrums that witches and sorcerers boiled up in medieval days. I hadn't allowed that most achievements in medicine have sprung from chance discoveries that must in their beginnings have seemed absurd to sceptics. If the flowers of a humble ditch plant could produce a priceless heart stimulant and a patch of mould on some beef broth could bring us penicillin, then I shouldn't have dismissed so casually a scientist's theory that a solution of frog spawn and bulrush seed would cure the rheumatism.

The first reports of improvement began to reach us within a week. Several patients taking the full treatment declared themselves better than they had been for years. The Directors seized eagerly upon these reports and wanted to announce them to the press for the sake of the publicity, but I urged them to caution and restraint. Superficial improvement might well have come from auto-suggestion: from faith. People anxious to emulate Lord Colindale might imagine themselves on the road to recovery, only to suffer relapse when the first effects of faith wore off. Premature announcements of sensational cures, afterwards to be contradicted, would do more harm than good.

But as the weeks went by such an overwhelming record of results came in that even a sceptic like myself became convinced.

An elderly lady who arrived from Toronto in a wheel-chair,

swathed in shawls and with two attendants, was playing clock golf within three weeks. An oil magnate from Texas who could scarcely raise an arm to feed himself won a coconut in the amusement park soon after beginning his treatment, and men who had walked with crutches for years were playing tennis; even dancing in the assembly hall within a few weeks of their arrival. Some cases failed to respond, but Lord Colindale's miraculous cure was repeated again and again.

These people needed no prompting from us to make their cures known to the world. They gave enthusiastic interviews to the reporters who came down to St Mary's for the latest news, frequently giving them 'before and after' photographs. Such testimony was far more effective than anything we might have issued as official propaganda and, as many of these interviews got headlines abroad, the Casino inquiry office was flooded with applications for treatment and accommodation in St Mary's. Jim Blundell's Coach and Horses was packed to capacity and everybody in the town with rooms available was booked for months ahead. St Mary's was a boom town: everybody gained in one way or another; property values soared as the chain stores moved in, and the thing that dazzled everybody was the belief that the boom was here to stay: to stay, it seemed, for ever. The supply of rheumatic people had no end.

Here to stay; here for ever. You heard the joyful words on every side, haunting those of us who knew the truth. Despite it all we were still impostors. Even if the waters of St Mary's raised the dead we were still criminals in the eyes of the law.

One day Dr Stagg came to the Manor House to talk things over with me. It was two months after the Casino opened, when doubt no longer remained about the astonishing properties of the water. He looked desperately tired, and he told me he couldn't bear the strain much longer.

Every evening he took samples from the pond to analyse in his laboratory: every evening he faced the nightmare of finding poisons that would force him to close the well, and he suggested we must now do the only right and proper thing.

'We can do it this way,' he said. 'We can announce that I sent a sample of the water to Professor Stein, who found the water contained substances that couldn't come from a mineral spring. We can say that we then made investigations and discovered the pipe to the duckpond. There's now such overwhelming proof of the water's value that people would still demand it – but we could then take steps to purify it and end this appalling risk.'

I told Stagg to put it to the Directors at our next meeting, but it led to a scene more violent than any that we had had. Jim Blundell blew up.

'It's a crazy, idiotic idea,' he shouted. 'Frog spawn and bulrush seed isn't the monopoly of our duckpond! You can get frogs and bulrushes anywhere, and once people know what happens when you mix 'em together, you'll have big companies making the stuff all over the world and we're finished!

'We can't take out a bloody patent for it! You'll 'ave people making their rheumatic cure in their own back gardens! A couple of frogs and a clump of bulrushes and they've got all they want!'

That was true. It was also true that such an announcement was bound to stir up Henry's murder in the minds of Scotland Yard. It would give them a hot clue: Inspector Morris would turn up again, and he wouldn't go away empty-handed next time.

Stagg didn't press the point. He knew from the start that he hadn't got a chance. In any case he was too tired and ill to fight Jim Blundell. He made the proposal because he believed it right: because he knew that he wouldn't be with us much longer, and nobody could take over his self-imposed duty of analysing the water after he had left us.

Jim Blundell was no doubt right. To lose our monopoly would have ended the prosperity of St Mary's and finished off the Company. To have done this to the people when they were just beginning to taste the fruits of success would have been more inhuman than to have done it before the Casino opened.

The proposal was rejected, and with it went our last chance of saving our integrity and peace of mind. It was also the last time we could ever discuss the problem at the Council table, for at this meeting the Vicar, the headmistress, and Mr Potter formally resigned from the Board, and the three Directors who filled their places knew nothing about the duckpond pipe and were never to be told.

The resignations, coming as they did after the project had been safely launched, caused no comment and the newcomers were delighted to join the Board of a Company bursting with success. We elected Lewis Watson, the Bank Manager; Farrell the Estate Agent and a Chartered Accountant named Gibbs; more useful than the people we had lost, and the Board was all the stronger.

We had some debate about whether to let them into the secret, but there wasn't any point in telling them. So long as they knew nothing about the duckpond pipe they were free of blame if it was discovered. Had we told them, there was no knowing what they would have done. So from the day they joined us the pipe officially ceased to exist.

A few weeks later Stagg was ill. The strain and the worry had caught up with him at last. He had a complete breakdown and was forced to give up his work and go on extended leave. I don't think we shall see him again in St Mary's.

Jim Blundell didn't conceal his relief at Stagg's departure. The doctor's daily analysis of the water had always been an irritation to him. In his view, Stagg's determination to close the well if he discovered contamination was a callous threat to the welfare of the people of St Mary's. 'He'd sooner wreck the town than give a few strangers the bellyache,' Jim Blundell said to me one day, and as the impressive list of cures built up, he had grown ever more impatient at Stagg's continual concern. His reasoning was simple. 'If we can cure them by the hundred,' he said, 'what's it matter if we kill a few here and there?'

But to me, and to men like Digby, Stagg's departure sharpened the edge of the torment that had dogged us from the day when it all began. Stagg had been a shield for us to hide behind. So long as he constantly tested the water we could at least persuade ourselves that nothing serious would happen. Now that he was gone, we were defenceless. He had told me once that if typhoid bacteria were to enter the well from one single source, hundreds of people might be infected within a few hours and deaths were bound to follow. That was the nightmare that was to haunt us, perhaps for the rest of our lives.

The new Medical Officer of St Mary's confined himself to his duties in the town. Had we told him the secret he might well have refused the responsibility and condemned the water out of hand. All we now have is the Borough Engineer, who keeps a supply of cane rods to clear the pipe if a fall in the level of the well suggests that it is blocked.

With the coming of winter we had expected a decline in visitors, but as people returned home to spread the news of their miraculous recoveries, new waves of patients arrived at the Casino to pack the town and swell the prosperity of our people.

Jim Blundell now goes about in a big Rolls-Royce. He is building an extension to The Coach and Horses with twenty additional bedrooms, and has invited me to spend a holiday in the luxury yacht he has bought for cruising on the Norfolk Broads. I declined with thanks. I couldn't think of anything more horrible than such a holiday. The Town Council is planning a large block of service flats to accommodate visitors at present forced to find rooms in neighbouring towns. The Casino Company is building an open swimming bath for our daily visitors who come in ever-growing crowds, and there are plans for a weekly display of fireworks all the summer.

I live in increasing seclusion in the Manor House. There are far more public functions now, but I attend only when I am bound to. It is an ordeal to get up and make speeches, and receive continual thanks for my 'surpassing generosity'.

In the New Year's Honours list I received the CBE for 'public services' and Jim Blundell got the OBE, which he wears on every conceivable occasion.

And every morning I scan the newspapers for the first reports of typhoid, or epidemics of mysterious origin that must inevitably lead finally to St Mary's Well. I hate to look. I hardly dare open the morning paper, but I cannot spend the day in peace until I have done it – if peace can ever again be the word for the days remaining to me.

I have told the story as best I can. I shall seal it and leave it tomorrow in the safe keeping of the Company solicitors.

If ever it has to be opened and read I can only hope that for what we have done we shall not be judged too harshly.

www.ingramcontent.com/pod-product-compliance
Ingram Content Group UK Ltd.
Pitfield, Milton Keynes, MK11 3LW, UK
UKHW040104010325
455690UK00002B/6